The Nois

THE NOISE OF TIME

Selected Prose

Osip Mandelstam

*Translated from the Russian
and with critical essays by* CLARENCE BROWN

NORTHWESTERN UNIVERSITY PRESS
EVANSTON, ILLINOIS

Northwestern University Press
Evanston, Illinois 60208-4210

First published 1965 by Princeton University Press as *The Prose of Osip Mandelstam.* Copyright © 1965 by Princeton University Press. Expanded edition published 1986 by North Point Press as *The Noise of Time.* Copyright © 1986 by Clarence Brown. Published 1993 by Penguin Books. Northwestern University Press edition published 2002 by arrangement with Clarence Brown. All rights reserved.

Printed in the United States of America
10 9 8 7 6 5 4 3 2 1

ISBN 0-8101-1928-5

Library of Congress Cataloging-in-Publication Data
Mandel'shtam, Osip, 1891–1938.
    [Prose works. English. Selections]
    The noise of time : selected prose / Osip Mandelstam ; translated from the Russian and with critical essays by Clarence Brown.
        p. cm. — (European classics)
    First published 1965 by Princeton University Press under title: The prose of Osip Mandelstam. Expanded ed. published 1986 by North Point Press and 1993 by Penguin Books under title: The noise of time.
    Includes bibliographical references and index.
    ISBN 0-8101-1928-5 (pbk. : alk. paper)
    1. Mandel'shtam, Osip, 1891–1938—Translations into English. 2. Mandel'shtam, Osip, 1891–1938—Criticism and interpretation. I. Brown, Clarence, 1929– II. Title. III. European classics (Evanston, Ill.)

PG3476.M355 A23 2002
891.78'308—dc21

                                                2001054425

The paper used in this publication meets the minimum requirements of the American National Standard for Information Sciences—Permanence of Paper for Printed Library Materials, ANSI Z39.48-1984.

Designed by David Bullen

Contents

Acknowledgments

All students of Osip Mandelstam owe their first debt of gratitude to Professor Gleb Struve and Mr. Boris Filippov, the editors of the *Collected Works*, which appeared in Russian in New York in 1955. For their many unselfish kindnesses to me, and for their interest and encouragement, I owe a further, entirely personal, debt. Professor Struve's scrutiny of certain parts of the translation greatly improved it. For many delightful conversations on the subject of his friend Osip Emilievich I am indebted to Artur Lourié. My colleagues Nina Berberova and Herman Ermolaev have patiently answered many questions, for which I am very grateful. The errors and infelicities that remain are to be blamed solely on my own stubbornness or ignorance. I thank Mrs. Mary Gutbrodt for her kindness in typing parts of the manuscript. For my wife's help in typing the final draft and in reading the proof, and for her other assistance, I am much obliged. I have been greatly aided by some who do not desire public acknowledgment.

Christmas 1964, Princeton, N.J.
C.B.

NOTE ON SECOND PRINTING
For many valuable suggestions incorporated in the second printing I am obliged to Simon Karlinsky, Sir Isaiah Berlin, and Donald Fanger.

January 1967
C.B.

A Note on the Illustrations

The drawing of Mandelstam by P. V. Miturich on p. 22 is discussed there. The drawing on p. 25, "Poets," is also by Miturich and also appeared in *Apollon* No. 4–5 for 1916.

The portrait of Valentin Yakovlevich Parnakh on p. 132, discussed on p. 49, is by Pablo Picasso. It appeared for the first time (and, if my search of the Picasso catalogues has been sufficiently thorough, for the only time) as the frontispiece to a book of Parnakh's poems (*Karabkaetsja akrobat*, Paris: Franko-russkaja pečat', 1922).

The rare photographs of Osip Mandelstam and the portrait of him by Lev Bruni have been kindly supplied by friends to whom I am very grateful. All of these appear here for the first time.

The map of St. Petersburg on pp. 18–19 is taken from Baedeker's *La Russie*, 1897.

A Note on the Transliteration

In the body of the text I have used the popular system of transliteration, the most explicit description of which is to be found in J. Thomas Shaw, *The Transliteration of Modern Russian for English-Language Publications* (University of Wisconsin Press, 1967). In the notes I have used the narrow transliteration now all but universally adopted for scholarly publication; occasionally, in the text, Russian words cited as words are rendered in this narrow system. Exceptions are made for words and names (moujik, Tchaikovsky) that have become familiar in other forms, and non-Russian names (Rubenstein, Hofmann) appear in their usual orthography. "Mandelstam" is the transliteration preferred by the writer himself. When place names contain an adjectival form of a name familiar in English I have used the English form (the Nicholas Station). A foolish consistency in this matter, however, would have produced the "Marie" Theater instead of the familiar Mariinsky. In quotations from other sources, except where noted, the original transliteration has been changed to conform to the style of this book.

Introduction:
The Prose of Mandelstam

The prose which is here offered to the English-speaking reader for the first time is that of a Russian poet.[1] Like the prose of certain other Russian poets who were his contemporaries—Andrey Bely, Velimir Khlebnikov, Boris Pasternak—it is wholly untypical of ordinary Russian prose and it is remarkably interesting. For reasons that have nothing to do with literature, it is also virtually unknown even, or especially, in Russia itself.

Osip Emilievich Mandelstam, a Jew, was born in Warsaw on the 15th of January, 1891, and died a political prisoner in a camp near Vladivostok in 1938. For years the end of his life was so obscured by rumor, conjecture, and deliberate falsehood that one could be sure only of the fact that he had perished. The date now officially given is 27 December and it is accepted by those close to the event, but there is one rumor left to haunt his biographer and to make it seem the part of prudence to precede the date of 27 December with the bleakly official formula "on or about." Except for details, however, we do seem now to have a large measure of truth about how Mandelstam spent his last days.

His troubles began in 1934. At that time, probably in the apartment of Boris Pasternak, Mandelstam read an epigram which he had written on Stalin. Whether the following excerpt, given here in the English version of George Stuckow, is from the actual poem itself or from another like it is not known, but its authenticity is asserted on good authority, and under the circumstances it is clearly actionable.

We live unconscious of the country beneath us,
Our talk cannot be heard ten paces away,
And whenever there is enough for half-a-conversation,
The Kremlin highlander is mentioned.
His thick fingers are fat like worms,

His words hit hard like heavy weights,
His cockroach's huge moustaches laugh,
And the tops of his boots shine brightly.[2]

It is unlikely that there were more than five of Mandelstam's close
friends within earshot of these verses. One of them reported the incident
to the appropriate authority, and that was the beginning of the end. Our
natural tendency toward revulsion at this act must be tempered by certain
circumstances. The man who did it was himself in trouble and was probably terrified that one of his associates would show greater and prompter
zeal than he, which would certainly have added to his difficulties. Besides,
in a recent work of reference his short biography concludes with an official
cliché which has lately begun to serve as the laconic epitaph for numerous
writers ("Illegally suppressed. Rehabilitated posthumously"), and he
perished even earlier than Mandelstam. Requiescat in pace.

The quarter of a century since Mandelstam's death has not seen him
restored to the canon of the elect, though there have been various signs
that his work would be published again. An announcement in *Voprosy
literatury* (Problems of Literature) for November 1958 (p. 256) declared
that his collected poetry would be published in one of the large volumes of
the distinguished series "Biblioteka poéta" (Poet's Library), and there
were other indications, some of them very encouraging, that his work
would be reissued, but little has yet come of it. So far as I have been able to
determine, the four poems printed in the almanac *Den' poézii* (Day of
Poetry) for 1962 constitute, with the exception of isolated quotations, the
whole extent of his rehabilitation. The bulletin *Novye knigi* (New Books),
No. 22 (1964), a prospectus of forthcoming books for the use of librarians
and the book trade, carried the announcement of an anthology called *Poéty
nachala XX veka* (Poets of the Beginning of the Twentieth Century),
scheduled for publication in an edition of 50,000 copies in the fourth quarter of 1964. Mandelstam is listed along with Balmont, Sologub, Annensky, Bely, Kuzmin, Voloshin, Khodasevich, and other poets for inclusion
in this work, which is to be one of the small-format volumes of the Poet's
Library. The announcement names V. N. Orlov, the editor-in-chief of the
entire series, as the editor of the anthology and since that same Orlov's
statement in *Literaturnaja gazeta* (Literary Gazette) for 27 June 1964
concerning proposed one-volume editions of Russian poets omits the
name of Mandelstam, it is to be presumed that the long-promised separate

collection of his work has been abandoned and that we are to receive only the few poems which the format and scope of the forthcoming anthology give one any grounds for expecting. The formulaic expression mentioned above has latterly been expanded to read "Illegally suppressed during the period of the cult of personality of Stalin," etc. Since it was the personal vindictiveness of the dictator himself that caused Mandelstam's tragic death, no one would seem more eligible for the posthumous amnesty awarded others. The reason for his continued exclusion is perhaps one of those curiosities of Soviet internal literary affairs about which it is seldom very rewarding to speculate.[3]

II

But even non-persons have biographies, though it may be extraordinarily difficult to establish them. Practically everything that we know of Mandelstam's early life comes from his own account in the pages that follow, and the detailed story of his mature years will be the subject of my forthcoming book on his life and poetry. In this introductory essay, therefore, I shall give merely the briefest sketch of his movements from the time of his emergence from the Tenishev School in 1907 at the age of 16 to the time of his death.

Mandelstam went at once to Paris, where, to our immense good fortune, he encountered Mikhail Karpovich (1888–1959), later Professor of Russian Literature at Harvard, who left what is the unique eyewitness account of Mandelstam during his first trip abroad.[4] It is worth quoting at some length:

"This happened in the distant past—nearly a half century ago. I was living in Paris at the time and attending lectures at the Sorbonne. I can give the exact day when I first met Mandelstam: 24 December 1907. As everyone knows, the French celebrate Christmas Eve in the same way that we greet the New Year. On that evening I was also 'making merry' in one of the cafés on the Boul' Miche along with a small group of Russian young people. At a separate table in our vicinity was sitting a certain youth who had attracted our attention by his rather unusual appearance. More than anything else, he looked like a young chicken, and that resemblance gave him a rather comic aspect. But along with that there was in his face and in his beautiful, sad eyes something very attractive. As soon as he heard that we were speaking Russian he became interested in us. It was clear that in the midst of the loud celebration going on about him he felt lost and alone.

We invited him to join us and he agreed with obvious pleasure. We learned that his name was Osip Emilievich Mandelstam.

"I was struck most of all by his extraordinary impressionability. It seemed that for him 'all the impressions of existence' were still really new, and to each of them he responded with his entire being. At that time he was filled with a youthful effusiveness and romantic enthusiasm which are difficult to reconcile with his later poetic character. In the future author of *Kamen'* (Stone) there was as yet nothing stony."

For all his ingrained habit of autobiography, Mandelstam was extremely uncommunicative about his family. Though there are, here and there, isolated portraits of individual relatives, there is nowhere in his published writings the slightest hint of what were the relationships among these people. Hence the value of Karpovich's observations on this side of his life:

"About his family Mandelstam almost never told me anything, and I did not inquire about them (the biographical interest in people . . . makes its appearance later in life). Only on one occasion—I do not remember in what connection—he gave me to understand that his relationship with his parents was not altogether satisfactory. He even exclaimed, 'It's terrible, terrible!' but since he was in general prone to overuse that expression, I immediately suspected him of exaggeration. And I still think that if Mandelstam's parents permitted him to live in Paris and occupy himself with whatever he wished they must not have been so indifferent to his wishes, and the family bonds did not lie so heavily upon him. In any case, he did not give one the feeling that he was constrained and bound. He was helpless in practical affairs, but spiritually he was independent and, I think, sufficiently confident in himself."

Our next glimpse of Mandelstam also reveals something of his relationship with his family. He turns up in the editorial office of *Apollon* accompanied by his mother, who apparently dragged the desperately embarrassed youth before the editor, Sergey Makovsky, for a showdown on his poetry. Years later, Makovsky, who emigrated to Paris, recalled the incident in a humorous memoir which makes the most of the dramatic contrasts involved: a sophisticated and erudite editor of one of the most elegant art journals of St. Petersburg, an awkward and mortified neophyte poet, and the loud and energetic wife of Emil Mandelstam, leather merchant.[5] To Mme. Mandelstam's amazement, Makovsky praised some of the poems, and her son's career had its beginning in one of those almost Dostoevskian moments of scandal which were so often to mark his later life.

Mandelstam circa *1910*

Mandelstam circa *1936*

The early poems of Mandelstam, published in *Apollon*, earned him an immediate though an exceedingly narrow fame. They secured his entree into the literary circles of the capital and he quickly became an intimate in the cafés and salons where the life of the mind was then being lived, or at least celebrated.

In 1910 he went abroad for the second time, on this occasion to Heidelberg, where he studied Old French, and to Switzerland. Mandelstam's poems reveal such a seemingly firsthand knowledge of Italy that there has been a persistent attempt to discover whether he was actually there at least for a time, probably during this trip. The evidence, however, is only in the poetry, and even though this has been exhaustively catalogued by Gleb Struve, it is still inconclusive.[6] Those like Artur Lourié and others who knew Mandelstam closely at the time tell me that he was never in Italy.

He returned to Russia to enter the University of St. Petersburg in the following year, after having crammed for the Greek entrance examination under the tutelage of the late Konstantin Mochulsky.[7] Whether he finished the University is not definitely known, though it seems unlikely. The *Literaturnaja éntsiklopedija* (Literary Encyclopedia) states that he did, but the date is not given, and there is no other evidence of his having received a degree.

Study abroad and the first stages of literary success had greatly altered the character of the shy, easily embarrassed youth pictured in the earliest reminiscences of him. Karpovich saw Mandelstam again, for the last time, in 1912 and found his aspect far more imposing. "He had grown some sidewhiskers à la Pushkin, and he already behaved himself like a *maître*."[8] It is worth recording, however, that Karpovich was speaking with Mandelstam on this occasion on the subject of poetry, a matter which he never treated lightly and in which he seldom deferred to the opinions of others. When his first book of poems, *Kamen'* (Stone), appeared in 1913 (at his own expense), his career was launched in earnest and his judgments more often solicited and given. There are numerous testimonies to Mandelstam's encounters with writers seeking his advice. When the poet Vsevolod Rozhdestvensky's memoirs first appeared in the magazine *Zvezda* (Star) it was clear that the nameless poet whom he described as a kind of *arbiter elegantiarum* was Osip Mandelstam.[9] The physical description as well as the magisterial manner tallied with other accounts so well that it was impossible to mistake the identity of the young man who delivered himself so gravely and even sternly of decisive opinions in the matter of rhythm and

imagery. But we need not rely on supposition alone, for when Rozhdestvensky's memoirs, *Stranitsy zhizni* (Pages of Life), appeared in book form
in 1962, Mandelstam's name was permitted to appear (p. 129)—a hopeful
sign. These memoirs relate approximately to the time (1915) when the
well-known artist P. V. Miturich made a drawing of Mandelstam, depicting him, in the pose of Whistler's mother, as a slender and rather haughty
young man whom one can well imagine as a member of the poetry jury
faced by Rozhdestvensky. The writer Veniamin Kaverin recalls a similar
interview with Mandelstam some five years later.[10] He had brought some
of his poems—his best, as he thought, because his most obscure—to Mandelstam for the purpose of hearing his judgment. A similar interview with
Viktor Shklovsky, the brilliant Formalist critic, who had not even inter-
rupted his exercise on a bicycle machine to deliver his ironic and withering
comments, had just left Kaverin rather downcast. But, though Mandelstam was no more encouraging to the personal ambitions of Kaverin, there
was something in his candid and passionate seriousness about poetry that

proved almost consoling. "Mandelstam spoke severely, convincingly, with passion. There was no room here for irony. It was important to him that I cease writing poetry, and his words were a defense of poetry against me and those dozens and hundreds of young men and women who were busying themselves with the game of words. . . ."

For all his characteristic gaiety and wit, poetry was for Mandelstam anything but a game of words. Though this book deals only with his prose, perhaps it would be appropriate to interrupt the narrative of his life at this point in order to characterize (however lamely at this remove from the original language) the poetry upon which his fame chiefly rests.

III

Mandelstam's career began at a time when literary taste was swinging, pendulum-like, away from the school of Symbolism which had dominated Russian poetry for some two decades. Symbolism, a term which covers some of the very best Russian poetry of the modern age, had brought with it in the 1890s a rejuvenation of poetic technique and an enormous refinement of poetic sensibility, but by the end of the first decade of this century its vitality had begun to wane and its inspiration to fade. The literary world, dominated exclusively by Symbolism for many years, saw the birth of several new "isms," each of them defined in large part by those features of Symbolism to which they were reacting negatively. Mandelstam's early poetry is written entirely in the spirit and manner of the Symbolists, the dominant masters of his formative years, but by the time the first collection of his poetry came out in 1913 he was already identifiable as one of the new group of Acmeists. The Acmeists, led at first by the gifted poet Nikolay Gumilyov, were no less attentive to matters of form and technique than their predecessors. This concern for the craft of poetry is emphasized in the name *Tsekh poétov* (Guild of Poets) given to the loosely organized meetings held for the purpose of discussion, instruction, and mutual criticism. It was the mysticism of the Symbolists, their fascination with the occult and the other world, to which the Acmeists objected. They offered instead a poetry of this world, a celebration of the rose, as they said, for its own petals and perfume rather than for its supposed symbolic link to love in this world or the next. The Acmeists were far from rejecting the religious values of the Symbolists, but they refused to turn poetry into a church or themselves into hierophants. Gumilyov himself, whose personality is largely identical with the earliest form of Acmeism, was a man of distinctly masculine Christianity, and the worldview of the Acmeists was declared to be manly, steady, and whole.

But if the Acmeists agreed in the demands to be made upon poetry, their answers to these demands were exceedingly various. Gumilyov's robust and colorful verse, filled with the exoticism of Africa and the clangor of all the wars of the West; Akhmatova's intimate, entirely feminine confessions; Mandelstam's recondite verbal elegance and the chaste architecture of his form—these were to be the leading representatives of the school.

Mandelstam's poetry also stands apart from that of his associates by virtue of its reputation for being extraordinarily difficult. As usual, much of the difficulty lies in the categorical expectations which readers bring to his work, but it is nevertheless true that he is not an easy poet. He is difficult in part because he refers to an immensely broad spectrum of culture and history as familiarly as a journalist might refer to the common news of the day. It may also be true that he is obscure to some because he requires of his reader, as Vladimir Pozner wrote, not only that culture which is acquired from books and museums but also that which is transmitted from father to son.[11]

For a modernist movement in verse, Acmeism was curiously conservative both in theme and technique. Mandelstam lived at a time when innovation in the prosodic elements of poetry was highly esteemed, but his rhymes and meters might, with few exceptions, seem familiar to the contemporaries of Pushkin. The diction of his slow, deliberately impeded lines occasionally recalled an even earlier age, that of Derzhavin. But the imagery, the life's blood of his poetry, was wholly of his time, and of ours.

One of the most characteristic subjects of Mandelstam's poetic art is art itself. He wrote numerous poems which have their inspiration in other works of literature, and if the formula *l'art pour l'art* describes his manner, the matter of his verse, as Viktor Zhirmunsky has noted, deserves Schlegel's rubric *die Poesie der Poesie*.[12] A taste for Racine, rare in Russia, lies at the basis of his famous poem on the *Phèdre*, from which he also translated a portion. The "other world" of which he speaks here is not the "beyond" of the Symbolists but the world of arrested gesture and formal purity and balance which he saw in the classical art of Racine. The poems of Homer, the novels of Dickens, the Gothic tales of Edgar Poe—these are some of the other sources which furnish the impulse for numerous poems.

It is so rare to find the art of architecture as a theme in Russian poetry that Mandelstam's attraction to it has been rather exaggerated. It is true, however, that some of his most successful lyrics are devoted to the great buildings of the world: the Hagia Sophia in Istanbul, the Cathedral of Notre Dame in Paris, the Admiralty in Petersburg, and the many churches of Moscow, the latter depicted in an exquisite poem as singers in a maidenly chorus. His poems on architecture are memorable also for his peculiar vision of buildings as organic structures, as processes of balance and tension, as a kind of joyous cooperative action to which each member contributes its share. This produces in the poem on Notre Dame, for example, a powerful tension between our sense of the cathedral as a massive, stationary structure and our sense of its continuous movement in the balancing of its parts. Through all of Mandelstam's poems on architecture, on religious ritual, on the Greek epics and the poems of Ossian, and on historical subjects there runs a single unifying element—the element of grandness, of monumentality and solemnity. There is about much of his poetry a swelling sense of stateliness. The movement is often that of ritual, but if this ceremoniousness of tone is characteristic of him, it is also true that he could mock such gravity by describing a tennis match in a solemn and elevated style.

IV

Mandelstam was not conscripted for the war, though it is unclear why he received the "white ticket" of exemption. Gumilyov enlisted at once, the Guild of Poets was disbanded, and the literary life of the capital was permanently altered. During some of the war years Mandelstam was in the south of Russia, mostly in the Crimea, where a large number of artists and writers had gathered. He found a haven in Koktebel, where Maksimilian Voloshin and his mother opened their dacha to many errant intellectuals, and also in Alushta at Aleksandr Aleksandrovich Smirnov's villa, which, together with several others nearby, bore the collective name *Professorskij ugolok* (Professors' Nook). The memoirs of Ilya Ehrenburg and of Marina Tsvetaeva provide much of our knowledge of this Crimean retreat.[13] By the spring of 1918 Mandelstam was back in the north. His extraordinary adventure in Moscow with the terrorist Blyumkin (described below, p. 49f.) was the occasion for another hasty withdrawal to the Crimea. His sojourn in Theodosia is described in the chapters under that name below. In 1920 he returned via Georgia to Petersburg, not without going through some of his usual misadventures. He was arrested by the military authorities on suspicion of being an enemy agent but was freed shortly thereafter. He tells this story in a brief magazine article called "The Mensheviks of Georgia."[14]

Post-war and post-revolutionary Petersburg, now Petrograd, was made habitable for intellectuals by the genius of Maksim Gorky, who was instrumental in having the former Eliseev mansion converted into a sanctuary for them. The House of the Arts, as it was called, figures largely in almost all the memoirs recalling those hungry and desolate years, but the most vivid evocation of the spirit of this extraordinary place is in Olga Forsh's novella, *Sumasshedshij korabl'* (The Mad Ship), the title of which is itself an image of the house.[15] Mandelstam was one of the inmates. His reputation, formerly confined to a limited circle of intimates, was now much broader and more secure. *Stone* had appeared in a second edition in 1916, and the poems which he had brought back from the south were known to all the residents of the House of the Arts long before their publication in his second collection, *Tristia*, in 1922. He managed to support himself and his wife (he married Nadezhda Yakovlevna Khazina in 1922)[16] by journalism, editorial work, and by translating for the publishing house *Vsemirnaja literatura* (Universal Literature), another of Gorky's enterprises. The summit of his career was the year 1928. In that year a collected edition of his poems appeared and so did all of the prose translated here (under the general title of *The Egyptian Stamp*). Soviet criticism of his work was still moderately mild, but the long night of the 1930s was already approaching. His last published work in the Soviet press was to *Journey to Armenia*, which appeared in the magazine *Zvezda* in 1933. On 13 May 1934 at No. 3 Furmanov Street in Leningrad Mandelstam was arrested for having written the epigram on Stalin that we have described and that, in effect, was the end of his public existence.

Shortly after the arrest Mandelstam was actually brought before Stalin himself for a personal inquisition—in its own sinister way perhaps the profoundest tribute ever paid by the Soviet regime to the power of Mandelstam's pen. Stalin's personal concern in the matter is further attested in the following curious episode, which is here reported as it was received directly from Boris Pasternak.[17]

"One day Mandelstam's wife came to Pasternak to beg him to do what he could to get Osip out of jail. This was the first news he had had of Mandelstam's arrest; the two had never been close friends (even their stylistic evolution, as Pasternak once remarked, had proceeded in opposite directions: Mandelstam's from clarity towards obscurity, Pasternak's from complexity towards simplicity). However, Mandelstam's wife begged him to do what he could, and Pasternak promised to try to help. It happened about this time that some high Government or Party dignitary died. In accordance with custom the body lay in state in the Columned Hall of the House of Unions, while Soviet notables stood guard of honor and the public filed past. Pasternak went to the Columned Hall to pay his last respects to the dead and noticed among the guard of honor someone he knew—I think it was Bukharin. He remembered Mandelstam's wife's request and stopped for a moment to ask Bukharin to see if he could do anything to help. Bukharin wasn't hopeful but said he would try. A few nights later a party was in progress in Pasternak's flat when the telephone rang. The voice at the far end asked if that was Comrade Pasternak; Comrade Stalin would like to speak to him from the Kremlin. A moment later a voice with a perceptible Georgian accent spoke: 'Is that Pasternak? This is Stalin.'

" 'Good evening, Comrade Stalin. By the way, this is not a leg-pull, is it?'

" 'No, no, this is Stalin, all right.'

"At the name of Stalin there was a hush in the room. Pasternak said, 'There are twenty-six people in the room and they're all listening. Does that make any difference?'

"Stalin said, 'No, that's all right. What's this about Mandelstam?'

" 'I'd like to do what I can to help him.'

" 'Do you think he's a very good poet?'

" 'You know, Comrade Stalin, you should no more ask one poet what he thinks of another than you should ask a pretty woman her opinion of another pretty woman's looks.'

" 'Then am I to take it you don't think much of him?'

" 'No, no, you've got me wrong. I'm a different sort of poet from him, that's all. I think he's a good writer.'

" 'Very well, thank you.' Pause. 'Why don't you ever come to see me?'

" 'I should have thought it was rather your place to invite me.'

"Stalin laughed and wished Pasternak a good evening and that was the end of the conversation. The next day Mandelstam was released. Pasternak had never heard from Stalin again."

But if Mandelstam was in fact released, as this account would have it, it was not for long. He was sentenced to three years of exile in Cherdyn, a small town near the upper reaches of the Kama and to the north of Solikamsk.[18] In Cherdyn he attempted to kill himself by leaping from a hospital window, but the result was no more than a broken arm. At this point his wife's appeals to the Central Committee were answered to the extent that Mandelstam was permitted to choose another place of exile. The permission is said to have come from Stalin himself. Mandelstam chose Voronezh.

To exile a poet is one thing; to prevent him from writing poems is quite another. It is largely owing to these later poems (and to the dates and places of composition with which they are marked) that we can follow some of Mandelstam's progress in the next few years. He was sent to Voronezh, and the major fund of his poems, recently received in the West and published in 1965 under the editorship of Gleb Struve and Boris Filippov, is divided into the "First Voronezh Notebook" and the "Second Voronezh Notebook." In the first the earliest dated poem is marked "April 1935" and the latest "Winter 1936." The span of the second notebook is from "Winter

1936" to "May 1937." That he may have been in Voronezh long before the first dated poem is hinted at by Ehrenburg, who writes, in the memoirs already cited, "I searched for him in Voronezh in the summer of 1934" (p. 496). This is, however, one of those maddening half-revelations for which Ehrenburg has a peculiar gift, so one cannot be sure.

In May 1937 the three years of Mandelstam's sentence expired and he and his wife returned to Moscow, where they lived temporarily in their former apartment. They were, however, not permitted the right of domicile in the capital and had to live in Kalinin, whence they went to Moscow from time to time. In the fall of 1937 they went to Leningrad, where they visited a number of old friends.

Almost exactly one year from the time of his release from Voronezh, Mandelstam was undergoing treatment at a sanatorium near Charuste, a small station not far from Tarusa, when he was arrested again (1 May 1938). He was charged with counter-revolutionary activity (this was the height of the Great Purge) and sentenced to five years in one of the concentration camps of the Far East. The journey from Moscow to Vladivostok (5,391 miles) was made in the stage-by-stage fashion that is customary in the deportation of large bodies of prisoners. The state of Mandelstam's health at this time can be judged by observing the photograph of the aged man on page 20, taken near the end of his life when he was only forty-five years old; by recalling the frightful experiences of his exile; and by the fact that he was under institutional care at the moment of his arrest. The effect of this latest calamity was to drive him to and, for a time at least, over the brink of insanity. The following is quoted from the communication of an anonymous correspondent, translated and cited by George Stuckow:

"Suspecting that his guards had received orders from Moscow to poison him, he refused to eat any meals (they consisted of bread, herring, dehydrated cabbage soup, and sometimes a little millet). His fellow deportees caught him stealing their bread rations. He was subjected to cruel beating-up until it was realized that he was really insane. In the Vladivostok transit camp his insanity assumed a still more acute form. He still feared being poisoned and began again to steal food from his fellow inmates in the barracks, believing that their rations, unlike his, were not poisoned. Once again he was brutally beaten up. In the end he was thrown out of the barracks; he went to live near the refuse heap, feeding on garbage. Filthy, with long, gray hair and a long beard, dressed in tatters, with a mad look in his eyes, he became a veritable scarecrow of the camp. Occasionally, he was fed by the camp doctors, among whom there was one who had known him in Voronezh and admired his poetry."[19]

A later account by George Stuckow is based on more recent information than the above, which it somewhat corrects. It contains a letter written by Mandelstam from Vladivostok, probably during the latter part of October 1938, to his brother Aleksandr Emilievich (addressed as Shura and Shurochka) and his wife, Nadezhda Yakovlevna (Nadenka, Nadya). While the letter is naturally that of a distraught and terrified man, it is not the product of a deranged mind:

"Dear Shura!

"I am in Vladivostok, USVITL [apparently an abbreviated form of the camp name; the last three initials stand for 'corrective labor camp'], barracks 11. I got five years for counter-revolutionary activity, by decree of the OSO [an organ of the NKVD, the secret police]. By stages from Butyrki [prison] in Moscow on 9 September, arrived 12 October. Health very weak, totally exhausted, terribly thin, almost unrecognizable, but as for sending clothes, food, money—I don't know if there's any point. Try anyway. Terribly frozen without warm things.

"Dear Nadenka, I don't know whether you're alive, my darling. Shura, you write to me right away about Nadya. This is a transit point. They didn't take me to Kolyma. May have to spend the winter.

"My dears, I kiss you.

                                                                    Osya

"Shurochka, I'll write some more. We've gone out to work these last few days. That's raised my spirits. People are sent from this place, a transit camp, to the permanent camps. I apparently got 'sifted' and will have to get ready for the winter. And please, send me a radiogram and some money by wire."[20]

This is Mandelstam's last prose.

He was not to live through the winter of which he speaks with such apprehension, and death came to him on or about 27 December 1938. Ilya Ehrenburg recalled Mandelstam with real warmth and, under the circumstances, considerable candor. Still, it is perhaps not to be wondered at that he should have averted his gaze from his friend's final agony, to which he lends a certain gentle, even "poetic," touch: "He was ill and had been sitting beside the fire reciting the sonnets of Petrarch."[21] There are other versions of a harder death.

V

A raznochinets *needs no memory—it*
is enough for him to tell of the books he
has read, and his biography is done.

The chapter on Vera Komissarzhevskaya in *The Noise of Time* begins in
the following characteristically oblique way: "My desire is to speak not
about myself but to track down the age, the noise and the germination of
time. My memory is inimical to all that is personal." Was it in fact? Certainly this declaration is not without value to the student of Mandelstam,
but I doubt that its plain meaning can be accepted uncritically. On the one
hand, there is that peculiar reticence about himself and his family that has
so often been noted in the memoir literature about Mandelstam. And no
reader of his autobiographical writings can remain unaware of the whole-
sale ellipsis which constitutes in large part the very aesthetic basis of his
work. Those who are more familiar with his personal history will be sensi-
tive to certain strange gaps, such as the failure even to mention the existence of his two brothers. Aunts, cousins, grandparents, and relatives too
distant for reckoning throng his pages. We are afforded little vistas into the
personal histories of governesses and workmen and shabby teachers of
Hebrew, but of Aleksandr and Evgeny, with the first of whom, at least, he
appears to have been quite close, there is not a syllable. In all of Mandelstam there is but one single reference to his wife, so obscure that the editors
of his collected works claimed in a literary polemic never to have heard of
her existence. His parents themselves are reduced to little more than their
pronunciations. Certainly no one can imagine Mandelstam emulating the
"Tolstoys and Aksakovs . . . with their epic domestic memoirs," which he
professed to find incomprehensible.

And yet, what is one to do with the plain fact of the matter: that all of
Mandelstam's prose is intensely and immediately personal when it is not
openly autobiographical? It is so densely imbued with his Self that one
tends soon to ignore this obvious and persistent element. It may be true
that his autobiographical writings, like those of Gorky, are conspicuous
for their continuous portraiture of other people, but those portraits are
conveyed to the eye of the reader through the prismatic vision of a consciousness whose presence we constantly sense. Mandelstam is always

there in his writing. This may be said even of his one known venture into what would at first appear to be fiction—*The Egyptian Stamp*. And his poetry, to which the word "impersonal" has so often been applied that it has become an unexamined critical cliché, requires only a closer and a more enlightened reading to be seen as the personal and intimate record that it is. He was preeminently the poet of the present moment, of the literal fact in all its particularity, believing that only the instant of the artist's perception has any chance of withstanding time's attrition, and it is just such poetry that is most closely linked to the actual personality and experience of the poet. It was, after all, the personal and immediate in his beloved Villon and even in Dante which Mandelstam regarded as the key to their permanence.

Mandelstam was possessed by the true taxonomical passion for sorting and arranging his impressions. It has been noted before that his people tend to be catalogued, and there is no more revealing example of this than the short "portrait gallery" of his classmates in the Tenishev School. Berkovsky spoke of this as Mandelstam's habit of returning all his little birds to their cultural nests.[22] But the same is true of all other phenomena in his artistic world. Objects, like people, have histories. They are the artifacts of a particular culture and derive from a specific time and place. Mandelstam may be conceived as a bemused stroller through his own personal waxworks, the museum of his past, where all the exhibits—from his mother's edition of Pushkin, through the brothers Krupensky, "connoisseurs of wine and Jews," to that "Marxist propylaea," Karl Kautsky's Erfurt Program—are lovingly maintained behind glass. But the glass which separates him from what he describes serves also to reflect his own image and, in his perception, to superimpose himself over all that he sees. The author's denial of any interest in that phantasmal likeness of his own face is a curiosity which reveals one facet of his psyche, but it will hardly dissuade the reader from observing that intense preoccupation with his own ego which is the very medium in which Mandelstam's prose exists.

The Russian title of *The Noise of Time* is *Shum vremeni*. Had the brief note of acknowledgment in the front of this book been really encyclopedic, it would have shown how abundantly I have availed myself of all the native Russian advice I could find in the task of turning Mandelstam into English, though this advice has not always been, as it could not be expected to be, in agreement. The translation of *shum* is difficult out of all proportion to the miniature size of this word. My first choice was "noise," and it found favor with some, but there was impressive insistence that *shum* is best rendered by "sound." On the point of yielding, I was stopped by that dean of scholiasts, Vladimir Nabokov, whose four-volume translation of and commentary on Pushkin's *Eugene Onegin* (New York, 1964) arrived in the nick of time. In his annotation of line 9 of One: xxxv—*Prosnulsja utra shum prijatnyj*, rendered by him as "Morn's pleasant hubbub has awoken"—Nabokov provides us with a characteristic little essay on the various nuances of *shum*. The transliteration in what follows is his:

"An analogous line occurs in *Poltava* (1828), pt. 11, l. 318: *razdálsya útra shúm igríviy*, 'morn's frisky hubbub has resounded.' Compare these epithets with those used by English poets, e.g., Milton's 'the busy hum of men' and John Dyer's 'the Noise of busy Man.'

"Generally speaking, the sense of *shum* implies a more sustained and uniform auditory effect than the English 'noise.' It is also a shade more remote and confused. It is at heart more of a swoosh than a racket. All its forms—*shum* (n.), *shumnïy* (adj.), *shumyashchiy* (part.), *shumet'* (v.)—are beautifully onomatopoeic, which 'noisy' and 'to noise' are not. *Shum* acquires a number of nuances in connection with various subjects: *shum goroda*, 'the hum of the city,' 'the tumult of the town'; *shum lesov*, 'the murmur of woods'; *shumyashchiy les*, 'the sough of forests'; *shumnïy ruchey*, 'the dinning stream'; *shumyashchee more*, 'the sounding sea,' the rote, the thud, and the roar of the surf on the shore—'the surgy murmurs of the lonely sea,' as Keats has it in *Endymion*, l. 121. *Shum* may also mean 'commotion,' 'clamor,' and so forth. The verb *shumet'* is poorly rendered by 'to be noisy,' 'to clatter.' " (Vol. 2, 143f.)

The solace which I find in this is not, of course, what Nabokov has to say about "noise," since he specifically rejects it in favor of "hubbub." It is the evidence of his uneasiness with the latter, which produces the delightful change-ringing on the various shades of *shum*. As in all such cases, the final choice is a matter of taste.

The relevance of these deliberations to Mandelstam's work is central. The insipid word "sound," which is virtually without overtones, cannot serve to describe the disjointed, elliptical style of these memoirs. If the faint but deliberate cacophony that arises from this jumbled juxtaposition of Finnish sleigh bells, strolling brass bands, the alpine chill of concerts by Hofmann and Kubelik, the wheezing of Yuly Matveich, and Vladimir Gippius's bellowing summons to the hack seems to the reader, as it does to me, inadequately reflected in "noise," let him contemplate in Nabokov's note some of the things to which Mandelstam's inner ear was attuned when he named his work *Shum vremeni*.

It is the type of autobiography that exposes the Self by showing its peculiar apperception of the people, the events, the large cultural and spiritual movements that have shaped it. It recalls that earlier masterpiece of evocative and reflective self-portraiture, Apollon Grigorev's *My Literary and Moral Wanderings*, now available to English readers in a new translation by Ralph Matlaw (New York, 1962). Much of the following paragraph from that work will sound familiar to readers of Mandelstam:

"I intend to write a history of my impressions rather than an autobiography; I choose myself as an object, as a complete stranger, I look upon myself as a son of a particular era, and consequently only what generally characterizes the era ought to be included in my reminiscences: whatever concerns me personally will be included only insofar as it characterizes the era." (p. 11)

The memoirs of both are instinct with a sense of place, and there is even a partial similarity in the places themselves. Grigorev's locale was the district in Moscow on the left bank of the Moscow River called Zamoskvoreche (literally: "beyond the Moscow"). It was in Grigorev's day a grimy quarter inhabited for the most part by the merchant class and notably lacking in the refinements of culture: a world made familiar in the dramas of Ostrovsky. The Jewish quarter of St. Petersburg, in the Kolomna district, had for Mandelstam much of the same significance. Baedeker's *Russia* (1914) notes this region of the city with a slightly averted gaze and offers no encouragement to the genteel traveler who might undertake a closer inspection, and in his story "The Portrait" Nikolay Gogol depicts the Kolomna of the early nineteenth century in equally unflattering terms. The nostalgia inspired in both writers by the settings of their early lives is, like that of John Betjeman, onomastic and toponymic. Their pages, especially Mandelstam's, are saturated with names of streets, parks, shops, buildings and builders, writers and their works. For both, literature is the preserve most often pillaged for allusion and example. Grigorev can dispense with a description of his grandfather since Aksakov's description of *his* grandfather is available and presumed to be familiar to readers.

Mandelstam's constant immersion in literary culture makes it the very currency of his prose. One has a sense of reading a document written for a close circle of acquaintances, all of whom share an immense fund of cultural resource, available upon demand. To expend these monies in the furtherance of his intellectual commerce with his readers, Mandelstam had only to breathe a word or two, to sign the briefest of chits. It is, to be sure, his native Russian literature to which he, like Grigorev, most often alludes, but his range is broader and more European in scope. The commentary to this translation assumes much of this knowledge on the part of the new readers to whom it is addressed, for had all the writers and characters and titles of Russian literature been noted, it would have been far too long. What is more, I think that a good deal of the effect of Mandelstam's prose comes from our feeling of sharing with this civilized Russian such large areas of thought and response which can be summoned before our consciousness without being too much insisted upon. The Russian modernists who flourished around the turn of the century are still, in spite of many excellent translations and studies, not yet really familiar below the level of the cultural elite in the West. This is true even of the extraordinarily gifted painters, whose way has never been blocked by the barrier of language. An awareness of how little cultural translation we require beyond that of language—infinitely less than we need in the case of our own contemporaries in the Soviet Union!—can serve only to increase our pleasure and our understanding.

If the Russians gave us the great masters of realistic portraiture, Tolstoy and Dostoevsky, with their incredible ability to create whole families of living human presences, more vital and memorable than most of our actual acquaintances, it was they who also produced Nikolay Gogol, that diabolically gifted puppet-master who causes his grotesque creatures to perform an endless *bouffonnerie* at the expense of the human race. Gogol's old friend, S. T. Aksakov, passed a two-word judgment on *Dead Souls* which has remained one of the most illuminating things ever said of that book: he called it a *sborišče urodov* (an assembly of monsters). It is to this tradition that Mandelstam belongs, though one must immediately add that, for all his Gogolian tendency to caricature, he was infinitely more kindhearted. This may arise partly from the fact that virtually none of the characters in the pages of Mandelstam was wholly imagined, not even in the apparent fiction, and the kindliness of his literary portraiture is in keeping with the image we have of him in life. Even his epigrams, however witty they may be, contain little acid. He seldom wrote of people whom he disliked, and it is extraordinary to find any animus whatever in his pages unless it be aroused in the defense of poetry, the one subject on which he was unfailingly serious. Indifference to poetry, or ingratitude for it, or the callow assumption that any drivel might be "dragged into prominence" in its name—this was intolerable and could be dealt with unmercifully.

But the ordinary human creatures resurrected in his prose could hardly have complained of the queer guise in which they are brought before us, so gentle and loving is Mandelstam's humor.

Could Yuly Matveich conceivably have objected to being portrayed as a sort of walrus wrapped in a beaver coat and with the improbably tender head of Bismarck on his shoulders? It seems most unlikely that these elements in his image could have outweighed the warmth and compassion which Mandelstam obviously feels for him. As in the case of the great fabulists, his pasquinades on the human race depend heavily on the equation of men with animals. The principal of the Tenishev School, Ostrogorsky, whose humor evidently delighted Mandelstam, was "a great scrofulous ape in a frock coat." Mandelstam is especially reminiscent of Gogol when he goes to the ultimate length of caricature: the reduction of a human portrait to one single feature. Thus Count Witte comes before us as a nose, and nothing more. The complex picture of Sergey Ivanych shows us the opposite extreme, for there are so many elements blended into the elaborate representation of him that one thinks rather of the technique of collage than of caricature. The controlling image is again that of an animal, this time the mythological chimera, a monster composed of the parts of various beasts, but if we dissect this monster we will find he consists of paper (he was an interlinear translation, he shed flimsy revolutionary tracts as he walked), of the police rock from which he had been chipped away, of cigarette smoke, and even of the delicious hot chocolate to which he was so passionately devoted. The face in this particular collage is composed of a crumpled student beret. Incidentally, would Beckett himself not envy the description of Sergey Ivanych's walk? "His walk resembled that of a man who had just been seized by the shoulder and led into the presence of some terrible satrap while trying to appear completely nonchalant."

Sergey Ivanych suffered a strange depletion of his revolutionary fervor after 1905 and went away to work in the Pulkovo Observatory. The chapter on him concludes: "If Sergey Ivanych had been transformed into a pure logarithm of stellar velocities or a function of space it would not have surprised me. He had to depart this world, such a chimera was he."

What is the technique here? It is essentially poetic—picturing one thing in terms of another. This device is so constant in Mandelstam that it becomes peculiarly his own, and one has almost a sensation of *déjà lu* when one encounters in the Soviet writer Vera Inber this purely Mandelstamian sentence, recalling what was said of Sergey Ivanych: "From his constant and long-standing communion with the cosmos our teacher Foma Narcissovich had acquired a nebulosity of expression and the circular movements of the stars."[23]

Mandelstam's approach to characterization is one of extreme concentration by virtue of which a human figure is pictured in terms of the surroundings. The epithet applied to the voice of the Petersburg cabby is "oaty," which is an absurdity to readers who have not understood Mandelstam's surrealistic technique of displacing modifiers on the principle of proximity. The horse of the cabby is not otherwise summoned into existence than by this single qualifier of his master's voice.[24] Mandelstam's relative, the literary historian Vengerov, is revealed to us smirking into his "dense *ant* beard." But the adjective for the word "ant" does not really characterize the beard itself so much as it does Vengerov's monumental tolerance for drudgery and his regular itinerary from apartment to card catalogue and back. The synagogue in the Kolomna District is characterized by the word "leonine," but that hardly describes the building itself, which was earlier compared to an "elegant exotic fig tree." Its presence in this sentence is to be accounted for by the near proximity of the name Samson: "The Cantor, like Samson, collapsed the leonine building. . . ." The entire building has been infected by the associations hovering about the name of Samson. There is a blending of the central object of vision with the qualities of the periphery, which, however, yields not a blur but a heightened intensity of awareness. In Mandelstam a man's occupation and preoccupation are all-important, for in this fictive world a man becomes, literally, what he does.

VI

"It is terrifying to think that our life is a tale without a plot or a hero, made up out of desolation and glass, out of the feverish babble of constant digressions, out of the delirium of the Petersburg influenza."

This sentence occurs toward the end of *The Egyptian Stamp*, the single example of Mandelstam's narrative prose and one of the few examples of surrealist fiction to be found in all of Russian literature. We might take these words as a clue to the pattern of the tale itself, which is composed in a kind of delirious key and consists of just such a feverish babble of constant digressions. In Mandelstam's serious writing it is the nearest approach to dealing directly with the bleak reality of his time and place, though it can seem, in the flaunting of its various opacities, to be as remote from that reality as poems like "Nashedshij podkovu" (The Finder of a Horseshoe) or the terrible "Grifel'naja oda" (The Slate Ode). It represents that reality in a fragmented, multifaceted manner which strives for an artistic equivalency to the fractured life of the period. The desolation and glass are those of Petersburg—temporarily Petrograd, though never recognized as such by Mandelstam—during the "Kerensky Summer" between the two revolutions of 1917.

Perhaps there were other reasons, too, for the elliptical manner. The central character strikes one almost at once as a familiar figure: here is one of the legion of "little men," the spineless or hapless but in any case heroically weak victims of Russian literature. We know him. But as we read, our familiarity with him seems to grow and to become more specific, our sense of his significance deepens, and we are at the end finally aware that this late descendant of Akaky Akakievich represents in the context of his time a statement which in a more naked form, shorn of the ambiguity of its many levels, might have been not only less poetic but certainly less prudent.

In noting that all of the prose translated here is personal and autobiographical, we must stress that the "fictional" *Egyptian Stamp* is no exception. To the best of our present knowledge, it is as close as Mandelstam ever came to creating a conventional plot, a purely imagined story, and it is my contention that even here he did not come so close as it may seem. For all the prismatic surrealism through which we see the background of the novella, it is still vividly the actual stone and glass of Petersburg. The same may be said of certain of the characters: they derive with hardly a change of name from actual acquaintances of Mandelstam. And it seems to me that the central event itself recapitulates, this time with considerably more disguise, an episode from Mandelstam's personal history.

His beloved Petersburg—the classical and eighteenth-century nature of which he caressed in his poetry with the Derzhavinian name "Petropol'"—has become animal: "loathsome as if it were eating a soup of crushed flies." Everything has gone to pieces, like the style of narration. Violence and lawlessness are unrestrained, since the government, "sleeping like a carp," has vanished. It is a background against which the impotence and futility of the dreamy little hero with the queer name of Parnok impress us all the more. But Parnok has the artist's antidote against horror—a retreat into his abstracted interior musing, the description of which vies with the external narration as the focus of the novella. There is in general an uneasy balance between the real and the imagined: Parnok's strabismal vision is forever half on one, half on the other. His inner thoughts are nostalgic, poetic, culture-laden; they sometimes descend into a fatigue-induced playing with the words that have snagged his attention.

Parnok loves music, and his presence alone in the foreground of the narration is sufficient to scatter musical images throughout the description of his surroundings. Another example of that saturation technique which we have already discussed is Parnok's entry into the Polish laundry, transforming it into a kind of Renaissance concert.

The narrative covers one day in the hero's life. There are two plot lines, both quite uncomplicated except in the manner of their telling, and there is no visible connection between them on the level of straight narration. In one, the frame of the novella, Parnok spends his day in the unsuccessful attempt to retrieve certain items of his clothing which seem to gravitate mysteriously into the hands of a certain Captain Krzyżanowski of the Horse Guards. In the second he tries vainly to prevent the mob murder of some unfortunate little man, like himself, who is accused of having stolen a silver watch.

Parnok's day, like Bloomsday, consists essentially of a journey through the city. He goes first to the tailor Mervis in a vain attempt to recover a morning coat, stealthily repossessed during the night for lack of payment. He is next briefly discovered in the chair of a barber who is rather more like an executioner than a barber. He then encounters an acquaintance, Father Nikolay Aleksandrovich Bruni, and goes with him to a Polish laundry, where he tries, again vainly, to retrieve some shirts. The laundry is Dantesque, an ominous tableau from Mandelstam's Inferno, where hot clouds of suffocating steam half reveal six twittering girls spraying water from their mouths onto the clothes to be ironed. When Parnok spies his shirts, the girls tell him that they belong to Captain Krzyżanowski, the first mention of that gray eminence whose presence is to be felt thenceforward in the story and who is finally to usurp even Parnok's place in it. Parnok turns up next in a dentist's chair, where he is having a tooth filled (things are forever being done to Parnok). It is from this vantage point that our hero hears a lynch mob outside in Gorokhovaya Street. Parnok—the little man par excellence, the rabbit-blooded Parnok—races out on a desperately quixotic adventure: to save the life of the nameless, faceless little man who is being taken to the Fontanka, where he will be drowned for some crime that is never specified. Parnok's mission has all the attributes of a nightmare. He must attract attention, that of the authorities, in order to stop the murder, and yet not attract the attention of the mob to himself. Nothing helps. The law has vanished. Parnok's single encounter with Captain Krzyżanọwski takes place, but the military officer, elegant and masterful in his uniform and with a lady on his arm, answers Parnok's pleas for help with a cool banality and vanishes into a café. The murder, we are to assume, takes place.

This is the midpoint of the story. All Parnok's important failures have taken place, and there is really nothing more for him to do. His external adventures are henceforth far less clearly described. The narrative dissolves into a series of evocative and shifting pictures, the function of which is extremely complex: to suggest the spiritual condition of Parnok by the musings and memories that shut actuality out of his mind and at the same time to reveal by a few hints some of the further events of the day. These episodes succeed each other in a curious mosaic pattern, the intrinsic charm of which seduces the attention from any direct concern with the events of the original narrative, which one feels to be taking its ordinary course just beyond or behind the language before us. This language has the qualities of Mandelstam's best poetry: condensation, form, grace, observation, wit. Were that its only reason for being, it would be sufficient, and the style in large measure *becomes* the plot of this *commedia erudita*. The foreground is momentarily occupied by a procession of deaf-mutes whose gesture-language is pictured as a literal weaving of the fabric of the air (Mandelstam had a singular fondness for textile images). They make their way across the vast Palace Square—the immense perspectives of Petersburg make it God's own setting for surrealism—and this tableau fades to an extraordinary passage in which the visual aspect of the musical notation of various composers is impressionistically brought to life. The illusion of third-person narrative is suddenly shattered by the author's own voice, which breaks in to cry, "Lord! Do not make me like Parnok! Give me the strength to distinguish myself from him." And so the novella proceeds: anecdotal family memoirs; here and there a glimpse of the characters and situations with which we started; orgies of metaphor, transmogrifying the objects of Parnok's vision and memory; the death of an Italian soprano accompanied by fire alarms which her expiring fancy transmutes into the overture of her London debut.

The rest of the objective narrative is this. Krzyżanowski and his lady go to a performance of *Giselle* at the Mariinsky. On the way there Krzyża-nowski somehow confuses Parnok with the victim of the lynch mob—an instructive error. Later the tailor Mervis is discovered hurrying through the street on an errand: to take Parnok's coat to (of course) Captain Krzy-żanowski. There is one last picture of Parnok. It is the evening of the day covered by the narrative, but he does not return home (he is, anyway, homeless). Instead, he occupies his worthless time with futile dreams of getting a position as a translator in the Foreign Ministry. It is his base genealogy that will prevent his being accepted there. Meanwhile, it is Cap-tain Krzyżanowski, his luggage packed with Parnok's coat and best shirts, who is to escape from the hallucination of Petersburg. He takes the express to Moscow, where he stops at the elegant Hotel Select.

If this account errs, it errs perhaps in imparting greater clarity and even obviousness to the story than is actually there on a first reading. But it will surprise no one to learn that the story itself, the primary surface narrative, hardly matters. It is no more the focus here than some of the equally trivial plots of Gogol are his focus.

The surface events of Parnok's day are indeed the surface, and below them one can discern at least two more levels: that of the literary tradition and that of autobiography. The former is the more important, and I deal with it first.

In a way, to be sure, any work that participates importantly in a specific heritage, a distinct one, may be said to contain by virtue of our examining it from that point of view the level of the "tradition." That is not what is intended here. *The Egyptian Stamp* not only forms a part of, while signif-icantly extending, one of the most viable and important themes of the Russian literary tradition, but it also uses specific earlier manifestations of that theme for the purpose of making its unique declaration. The chief among its sources is Dostoevsky's weird tale *Dvojnik* (The Double). But since it is generally acknowledged that Dostoevsky's tale is very much in the debt of an even weirder tale, Gogol's *Nos* (The Nose), then clearly Mandelstam's work depends not only on *The Double* but also on *The Nose*.

Dostoevsky's early apprenticeship to his master Gogol is well known. *Bednye ljudi* (Poor Folk), which made Dostoevsky's fame in 1846, is so clearly an answer to Gogol's *Shinel'* (The Overcoat) that he even goes to the length of having his characters read and comment upon the earlier work. The importance of *The Nose* for *The Double* is, however, not made so patently evident. It lies rather in the fact that Dostoevsky reproduced in broad outline the essential framework of the plot: the split in identity of the central character. His Mr. Golyadkin is, like Gogol's Kovalyov, a civil servant hounded by real and imagined enemies who prevent his getting on in the struggle up the ladder of civil service ranks. Mr. Golyadkin, unlike Kovalyov, is clearly mad, a fact which he himself suspects from the outset, and he becomes more so in the course of the narrative until, in the final scene, he is being driven off to the lunatic asylum as his double bounds along beside the carriage with expressions of feigned solicitude. This double, this antagonistic other self, is Dostoevsky's equivalent for Kovalyov's fantastic nose, which detaches itself mysteriously (perhaps cut off by the barber, but perhaps not) and takes up its independent existence in a civil service rank higher than that of Collegiate Assessor Kovalyov himself. Like the nose, the second Mr. Golyadkin is as great a success in the constant internecine war of the civil service as the first Mr. Golyadkin is a failure. He shines at just those enterprises at which his original would most like to shine: he is, in fact, as much the projection of Mr. Golyadkin's inner self as the nose was an actual part of Kovalyov's outer self. And in both cases it is the self as its own worst enemy. In addition to all this, which amounts to nothing less than that "serious idea"—the antagonism of the self—to which Dostoevsky was later to ascribe such central importance, there are little touches betraying his preoccupation with Gogol's earlier treatment of the theme: Golyadkin, repeating the identical actions of Kovalyov, arises from sleep at the beginning of the narrative and fusses about before a mirror, anxious lest a pimple might have appeared on his face overnight.

The Nose and *The Double* represent merely one pair of closely linked mutations of the theme. The little wretched self-divided hero has of course many incarnations in the history of Russian literature, beginning, it has been suggested, as far back as the hapless youth in the seventeenth-century *Tale of Gore Zlochast'e*.[25] Mandelstam's hero Parnok belongs in this line, but his closest relative is the one nearest to our modern sensibility: Mr. Golyadkin. And the progenitor of both is Gogol's *The Nose*.

For all its vastly more complex and sometimes baffling structure and symbolism, *The Egyptian Stamp* presents the identical basic situation that we find in the works of Gogol and Dostoevsky: the hero, a helpless little man, finds his own identity split in two, the second half being endowed with all those attributes of power and invulnerable knowledge of the world lacking in the first. And the double uses his superiority to antagonize and persecute the hero. To put it briefly, Parnok is to Captain Krzyżanowski as Kovalyov is to the Nose and as Mr. Golyadkin the Elder is to Mr. Golyadkin the Younger. Mandelstam, like Dostoevsky in *Poor Folk*, makes his intention unmistakably clear to the reader by actually mentioning the hero of his model, and, moreover, by including that hero precisely in the list of Parnok's *ancestors*:

"Yes, with such relatives one could not go far. But—wait a moment— how is that not a pedigree? How not? It is. What about Captain Golyadkin? And the collegiate assessors, to whom 'the Lord God might add intelligence and money'? All those people who were shown down the stairs, publicly disgraced, insulted in the forties and fifties of the last century, all those mutterers, windbags in capes, with gloves that had been laundered to shreds, all those who do not 'live' but 'reside' on Sadovaya and Podyacheskaya in houses made of stale sections of petrified chocolate and grumble to themselves: 'How is that possible? Not a penny to my name, and me with a university education?' "

It is interesting to note that in the original version of this passage the name Golyadkin appeared without any military rank. Both Mr. Golyadkin and his Double held the rank of Titular Councilor, the ninth of the fourteen civil service grades, equivalent to the military rank of Captain of Infantry (*kapitan*) or Captain of Cavalry (*rotmistr*). Krzyżanowski is a Captain of Cavalry, and when Mandelstam republished the novella in book form he added the word "Captain" before Golyadkin's name (it is not there in Dostoevsky), thus clearly reinforcing the desired association.

But Parnok recalls Mr. Golyadkin in other ways, in his habits and even in certain verbal responses. Mr. Golyadkin, waiting for two hours on the cold landing of the back stairs in a torment of indecision before breaking uninvited into the ballroom, comforts himself with little, random, irrelevant thoughts:

"Having just quoted, as has already been said, the very pertinent phrase of the former French minister, Villèle, Mr. Golyadkin, for what reason is not known, immediately recalled the former Turkish vizier Martsimiris, as well as the beautiful Margravine Luise, about both of whom he had also read at some time or other in a book."[26]

After entering the brilliant company at the dance being given by his

superior, Mr. Golyadkin, immediately conspicuous, is racked by self-con-
sciousness and embarrassment. As Parnok was later to do, he retreats into
inconsequence, into a purely verbal innocence and innocuousness:

" 'That gentleman is wearing a wig,' thought Mr. Golyadkin, 'and if he
were to take it off, his head would be just exactly as naked as the palm of my
hand.' "27

This prefigures the identical habit of Parnok. Racing down the stairs
into the street where the lynch mob is carrying its victim to the Fontanka,
he soothes his terror with just such an irrelevancy: "Buttons are made of
animal blood!" Earlier Parnok had "managed to think" of the mob: "All
these people are brush salesmen."

Golyadkin moves by short, quick steps—the gait of Parnok, as is often
noted. The central event in Golyadkin's wretched little history is his ig-
nominious expulsion from the ball, and it is just such expulsion, again
translated into the surrealistic idiom, that is the fate predicted for Parnok:

"They will throw you out one of these days, Parnok, throw you out with
frightful scandal and shame . . . they'll take you by the arm and pf-t-t! . . .
out of the Symphony Hall, out of the Society of Friends and Amateurs of
the Last Word, out of the Circle for Grasshopper Music, out of the salon
of Mme. Bookbinder . . . who knows where else? . . . but out you will go,
disgraced, vilified. . . ."

Parnok and Krzyżanowski fall easily into the paradigm prescribed by
their earlier shapes in the tradition. Parnok's dream is to get a position in
government service, but Captain Krzyżanowski, as the proprietress of the
laundry relates, is not only a success in the service of the government but
even a hero. Parnok is attracted to women after his fashion, but on sensing
their distress in his presence retreats into "wild, bombastic, twittery language." Krzyżanowski, on the other hand, has a lady whose "criminal,
pink little ear" is receptive to "the sweet nothings of the Horse Guard."
Parnok's pitifully limited aim during the day in which we follow his activities is to recover his coat and shirts, but it is Krzyżanowski who, without
even trying or seeming to care, gets possession of them and carries them
off to Moscow.

It is clear that certain of Mandelstam's secondary characters are also
drawn from the two sources dealt with here. What is the barber in *The
Egyptian Stamp* but a descendant of the barber in *The Nose*? His lavatory
is a chopping block, and he is presented as an executioner, a characterization that can be accounted for (given the correspondences already pointed

out) only by his being modeled after Gogol's Ivan Yakovlevich, whose shop sign advertised his surgical services and who was, indeed, suspected of having cut off Kovalyov's nose. The presence of the dentist is also probably to be explained by the doctor in each of the earlier works, though the question of why it was precisely a dentist who was chosen is perhaps to be explained by Mandelstam's own pathological dread of dentists, of which more later.

But there is more to the lineage of Parnok and his story. If the parallels with *The Nose* and *The Double* account for some elements of the story (they would appear to account almost entirely for Krzyżanowski), they leave others unexplained. I do not expect to discover some earlier incarnation in Russian literature for each personage in Mandelstam's tale, but, still, the tailor Mervis plays a central enough part to invite some speculation. Who is he?

Among the works offered as belonging more or less significantly to the general background of *The Egyptian Stamp*, Berkovsky mentions Pushkin's *Mednyj vsadnik* (The Bronze Horseman), Gogol's *Zapiski sumasshedshego* (Notes of a Madman), and Dostoevsky's *The Double*. In a brief prefatory note to their French translation of the novella, D. S. Mirsky and Georges Limbour mention Dostoevsky's *Idiot* and Tolstoy's *Anna Karenina* as well as *The Double*. Viktor Shklovsky mentions *The Bronze Horseman* and *The Double*.[28] It is remarkable that these lists draw our attention to certain liaisons which, while genuine, are far more tenuous than those with a work which they neglect to mention: Gogol's *Shinel'* (The Overcoat). After *The Double*, this is surely the most important literary source of Mandelstam's tale. For one thing, it answers the above question about Mervis.

The parallel with *The Overcoat* is striking indeed. It is enough to point out that Gogol's story is about Akaky Akakievich Bashmachkin, a kind of archetype of the civil servant—desperately poor, terrified of his superiors, the butt of his fellows—whose entire being is concentrated toward one end, the possession of an overcoat; that he is at the mercy of a malign tailor named Petrovich; and that he is finally robbed of his precious coat to realize how important are the links between it and *The Egyptian Stamp*. Mandelstam's central plot is, after all, about a little man striving without success to get back a coat of which he has been robbed. There is something about that coat itself that recalls Gogol's story: it is a *vizitka*, a morning coat or cutaway, which we may imagine as rather out of place in the grim milieu of this story, and which, moreover, is above Parnok's station in life. So was the overcoat of Akaky Akakievich too grand for him. It may be that for Dostoevsky, attacking Gogol's conception, the overcoat was a contemptible, unworthy object of human desires; but for Akaky himself, we must remember, it was almost too lofty an object for his aspirations.

The coat is functional in another way. It provides an organic link between the two principal streams of the tradition to which Mandelstam is adding a modern instance. I take Pushkin's Evgeny in *The Bronze Horseman* and Akaky Akakievich as typical of one stream: the little loser overwhelmed by large, exterior, objective forces—the very elements themselves, the consequences of the Petrine transformation, the inhumanity of the social structure. Kovalyov and Golyadkin represent the other stream: the antagonists are their other selves, parts of their divided personalities. This neat dichotomy must not be made to bear more than it can bear; if we look closely we see that there are elements of the first in the second and vice versa. To define the hero-victims by their antagonists is not to say the last word about them. But essentially it holds that we are dealing with undivided as against divided central characters, and the coat serves to unify this tradition in Mandelstam's novella. The goal of Parnok's desire is that of Akaky's, and it is carried off in the suitcase of his antagonistic double.

Parnok bears the greatest resemblance, as I have indicated, to Mr. Golyadkin; but there is at least one feature that reminds us of Akaky Akakievich: "At the beck and call of my consciousness are two or three little words: 'and there,' 'already,' 'suddenly.'" This recalls the unfortunate Akaky's almost unintelligible speech, consisting for the most part of prepositions, adverbs, and entirely meaningless particles.

Mervis, then, the tailor of Parnok's too-grand coat, is the direct spiritual descendant of Gogol's Petrovich. And he even bears a certain physical resemblance. The latter was blind in one eye and his face was disfigured by pockmarks. Of his tailor Mandelstam writes: "I must confess that I love Mervis—I love his blind face, furrowed by wrinkles that see." Petrovich's shrewish wife is not represented by Mervis's wife, who congratulates her husband on his cleverness in stealing back Parnok's coat, but her characteristics, like the characteristics of her smoke-filled kitchen, would seem to have been transferred to the furious proprietress of the laundry and her steamy shop, where Parnok also goes in his futile search for his clothes.

If Mandelstam's story is an ingenious combination of numerous elements from earlier works, the question why this is so may prove interesting. Are we to suppose him so poor in invention that he was compelled, in his only attempt at contriving an objective narrative, to borrow characters and situations from his predecessors? I do not think anyone even slightly acquainted with Mandelstam's work could accept that explanation. He had in fact an astonishingly inventive mind. One's feeling in reading him is constant and unflagging amazement—amazement precisely at the novelty and originality of his vision, and the uniquely personal character of his conception of the world, so personal that his individual imprint on whatever he created is immediately recognizable as "Mandelstamian." There can be no argument with Berkovsky's remark about his "lofty arrogance" in approaching the world of objects as the "last name-giver."[29] For the answer we must look rather to the complexity of Mandelstam's vision. Audacity of purpose, not paucity of invention, led him to utilize for his own special aims Gogol's and Dostoevsky's themes and characters. In order fully to grasp this complexity and audacity, it will be necessary to turn to the third of the principal levels of *The Egyptian Stamp*: the elliptical and elusive reference to Mandelstam's own life.

One must deal here with allusion, often cryptic enough, with "tone," and with scattered, fractional details which, taken separately, could scarcely be regarded as conclusive, but together impress one with the extent to which Mandelstam was writing of himself. We know little of his life, as I have said, but it is clear that we know quite enough to see that a good deal of it has found its way into the ostensible fiction which we are considering.

There are two sorts of autobiographical reference in *The Egyptian Stamp*. The first is thoroughly private and consists of occasional references to and verbal echoes from his own work, especially from *The Noise of Time*, and also of some of the personal characteristics of Mandelstam which we find abundantly in the memoir literature devoted to him. An example of this kind of reference is to be seen in the last episode of Chapter VI. Captain Krzyżanowski and his companion are strolling along Ofitserskaya, where they drop into Aboling's lamp store, but we are told that "they never stopped by Eylers's flower shop." Why do we require this bit of negative information? In the chapter entitled "Finland" in *The Noise of Time* Mandelstam mentions his family's constant move from apartment to apartment. One of their apartments was located on Ofitserskaya above that same Eylers's flower shop. Is this autobiographical? I think that it is. Mandelstam, as this novella and his poetry show, had an acutely developed sense of place. A predominant mood in his work is that of nostalgia, an elegiac sense of the past, and Mandelstam's nostalgia, as we have noted, was heavily dependent upon the actual names of places and things in Petersburg. There were a number of flower shops bearing the name of Eylers in Petersburg, for they belonged to one chain, but there was only one on Ofitserskaya, and it was over that one that the Mandelstams lived. It had for him a purely domestic and personal connotation, like a family joke which means nothing to an outsider. The grandmother of Giselle is said to be pouring out milk, "probably almond." This is doubtless a verbal echo of the passage in *The Noise of Time* about his own grandmother and the "bitter, almond taste" of the dainties which she was forever offering. The scalpers behind the Mariinsky Theater, which was on the edge of the Jewish quarter in Petersburg, have their predecessors in the earlier work.

Whence the Polish laundry so vividly described by Mandelstam? The laundries of Petersburg were not traditionally or stereotypically operated by Poles as they are supposed to be by Chinese in the United States. We find the source in a passage from the memoirs of Mandelstam's friend, the cubo-futurist Benedikt Livshitz:

"By the way, it was none other than Mandelstam who disclosed to me the mysteries of 'savoir vivre' in Petersburg, beginning with the secret of how to obtain credit at the Stray Dog cabaret and ending with the Polish laundry where one could, by paying triple the regular price, get a shirt beautifully washed and stiffly starched in an hour's time—a really invaluable convenience in view of the meagreness of our wardrobes."[30]

It should be noted that this identifies not only the Polish laundry but even the practice of labeling one's wash "urgent," a habit which the outraged proprietress mentions in her general indictment of Parnok.

Not only the Polish laundry, but one of the central figures in the scene at the laundry—Father Nikolay Aleksandrovich Bruni—is also drawn from the personal life of the author. This is the actual name of a priest who was a close friend of Mandelstam. He was the brother of the artist Lev Bruni, who painted a portrait of Mandelstam, and a member of the prominent family which included the more famous artist Fyodor Antonovich Bruni (1799–1875), known for his immense academic canvases on biblical and historical subjects. A member of the Academy and at one time director of the Academy of Fine Arts, F. A. Bruni was the son of an Italian painter who immigrated to Russia. He was celebrated for his decorations in St. Isaac's Cathedral in Petersburg. It was undoubtedly this long family association with painting which suggested to Mandelstam the conclusion of the scene in the laundry: "All this cries out to be painted on a ceiling."[31]

What is perhaps still more surprising is that the central character himself, Parnok, actually existed. His real name was Valentin Yakovlevich Parnakh, and the slight change in names is to be explained as follows. Parnakh, a Jew, was the brother of the minor poetess and critic Sofia Parnakh, who wrote under the nom de plume of Andrey Polyanin and who legally changed her surname, perhaps in order to escape the disadvantages of its conspicuously Jewish sound, to Parnok, a name which is neither Jewish nor Russian, but merely strange. Parnakh left Russia and lived for a long time in Paris, where he published several books of his poetry in the early 1920s. His principal concern as a writer, however, was the dance; he published a brief history of the dance and wrote widely for dance periodicals. In Paris he spelled his name both "Parnakh" and "Parnac." It is altogether possible that Mandelstam was under the impression that he had, like his sister, changed his name; but it is also possible that he simply preferred the new name for its strange quality, for its queer appropriateness to the literary character. The Parnok of the story seems, though, to have been drawn rather literally from his model. Small of stature, slight of build, he is described by those who knew him as a nervous, restless little eccentric whose salient feature seems to have been his conspicuously sharp, shiny little shoes—the little "sheep hooves" so often ascribed to the fictional Parnok.[32] Picasso's portrait of him—luckily representational—shows a narrow-shouldered man with a rather large head, thrown back, as it chances, in exactly the haughty gesture which all memoirists of Mandelstam recall in their subject. There is, in fact, a striking resemblance between the portraits of Mandelstam by Miturich and Bruni and the portrait of Parnakh by Picasso.

Parnok would seem to be complicated enough, what with his complex literary genealogy and now his real-life source, but we have not yet come to the end. For Parnok was, finally, Mandelstam. This might suggest itself soon enough to anyone familiar with the reminiscences devoted to Mandelstam, where he is pictured in ways that make not only his physical but even his spiritual similarity to Parnok unmistakable. He was also small and rather frail. Nearly everyone who wrote of his appearance seems to have been struck by one aspect of it: he reminded most people of a bird. In fact, he seems to have reminded himself of a bird, for that is the way he pictures himself in the chapter from *Theodosia* called "The Old Woman's Bird."

He walked with an eccentric, bouncy little step. He was painfully shy, excessively prone to take offense, terrified of unboiled water, and suffered from such an inordinate fear of dentists that he preferred to let his teeth rot in his head rather than submit to treatment. (Hence, I presume, the transformation of the doctor of his models into a dentist, and also the acidly sardonic treatment of him—"I love dentists for their wide horizons. . . .")[33]

In dealing with the literary sources of this tale, I have, it will be observed, treated only one of the two plot lines, that of the lost clothes. There is nothing in the other works that will account for the central episode: Parnok's paradoxical heroism in trying to save a nameless, faceless victim from the fury of a lynch mob. For this, we must go to Mandelstam's own life.

The principal authority for the *details* of the following story is, I must warn the reader, Georgy Ivanov, whose writings about Mandelstam contain a remarkable amount of fancy along with fact (as I shall undertake to show in a later study).[34] But the anonymous informant to whom I referred above has assured me of the basic veracity of this particular story, and of other stories which tend to lend this one plausibility.

Shortly after the Revolution, Mandelstam—so Ivanov's story goes—was at a drinking bout attended by both Bolsheviks and Left Socialist Revolutionaries during the period of their collaboration. Mandelstam was there because it was a place where sweets, his nearly pathological appetite for which is well documented, could be obtained. One of the most prominent of the Left SR's, Blyumkin, the future assassin of the German ambassador, Count Mirbach, was engaged in the macabre task of filling in blank death warrants (already signed by Feliks Dzerzhinsky, the head of the Cheka) with the names of "counter-revolutionaries," which he was drunkenly and haphazardly transferring from other lists. Mandelstam was naturally terrified of the leather-jacketed Blyumkin and his grim task, but, after what one may suppose to have been agonies of resolution, he leaped from his seat, snatched the warrants from Blyumkin's hands, tore them to bits before the astounded gaze of everyone, and raced headlong from the room. Ivanov alleges that Mandelstam told him later that he had wandered about in the snow of that Moscow night, recited poetry, his own and others', smoked, and finally, at dawn, sat on a bench beside the river and wept.

When it finally became light he got up—here the story, already fantastic enough, takes a turn that puts one's powers of belief to the severest test—

and went into the Kremlin to the apartment of Kameneva, the sister of
Trotsky and the wife of Lev Borisovich Kamenev, one of the most power-
ful Bolsheviks of the Revolution, where he waited for that lady to wake up.
When she did, he was admitted, warmly received, told to wash up, given
tea, bundled into the overcoat of Lev Borisovich himself, and taken off by
Kameneva for an interview with the signer of the ill-fated death warrants,
Feliks Dzerzhinsky. Dzerzhinsky received them at once and, on hearing
Kameneva's account of what had happened, thanked the speechless poet
who stood before him and ordered into the telephone that Blyumkin be
arrested immediately in order to be tried before a summary court within
the hour. He then told his visitors that Blyumkin would be shot that same
day. Mandelstam, according to Ivanov, attempted to stutter out a plea that
Blyumkin be merely exiled and not executed, but Kameneva led him away
before he could get it out. She took him to his apartment, gave him some
money, and advised him to remain concealed for at least two days.

Blyumkin was arrested at noon. At two o'clock some well-wisher telephoned Mandelstam the information that Blyumkin was free and searching the entire city for him. At this juncture Mandelstam disappears from
our view as he did, mercifully, from that of Blyumkin.

Once more, whether or not the dramatic *details* of the foregoing were
fabricated by Ivanov, the fact remains that the essential outline of this story
has the independent corroboration of others whose testimony is more reliable. In addition to the anonymous support which I have already mentioned, I am told by my colleague Nina Berberova that Mandelstam's
amazing heroism was discussed in Berlin in 1922 by Ilya Ehrenburg and
Vladislav Khodasevich.

It seems to me that in this curious blend of literature and reality, the
episode of Parnok's attempt to forestall an unjust execution comes from
reality: it is a lightly concealed recapitulation of Mandelstam's moment of
reckless heroism, an event which must have impressed itself deeply within
his consciousness. It has no precedent in the literary sources, and while
not everything in the story must be assumed to mirror something in art or
life, it is true that we have found the source of most of the important elements, which must strengthen our confidence that we have found it in this
case, too.

It will be further strengthened by continuing the evidence of the autobiographical nature of *The Egyptian Stamp*. The entire tone of the story is
thoroughly Semitic. Parnok is a Jew. The "melancholy, bewhiskered si-

lence" in Jewish apartments is precisely the atmosphere described in Ivanov's picture of the gloomy meals in the apartment of Mandelstam's parents.[35] Practically every proper name encountered is Jewish: Shapiro,
Kaplan, Grusenberg, Babel, and so on. Unnamed characters are specified
as Jewish; the watchmaker, for instance, is Jewish and resembles Spinoza.
Memory is personified as a sick Jewish girl. The contralto of Mme. Mervis
flows like Jewish honey. The swarming, shifting, baffling scenes of *The
Egyptian Stamp* are, indeed, nothing less than that "Judaic chaos" which
Mandelstam portrays in *The Noise of Time*.

But I have called such references to his life "private," for they are revealed only by a special knowledge of Mandelstam's personal life and by
the most sedulous collation of his published works. He could hardly have
expected his audience to remark the significance of such things as the mention of Eylers's flower shop on Ofitserskaya. But that he did intend his
readers to be aware of the autobiographical elements in *The Egyptian
Stamp* is evidenced by a second, more explicit type of reference to himself. The narrator of the story is ubiquitously present, like the ironic and
whimsical narrator of Gogol's tales. He refers to his pen (the symbol of the
very process that is creating the story before our eyes), which he has some
trouble in subordinating to his will, and to the manuscript itself: "Destroy
your manuscript, but save whatever you have inscribed in the margin out
of boredom, out of helplessness and, as it were, in a dream."[36] The most
explicit implication of himself in the whole story is the already noted *cri de
coeur*: "Lord! Do not make me like Parnok! Give me the strength to distinguish myself from him." This altogether ironic entreaty is echoed in the
still more ironic exclamation: "What a pleasure for a narrator to switch
from the third person to the first!" The irony is that he has inserted first-
person narration throughout. Such inserted anecdotal reminiscences as
those about Shapiro, the sooty lamp, Geshka Rabinovich, Aunt Vera, the
little domestic dictionary are all, in the strictest sense, continuations of the
autobiography in *The Noise of Time*.

The Egyptian Stamp would thus appear to be, to adopt one of E. M.
Forster's phrases for the novel as a genre, "a queer blend of Poetry and
History"—not, though, just any poetry and history. Let us ask why this
particular poetry—the narrow, though dual, theme from Russian literature to which Mandelstam added his surrealistic extension—and why this
particular history, his own and that of his times. Surely the significance of
the novella is heightened by the date of its appearance, 1928, and by the

time in which it is set, the "Kerensky summer" of 1917. Like many other men of good will, Mandelstam believed at first in the inevitability of the political upheaval of the Revolution and welcomed it. With negligible exceptions, however, the Revolution left virtually no overt trace on his creative work, a fact which hostile critics never omitted from their charges against him. But one cannot read Mandelstam's poetry—even that written as early as 1918 (e.g., "Sumerki svobody" [The Twilight of Freedom])—without receiving an immediate and clear sense of his overwhelming sadness. I think one may interpret part of the meaning of *The Egyptian Stamp* as Mandelstam's intensely personal protest against what had become of the promise of the Revolution. The pathetic hero, Parnok-Mandelstam, heavy with the literary tradition of which he is emblematic, scurries over the face of his beloved Petersburg in search of more than his clothes: he seeks his very identity and the redemption of a promise that has failed. But this "concert-going" intellectual is at the mercy of a part of himself that has gained power over him, the strutting military officer, Captain Krzyżanowski. In an agony of terror before the frenzied mob and the "maniacal automobiles," he vainly seeks to get in touch with forces that might restore the legitimacy of the past, but he foresees, in a moving and prophetic passage, the very "desolation and abyss" that await him.

One senses in the story a rhythmic alternation between the present and the past. The foreground of present time is ringed about with images of horror, while the past is always recalled with affection and longing. The little inserted episode about the death of Angiolina Bosio (p. 157) can serve as a model of this. As the singer is dying, a fire brigade rushes past on the Nevsky with a terrible clangor and din; her guttering consciousness transforms this into the overture of *I due Foscari*, the opera of her London debut, and she lifts herself from her bed in an attempt to respond one last time to her cue. Parnok's inner musing in most cases amounts to just this: a mastery of the unthinkable present by wrapping it round with warm little visions and cultured musings on the past.

An analysis of the remarkable style of *The Egyptian Stamp* falls outside the scope of this brief study, in which my aim has been to deal with the sources of the tale, but at least one of the aspects of that style must claim our attention because of its immediate relevancy to what has just been said.

Mandelstam's novella might serve as a veritable textbook of one of the "devices" of literary art, which received its name and formulation in the writings of the Russian Formalist school of criticism: *ostranenie* (making strange). First labeled and analyzed by Viktor Shklovsky, this is a poetic technique for compelling the reader to perceive the familiar external world in a new way. Thus, as Shklovsky pointed out, when Tolstoy in *War and Peace* describes an evening at the opera in the naïve terms of a young girl's vision, without any of the aesthetic sophistication or technical terminology usually associated with such a scene, he renovates our very perception, fatigued by long familiarity, of what we thought we knew.[37]

But Mandelstam's use of *ostranenie* is not that of Tolstoy. Far from presenting the visual world in its primeval state, stripped bare of the accretions of sophisticated terminology, Mandelstam rather increases the complexity and enriches the image of whatever he portrays, "making it strange" by the startling juxtaposition of images from widely different, and usually opposed, areas of life. Thus bast mats are likened to the chasubles of priests; a drawbridge is perceived as a wooden, stone-bound book; the flames of blowtorches are white, shaggy roses; a personified Dawn breaks her colored pencils, which gape like the beaks of nestlings; a page of music is a revolution in an ancient German city. The incongruity of such metaphors, as Berkovsky noted, represents the very essence of Mandelstamian prose style. What Berkovsky did not point out, however, and what it is essential to realize in order to understand the significance of this device for the total meaning of *The Egyptian Stamp*, is that there is a *patterned* selection of the incongruous images that are juxtaposed. Incongruity can be achieved in any number of ways, but Mandelstam achieved it over and over again in only one way, the significance of which must therefore be marked.

To be more specific, in an overwhelming number of instances one component of the incongruity is drawn from a semantic area that can be characterized by the adjectives "massive," "lethal," "threatening," "hot," "revolting," while the other comes from the area of the "frail," "delicate," "cold," "defenseless," "beautiful." Here is a selection of certain contrasts to exemplify what is meant:

pistols fire into chinaware / cold, white flame / white blood / airy outline of Europe: blunt boot of Africa / steamship engines checked by roulades and tremolos / golden vultures rending a singer / tornado sweeping away a family like a little feather / the lemonade government / airplane drilling a hole in the azure / irons like battleships travel over the whipped cream of frilly clothes / mother-of-pearl filth / scarlatina tree in enema groves / chicken pistons of a locomotive / a railroad station for fat roses / Parnok is a lemon seed in a crevice of granite / starling houses in boiling pitch / palaces like silken cowls / the mummy of a flower / flame of torches lick the mirror / white bark, tender as a bridal veil / terror in a white cotton glove.

The omnipresence of this pattern of imagery in the story is clearly to be identified with the basic dichotomy which informs *The Egyptian Stamp*. Parnok—the frail, delicate, utterly defenseless hero—belongs to the same world of imagery as the bridal veil, silken cowl, flowers, mirrors, and green branch; while to the other world, the world of threat and danger, belong Captain Krzyżanowski, the locomotives, the flames, the tornado, the vultures, battleships, and filth.

If art lives, as the Formalist critic Boris Eichenbaum wrote, "by interweaving and contrasting its own traditions, by developing and refashioning them on the principles of contrast, parody, shifting and sliding,"[38] it is clear that the meaning of *The Egyptian Stamp* will be in the final analysis artistic.

Mandelstam was attempting to do what is done successfully only in the greatest art: to advance the frontier of vision by creating something new out of the resources of a strong tradition. It is our recognition not only of the familiar tradition in the helpless little figure of Parnok driven to the edge of madness in his search for identity and compassion, but also of what that tradition becomes, how it is transformed in its radically new statement, that lends profound significance to *The Egyptian Stamp*.

VII

As I have indicated, Mandelstam is a unique prose stylist. But since to present any writer in translation is to present him bereft of his style, perhaps some atonement can by made by a few comments on what impression this style makes in the original Russian.

He composed word by word, sentence by sentence, paragraph by paragraph. "Lapidary" as a qualifier of style has lately fallen into disrepute, but it is not one which the author of *Stone* could have rejected. Each of the elements of his prose was carefully polished, hefted for balance, weighed and tested before the next was undertaken. Most paragraphs give the distinct impression of a new start, a fresh adventure, something written in another key. Individual sentences have a grace, rhythm, and wit that render them unforgettable.

For example, the two sentences beginning at the words "Wandering musicians . . ." on page 87 are one in Mandelstam's Russian, and whatever the translation may convey, I ask the reader to believe that the original must have cost its author considerable pain. Nothing comes out this right by accident. The wretched little brass bands wander through Mandelstam's syntax as they did in life, now faster, now slower, now miraculously in time for a few measures, and ending with a fine, brave flourish: ". . . of the splendid Karolina." About his prose as about his poetry there is a peculiar material quality, an almost palpable substance and texture, and this plasticity of his language can often be observed when he renders, as in this sentence, physical movement. In the first paragraph of "The Harbor Master" one reads: "There beyond the salt marshes there was no longer any starch, there were no washerwomen, no glad subordination, and it would be impossible there to have that springy step, as after a swim, that permanent excitement: the blended sense of well-bought currency, of clear government service and, at the age of forty, the feeling of having passed one's exams." It is a typically Mandelstamian sentence in a number of ways, but it is especially so when the gait of the harbor master is described. In Russian, Mandelstam alliterates on *p*, spaces the ictus with an almost verse-like regularity, and the result is not so much talk about the bouncy step of Sarandinaki as it is a rhythmical imitation of it: "éta poxódka, uprúgaja, kak pósle kupán'ja. . . ." The first sentence of "Mazesa da Vinci" deals with horse-drawn vehicles clattering up the cobble-stoned streets of Theodosia and ends with a curious statement which can be translated literally "there were enough hooves for four blocks." But the actual sense of the statement is probably the secondary and not very important result of a little rhyming tune, which caught Mandelstam's fancy to the exclusion of everything else: ". . . kopýt xvatálo na četýre kvartála." It is no accident that, in his essay on Dante, Mandelstam apprehends the rhythmic cadences of the *Divine Comedy* first of all as a literary sublimate of the physical motion of walking:

"The question occurs to me—and quite seriously—how many shoe soles, how many ox-hide soles, how many sandals Alighieri wore out in the course of his poetic work, wandering about on the goat paths of Italy. The *Inferno* and especially the *Purgatorio* glorify the human gait, the measure and rhythm of walking, the foot and its shape. The step, linked to the breathing and saturated with thought: this Dante understands as the beginning of prosody. In order to indicate walking he uses a multitude of varied and charming turns of phrase."[39]

I think that it is in the light of the foregoing that one has to read one of the many asides on literature in *The Egyptian Stamp*:

"The railroad has changed the whole course, the whole structure, the whole rhythm of our prose. It has delivered it over to the senseless muttering of the French moujik out of *Anna Karenina*. Railroad prose, like the woman's purse of that ominous moujik, is full of the coupler's tools, delirious particles, grappling-iron prepositions, and belongs rather among things submitted in legal evidence: it is divorced from any concern with beauty and that which is beautifully rounded."

Does this not reveal one of the principal concerns of Mandelstam as a prosaist? We are to understand the pernicious effect of the railroad, I think, as referring not only to the mechanization of modern life, the distance we have come from simple walking, but to all that beefy, oily, hot massiveness that forever threatened Mandelstam's fragile equilibrium. His prose could never be submitted as legal evidence in any imaginable court, for its aim is beauty and to be beautifully rounded. Its only testimony is to that ineffable satisfaction that comes when sentences wave like flags and strut like peacocks and roll trippingly off the tongue.

A part of the impression of density and close-knittedness, of that plasticity which I am seeking to describe, must certainly come from the associative habits by which Mandelstam proceeded. Words beget words, images beget images. One constantly hears in the mind's ear verbal echoes of what has just preceded. Or, to change the figure, certain images and sounds seem to plop into his prose and propagate ever widening circles.

The second paragraph of "Sergey Ivanych" is dominated by the image of paper. First, men are said to fall into categories of bound paper: books, newspapers, and interlinear translations. Then Sergey Ivanych's cold-stuffed head is said to rustle with pages of flimsy. In Russian, flimsy is called "cigarette paper," and this mention of cigarette leads to a remark about Sergey Ivanych's cigarette, rolled out of illegal paper, and so on.

The fifth chapter of *The Egyptian Stamp* concludes with a rather hallucinatory cacophony of bits of conversation, the author's voice, and disembodied snatches of doggerel. In the midst of it occurs this paragraph: "The January calendar with its ballet goats, its model dairy of myriad worlds, its crackle of a deck of cards being unwrapped. . . ." The word "ballet" appears because this is in the context of talk about *Giselle*, but it is applied to goats because it refers to the saltant image of a goat, which is the tenth (or strictly speaking the eleventh) sign of the zodiac, Capricorn, covering the period from December 21 to January 20, and represented on the calendar. A few lines later these associations lead us to the final paragraph, opening with the words "The Petersburg cabby is a myth, a Capricorn. He should be put in the zodiac." In analyzing the means by which the cabby is somehow woven into the web of associations started at the January calendar, we have passed other complex and interlocking elements, such as the dairy summoned up by the goats, and, most remarkable of all, the crackle of the new deck of cards, an image produced not only by its obvious association with the first sheet of a new calendar, but also by the rich mythological links with card playing and even by the sharp wintry sound, as of the snow crust being broken, frequently referred to by Mandelstam.

To be convinced of how thoroughly conscious a device this is, one has only to turn once again to the essay on Dante. It is a characteristic of Mandelstam's criticism and another indication of its wholly personal nature that it often throws at least as much light on his own poetic practice as it does on the subject at hand. In discussing the flight made by Dante and Virgil on the back of the winged monster Geryon in Canto XVII of the *Inferno*, Mandelstam declares it to be a prime example of what he calls the "transformability of poetic material." By this phrase he means the process which we have just been examining: the subtle chain of association and implication which causes one image to give birth to another and that to a third, imparting to the whole a sense, however unconscious, of inevitable rightness and logic.

The impetus of association in Mandelstam's prose springs not only from the sense but also from the sound of the words. Rhyme is heuristic, as the great American linguist Edward Sapir once pointed out,[40] and it can hardly be doubted that Mandelstam was often led to new discoveries of theme and manner by nothing more than the reverberations which particular words set going in his inner ear. The following strange little passage may serve as an intensely concentrated instance of this: "Garbage in the squares . . . Simoom . . . Arabs . . . 'Semyon simpered to the proseminar.'" The word for garbage is *músor*. This has a near phonetic identity with *mussón*, which means "monsoon," the seasonal wind of the Indian Ocean and southern Asia which alters its direction according to the time of year. *Mussón* itself, however, is one of those temporary bridges of thought which Mandelstam was forever burning behind him. It does not appear in the text. What does appear is its influence in prompting the association with another wind, the *samúm* (simoom), the pestilential, sand-laden wind of the Arabian desert. Hence—*araby* (Arabs). The consonantal structure of *ṣamúm* is such that it produces in turn its near phonic relative, the proper name *Semyon*, and this cues the pyrotechnic punning of the final sentence: *Prosemenil Semën v proseminarij*. (See n. 15, p. 237.)

In the following passage, a resemblance in sound has again pointed the way for the sense to follow: "Pust' trudnejšie passaži Lista, razmaxivaja kostyljami, *volok*ut tuda i obratno požarnuju lestnicu. Rojal'—éto umnyj i dobryj komnatnyj zver' s *volok*nistym derevjannym mjasom. . . ." (Let the most difficult passages of Liszt, waving their crutches about, *drag* the fire ladder there and back. The grand piano is an intelligent and good-natured house animal with *fibrous*, wooden flesh. . . .) Between these two words there does exist a distant etymological relationship, but one can be confident that it was the sound alone which prompted this connection.

There are many examples of such association in the pages of Mandelstam. I will mention one more. In the first paragraph of "The Concerts of Hofmann and Kubelik" there is a sentence that goes "I can recall no other musical experiences . . . that might be compared with these *Lenten* orgies in the *white-columned* hall." In Russian, the italicized words read: "s étimi *velikopóstnymi* órgijami v *belokolónnom* zále." The words *velikopóstnyj* and *belokolónnyj* are, in the first place, of similar morphological construction, being compounds of modifier plus substantive plus adjectival suffix, and they are also in similar syntactic position. They are identical in stress pattern: – – – ′ –. Finally, and most importantly, these identities are supported by an alternation of vowel and consonant which causes the second word to be perceived by the reader as a kind of phonic shadow of the first. I am speaking, of course, of the pronunciation. In ordinary prose, such repetitions would be avoided, but Mandelstam's prose subsists on the flourish, the almost physical gesture of this and similar passages.

As a miniaturist and digressionary, Mandelstam stands in the tradition of Gogol. His poetic gift for condensation and precise observation can be seen in his skill at making a few lightning strokes of narrative shorthand render up a complete little story:

"Somewhere in the Ile de France: grape barrels, white roads, poplars— and a winegrower has set out with his daughters to go to their grandmother in Rouen. On his return he is to find everything 'scellé,' the presses and vats under an official seal, the doors and cellars closed with sealing wax.

The manager had tried to conceal from the excise tax collectors a few pails of new wine. They had caught him in the act. The family is ruined. Enormous fine. And, as a result, the stern laws of France made me the present of a governess."

This surefooted little paragraph moves without a single false step through a tangled growth of incident and scene and comes out—to our surprise—at the place where it had started: an account of the French governesses and maids whom he knew as a child.

Such narrative asides are frequent, and give to the pattern of Mandelstam's prose an effect of mosaic and montage. Mandelstam uses this technique not only in his larger composition but also in individual sentences. Thus the "chaos of Judaism" is pieced together for us in a mosaic sentence: "The chaos of Judaism showed through all the chinks of the stone-clad Petersburg apartment: in the threat of ruin, in the cap hanging in the room of the guest from the provinces, in the spiky script of the unread books of Genesis, thrown into the dust one shelf lower than Goethe and Schiller, in the shreds of the black-and-yellow ritual." And it is sharply contrasted with the Russian reality surrounding it in the next sentence, which turns out to be another mosaic: "The strong, ruddy, Russian year rolled through the calendar with decorated eggs, Christmas trees, steel skates from Finland, December, gaily bedecked Finnish cabdrivers, and the villa."

In the different employment of this technique we can see one of the principal differences between *The Noise of Time* and *The Egyptian Stamp*, for in the latter the process of disintegration has greatly advanced, the individual pieces of the mosaic tend to be smaller, less uniform, and more widely spaced. In fact, were it not for the hopelessly pejorative sense attaching to the word, the most appropriate term for this aspect of Mandelstam's style would be "decadence," for it is precisely the tendency toward decomposition that Paul Bourget saw as the fundamental element in the decadent style: "Un style de décadence est celui où l'unité du livre se décompose pour laisser la place à l'indépendance de la page, où la page se décompose pour laisser la place à l'indépendance de la phrase, et la phrase pour laisser la place à l'indépendance du mot."[41]

This is not at all to say that the totality of the impression is diffuse. However lavish the attention which Mandelstam devoted to individual words, phrases, and pages, these elements unite at last to leave the reader with a vision of reality that is single and whole. The experience transfigured in these chapters of lightly fictionalized memoirs and documentary fiction is of course not external, but how vividly is the inner life of an epoch, the *noise* heard in the mind, made to live in our own imaginations! There are many accounts of what took place in the external Petrograd of the Kerensky summer; Mandelstam's novella transmits the inner experience of the death of Russian culture. Relatives and bystanders may have that circumstantial and detailed knowledge of a man's death which is commonly accredited as real, but the dying man himself, as Emily Dickinson knew, is bemused by the buzz of a fly.

In Soviet parlance, of course, decadence is a standard term of abuse, and though the critic M. Vitenson did not use it, he had in mind something like Bourget's definition when he wrote the following sinister paragraph in 1934: "Criticism must realize that the artistic method of isolating the events represented, an isolation that consists of separating the part from the whole, such as is now practiced by certain writers (K. Vaginov, V. Shklovsky, O. Mandelstam), leads to a distortion of reality. This method . . . is a new tactic of the class enemy in literature."[42]

One of Mandelstam's essays has acquired, in consequence of his hard fate, a peculiar poignancy. This is the one entitled "O sobesednike" (On the Interlocutor), where he confronts a problem that is central to every writer: that of the audience. His conclusion is that a poet must out of necessity address himself to some future reader. It is impossible to be truly free if one is fettered by the knowledge that some particular, familiar, contemporary audience is listening. Only by addressing his unknown, merely presumptive reader in posterity is the poet able to achieve that continuous sense of surprise which Mandelstam saw as the essential ingredient of all true art. Though Mandelstam also wrote, in one of his later poems, "I will be inclosed in some alien speech," it is hardly likely that he could have expected to be speaking, after a lapse of some forty years, to the readers of this book in their own language. But it was in the same essay that he himself observed how providential is the force that drives the mariner's message in its glass bottle across no matter how wide a sea into the hands of the one who is destined to find it.

Introduction to the
Second Edition

I

After an interval of a mere score of years—not very long, given one's altered perspective on the passage of time—it is surprising to detect in the preceding pages so large a measure of furtiveness and speculation, such avid grasping at every straw of evidence. But it could scarcely be otherwise, for I was writing at a moment when the ban on mentioning so much as the name of the poet had only begun to be cautiously and sporadically lifted. In the journal publication of his memoirs in 1958 the writer Rozhdestvensky could only hint at the identity of his admired mentor, but by the time of their book publication in 1962 it was permissible to print the name: Mandelstam.

Or consider the note on the poet's wife (p. 27 above). Not even the editors of Mandelstam's *Collected Works*, who knew more of his life than anyone else in the West, had so much as heard of her existence when they began their work. One relied helplessly upon the mendacities of Georgy Ivanov or the more reliable but elliptical memoirs of Anna Akhmatova.

Today Nadezhda Yakovlevna Mandelstam (née Khazina; 1889–1980) is, if anything, more widely known throughout the world, and indisputably more widely read, than her husband. Her two books, *Hope Against Hope* (1970) and *Hope Abandoned* (1974), have been translated into every major language and hailed, especially the first, as transcendent masterpieces. Her relationship to Osip, both during his life and after it, was the picture of devotion, and her memoirs of their shared life and her subsequent life alone provide us with an account of his days that is no less rich, vivid, and detailed than it was unimaginable in the early 1960s. For all of her stubborn keeping within the shadow of her husband, history seems already to have accorded them equally the title of Russian writer.

II

Before describing further the changes in Mandelstam's posthumous existence, let me attend to one or two details of the preceding introduction that require emendation in the light of subsequent events.

I am happy to continue mute, in deference to Nadezhda, as to the identity of the individual alluded to on p. 14. Though he witnessed and wrote down the epigram on Stalin, she exonerates him from the role of informer (*Hope Against Hope*, pp. 146f).

The collection of Mandelstam's poems mentioned on the same page appeared in 1973, three years after the immense delay in its publication was held up to international ridicule in his widow's memoir.[1] It was edited by Nikolay Khardzhiev and introduced by Alexander Dymshits.[2] While its symbolic significance is great indeed, certain details of its publication have a forlornly familiar ring. The edition, for instance, was a risible 15,000, and well over half of that was sent abroad to earn hard currency. The balance vanished from the bookstores within minutes of having been put on sale, and today it is still rarer on the shelves of Soviet bibliophiles than the New York edition, however dangerous the possession of the latter might be.

Was Mandelstam never in Italy? So I write on p. 8, relying upon what I took to be the trustworthy evidence of Anna Akhmatova, though the person whom I cite (truthfully enough, since he said the same) was my fellow townsman in Princeton, Artur Lourié, who had known Mandelstam well. It is typical of those days that I was anxious to protect the still living Akhmatova by suppressing all evidence of my extensive interviews with her (quite illegal in Soviet terms in 1962).

Nadezhda confirms what, on the basis of the poetry alone, everyone had long supposed, that Mandelstam *had* visited Italy:

M. in fact went to Italy twice, in the days when he was a student at Heidelberg and the Sorbonne. But these lone trips, short and superficial (they only lasted a few weeks), left him with a feeling of frustration ("It's as though I'd never been there," he said once) (*Hope Against Hope*, p. 247).

A somewhat different account of Pasternak's famous telephone call from Stalin (p. 27) can now be found in Isaiah Berlin's memoirs *Personal Impressions* (New York: Viking Press, 1981), pp. 181–82; but the definitive report of that episode is in Nadezhda's memoir (*Hope*, p. 145ff). While the conversation itself is not significantly different in her version, the circumstances of the call are. The essential difference is that Stalin had already commuted Mandelstam's sentence, so that Pasternak's replies, whatever their exact text might have been, could have had no material effect on his friend's fate. The Kremlin, in the person of Stalin's secretary, informed Pasternak that there was no reason to keep the call confidential, which he was far from doing, for he spread the news so indefatigably that all Moscow knew of it within days. That, says Nadezhda, was the point. The miracle of Mandelstam's reprieve was no miracle unless it had admirers. The telephone call testified to the dictator's solicitude for poets and to his generous and forgiving nature.

For those interested in Mandelstam's life, Nadezhda's two volumes provide an immense enlargement of resource. As for his work, the enlargement of resource, if one counts pages alone, is even greater.

The 1965 version of this book depended upon the first collection of Mandelstam's work to have appeared since 1928. Edited by Gleb Struve and Boris Filippov, it was published in New York in 1955 by the Chekhov Publishing House and contained some 180 poems together with the autobiographical prose and the novella translated here. That small volume has now been replaced by a virtually complete *Collected Works*, edited by Struve and Filippov, which was originally planned as two volumes, then grew to three, and has now almost certainly concluded with a fourth, supplementary volume, while the first two volumes have each appeared in second, greatly enlarged editions. The complex details can be left to a note.[3]

III

It remains to say a few words, however impressionistically, about the changes that have occurred in the public perception of Mandelstam, keeping always in mind that one is speaking about that segment of the public that is conversant with Proust and Joyce.

In the late 1950s and early 1960s the name of Mandelstam was known in the West only to specialists in Russian literature, and by no means to all of them; nor could one take for granted that those who knew the name knew anything further about him. Today, if one may without undue levity leap to a contemporary fact on another level, the name *Osip Mandelstam*, especially the first, occurs regularly as a solution to clues of the *New York Times* crossword puzzle. Solvers are at least expected to be able to look up the answer, which seems to me as revealing in many ways as the dry statistics concerning the scholarly books and articles. There are soberer comparisons.

He is, for instance, accorded a respectable amount of space in Margaret Drabble's much-praised new edition of the *Oxford Companion to English Literature* (which, like its predecessors, includes foreign writers of sufficient prominence to be of interest even to readers chiefly concerned with literature in English). This is to say that Mandelstam enjoys among a cultivated body of readers something like the—dreadful but expressive word—status accorded Jorge Luis Borges, Heinrich Böll, Boris Pasternak, and similar writers of truly international reputation.

Unmentionable in his own country and once all but unmentioned abroad, Mandelstam is now virtually unavoidable. Studied, taught, anthologized, even imitated, he has found with amazing rapidity that "reader in the future" for whom he always conceived himself to be writing.[4]

A NOTE TO THE 1993 EDITION

In Moscow, in January, 1991, a hundred years after Mandelstam was born in Warsaw, and fifty-five after he died in Soviet captivity in one of the camps on the eastern rim of the USSR, I addressed an audience gathered to celebrate his Centenary. I was there by invitation of the Academy of Sciences of the USSR and stood on a platform in the large hall of the Union of Writers of the USSR. Not far away, there had been a ceremony to unveil a memorial bust of Osip Mandelstam on the street wall of the Dom Gertsena, the House of Herzen, where the poet and his wife had for a period been grudgingly housed. For musical accompaniment, a band had played the State Anthem of the USSR. During the celebration of Osip Mandelstam's Centenary, which lasted for days, and even moved on to the city that was shortly to resume its ancient name of Saint Petersburg, his portrait appeared in newspapers, in placards on the side of kiosks, even on commemorative postcards.

I found his last appeal for help (p.30) in a Russian newspaper in New York. The rough scrap on which it is written now lies a few hundred yards from here, in the Princeton University Library, along with the rest of the poet's archive, donated by Nadezhda Mandelstam. Princeton sent photocopies of parts of it to the State Literary Museum in Moscow, where an exhibit occupied two entire floors at the time of the Centenary. Important pieces of the exhibit were kindly supplied by the KGB.

Today, the USSR has ceased to exist.

The Noise of Time

I. Music in Pavlovsk

I remember well the remote and desolate years[1] of Russia, the decade of the Nineties, slowly slipping past in their unhealthy tranquillity and deep provincialism—a quiet backwater: the last refuge of a dying age. At morning tea there would be talk about Dreyfus, there were the names of Colonels Esterhazy and Picquart, vague disputes about some "Kreutzer Sonata" and, behind the high podium of the glass railroad station in Pavlovsk,[2] the change of conductors, which seemed to me a change of dynasties. Immobile newsboys on the corners, without cries, without movements, awkwardly rooted to the sidewalk—narrow droshkies with a little collapsible seat for a third passenger—and, all in all, I picture the Nineties in my mind in scenes scattered apart but inwardly bound together by the quiet misery and the painful, doomed provincialism of the life that was dying.

The ladies' wide bouffant sleeves, luxuriously puffed up at the shoulders and pulled tight at the elbows, and their wasp waists; the moustaches, imperials, carefully trimmed beards; men's faces and haircuts such as one could find now only in the portrait gallery of some run-down barbershop where there are pictures of the "Capoul cut" and the "coq."

What, in a word, were the Nineties? Ladies' bouffant sleeves and music in Pavlovsk: the balloons of the ladies' sleeves and all the rest revolve around the glass railroad station in Pavlovsk, and Galkin,[3] the conductor, stands at the center of the world.

In the middle of the Nineties all Petersburg streamed into Pavlovsk as into some Elysium. Locomotive whistles and railroad bells mingled with the patriotic cacophony of the *1812 Overture*, and a peculiar smell filled the huge station where Tchaikovsky and Rubinstein reigned. The humid air from the moldy parks, the odor of the decaying hotbeds and hothouse roses—this was blended with the heavy exhalations from the buffet, the acrid smoke of cigars, a burning smell from somewhere in the station, and the cosmetics of the crowd of many thousands.

As it turned out, we became "winter people" in Pavlovsk, that is, we lived the year round in our *dacha* in that old ladies' town, that Russian demi-Versailles, the city of court lackeys, widows of high officials, red-headed policemen, consumptive pedagogues (it was thought more salubrious to live in Pavlovsk), and grafters who had raked together enough money for a detached villa. Oh, those years—when Figner[4] was losing his voice and the double caricature of him passed around from hand to hand: on one side he was singing and on the other stopping up his ears. When carefully bound volumes of *The Field*, *Universal Virgin Soil*, and the *Foreign Literature Herald*, crushing book stands and card tables beneath their weight, were to constitute for a long time to come the basis of the libraries of the petty bourgeoisie.

There are nowadays no encyclopedias of science and technology like those bound monsters. But the *Universal Panoramas* and *Virgin Soils* were true fonts of knowledge of the world. I loved the "miscellany" about ostrich eggs, two-headed calves, and festivals in Bombay and Calcutta, and especially the pictures, the huge, full-page pictures: Malayan swimmers bound to boards and skimming through waves the size of a three-storied house; the mysterious experiment of a M. Fouqué: a metal sphere with an enormous pendulum skimming around it in the midst of a throng of serious gentlemen wearing neckties and pointed beards. I have a feeling that the grownups read the same thing as I, that is, mainly the supplements, the immense, burgeoning literature of the supplements to *The Field* and the rest. Our interests were, in general, identical, and at the age of seven or eight I was fully abreast of the century. More and more often I heard the expression *fin de siècle*, the end of the century, repeated with frivolous hauteur and with a sort of coquettish melancholy. It was as if, having acquitted Dreyfus and settled accounts with Devil's Island, that strange century had lost all meaning.

It is my impression that the men were exclusively absorbed day and night by the Dreyfus affair, while the women—that is, the ladies with the bouffant sleeves—hired and fired the servants, an activity that provided inexhaustible food for lively and delightful conversations.

On Nevsky Prospekt in the building of the Roman Catholic Church of St. Catherine there lived a respectable little old man named père Lagrange. One of the functions of His Reverence was to recommend poor young French girls who were seeking positions as governesses in respectable houses. Ladies came to consult père Lagrange straight from the Gostiny Dvor[5] with their parcels in their hands. He would come out in his decrepit way, wearing his shabby cassock, and affectionately banter the children with unctuous Catholic jokes, spiced with French wit. The recommendations of père Lagrange were taken very seriously.

The famous employment office for cooks, nursemaids, and governesses on Vladimir Street, to which I was rather often taken along, resembled a genuine slave market. Those who were looking for a place were led out in turn. The ladies sniffed them over and asked to see their references. The recommendation of some totally unknown lady, especially if it were the wife of a general, was regarded as sufficiently weighty; but it sometimes happened that the creature who had been led out for sale, having carefully examined the buyer, would make a rude noise right in her face and walk away. Then the intermediary in this slave traffic would come running up with apologies and talk about the decline of manners.

Once again I glance back at Pavlovsk and take morning strolls through all the walks and parquets of the station, where over a foot of confetti and serpentin has collected overnight—remnants of the storm which used to be called a "benefit performance." Kerosene lamps were being converted to electricity. The horsecars still ran along the streets of Petersburg behind stumbling nags out of *Don Quixote*. Along Goroxovaya as far as the Alexander Garden one could see the *karetka*, the most ancient form of public vehicle in Petersburg. Only on the Nevsky could one hear the clanging bells of the new express trams, painted yellow rather than the usual dirty wine color, and drawn by enormous, sleek horses.

II. *Childish Imperialism*

The equestrian statue of Nicholas I across from the State Council Building was guarded by a grenadier, mossy with age, who would march in a ceaseless circle around it, winter and summer, with a shaggy sheepskin cap pulled down over one eye. His headdress resembled a mitre and was practically as large as a whole sheep.

We children would strike up conversations with this decrepit sentry. It was a disappointment to learn that he was not, as we had thought, a veteran of 1812. But he informed us that the other old codgers like himself were sentries, the last to have served under Nicholas, and that in the entire company there remained only about five or six of them.

The entrances to the Summer Garden—both the one near the river, where the railing and the chapel are located, and the one across from the Engineers' Palace[6]—were guarded by cavalry sergeant majors bedecked with medals. They determined whether a person was suitably dressed. Men in Russian boots they drove away, nor would they admit persons in caps or in the attire of the lower middle class. The manners of the children in the Summer Garden were extremely ceremonious. After a whispered consultation with a governess or nurse, some bare-legged child would approach the park bench and, after a bow or a curtsey, would pipe, "Little girl (or little boy—such was the official form of address), would you not like to play 'London Bridge' or 'Hide and Seek'?"

After such a beginning, you can imagine how merry the game was. I never played, and the very etiquette of introductions struck me as forced.

As it turned out, I spent my early childhood in Petersburg under the sign of the most authentic militarism, but it was really not my fault: it was the fault of my nurse and of the Petersburg street of that period.

We would take our walks along the deserted stretch of Bolshaya Morskaya Street, where one finds the red Lutheran church and the wood-paved embankment of the Moyka.

Thus we imperceptibly approached the Kryukov Canal, the Dutch Petersburg of ships' berths and Neptune arches with marine emblems, and the barracks of the crew of marine guardsmen.

Here on the green roadway over which no vehicles ever passed, the marine guards held their drills, and the brass kettledrums and the drums shook the waters of the quiet canal. I liked the physical selection of the men—they were all taller than the normal height—and my nurse completely shared my tastes. Thus we selected one sailor, the "black mustache," as we called him, came regularly to look at him personally, and, when we had picked him out of the formation, would not take our eyes off him till the end of the exercises. And I say now, without a moment's hesitation, that at the age of seven or eight all this—the whole massif of Petersburg, the granite and wood-paved quarters, all the gentle heart of the city with its overflow of squares, its shaggy parks, its islands of monuments, the caryatids of the Hermitage, the mysterious Millionnaya Street, where there were no passers-by and where only one small grocery store had wormed itself in among the marble, but especially the General Staff Arch, the Senate Square, and all Dutch Petersburg I regarded as something sacred and festive.

I do not know with what imaginary inhabitants the fancy of young Romans used to people their capital, but as for me, I filled these fortresses and squares with a sort of unthinkably ideal, universal, military parade.

It is characteristic that I did not for a moment believe in the Kazan Cathedral, for all the tobacco twilight of its vaults or its forest of bullet-riddled banners.[7]

That place was also unusual, but of it more later. The stone horseshoe of the colonnade and the wide, paved court with its guard chains were meant for riots, and for my imagination this place had no less interest and significance than the May Parade on the Field of Mars. What will the weather be like? Won't they put it off? Will it even take place this year? But they have already laid out boards and planks along the Summer Canal, the carpenters are already hammering on the Field of Mars, and the grandstands are already swelling up like mountains, dust is roiling over the mock attacks, and the infantrymen, spaced apart like stakes in the ground, wave their banners. The platform was erected in three days. Such rapid construction seemed to me miraculous, and the dimensions of it overwhelmed me like the Coliseum. I visited the site daily, marveled at the graceful ease of the work, ran up and down the stairs feeling as if I were on the stage, a participant in the next day's splendid spectacle, and envied the very boards themselves, which would probably see the attack.

If one could only hide in the Summer Garden unnoticed! There would be the Babylonian uproar of hundreds of orchestras, the field, sprouting bayonets like ears of corn, the acreage patterns of the formations of foot and horse, as if they were not regiments but standing fields of buckwheat, rye, oats, and barley. The covert movement between the regiments along the interior clearings in the ranks. And more—the silver trumpets, the bugles, the bedlam of shouts, drums, and kettledrums. To see the attack of the cavalry!

It always seemed to me that in Petersburg something very splendid and solemn was absolutely bound to happen.

I was in ecstasy when the lanterns were draped in black crepe and black ribbons were strung up on the occasion of the death of the heir to the throne. The mounting of the guard at the Alexander Column, the funeral pomps of some general, the "progress"—such were my daily diversions.

"Progress" was the name then used for the trips of the Czar and his family through the streets. I acquired great proficiency in learning of these events beforehand. At the Anichkov Palace at a certain time members of the palace constabulary would come crawling out like red mustachioed cockroaches: "Nothing special, ladies and gentlemen. Move along, please. . . ." But the house porters were already scattering yellow sand with their wooden scoops, the constables' mustaches had been dyed, and along Karavannaya and Konyushennaya policemen had been spilled like peas.

It amused me to overwhelm the guards with questions about who was going to come out, and when, but they never dared to tell. I must say that the fleeting glimpse of the emblazoned carriage with the little golden birds on the lanterns or of the English sleigh drawn by trotters covered with nets always left me disappointed. The game of the "progress" seemed to me, nevertheless, rather fun.

The Petersburg street awakened in me a craving for spectacle, and the very architecture of the city inspired me with a kind of childish imperialism: I was delirious over the cuirasses of the Royal Horse Guard and the Roman helmets of the Cavalry Guard, the silver trumpets of the Preobrazhensky band; and after the May Parade, my favorite distraction was the regimental festival of the Royal Horse Guard on Lady Day.

I also remember the launching of the battleship *Oslyabya*, its sliding like some monstrous sea caterpillar down into the water, the cranes, and the ribs of the covered slip.

All this mass of militarism and even a kind of police aesthetics may very well have been proper to some son of a corps commander with the appropriate family traditions, but it was completely out of keeping with the kitchen fumes of a middle-class apartment, with father's study, heavy with the odor of leathers, kidskin and calfskin, or with Jewish conversations about business.

III. *Riots and French Governesses*

It was always known in advance when the students would riot in front of the Kazan Cathedral. Every family had its student informer. The result

was that these riots were attended—at a respectful distance, to be sure—
by a great mass of people: children with their nurses, mamas and aunts
who had been unable to keep their insurrectionaries at home, old civil
servants, and simply people who happened to be walking idly about. On
the day appointed for the riot the sidewalks of the Nevsky teemed with a
dense throng of spectators all the way from Sadovaya to the Anichkov
Bridge. This mob was afraid to approach the Kazan Cathedral. The police
were hidden in courtyards—for example, in the courtyard of the Roman
Catholic Church of St. Catherine. The Kazan Square itself was relatively
empty; across it would pass small knots of students and actual working
men, the latter being pointed at with fingers. Suddenly, from the direction
of the Kazan Square, there would burst forth a protracted, crescendoing
yell, something on the order of a steady "oo" or "ee," which became an
ominous howling, growing nearer and nearer. At that moment the spectators scattered and the crowd was crushed back by the horses. "Cossacks!
Cossacks!"—the cry spread like lightning, faster than the Cossacks themselves. The "riot" itself, strictly speaking, was cordoned off and led away
to the Mikhaylovsky Manège, and the Nevsky emptied as if it had been
swept with a broom.

My first conscious, sharp perceptions were of gloomy crowds of people
in the streets. I was exactly three years old. It was 1894 and I had been
brought from Pavlovsk to Petersburg for the purpose of seeing the funeral
of Alexander III. A furnished room had been rented on the fourth floor of
some house on the Nevsky, opposite Nikolaevskaya Street. On the evening
of the day before the ceremonies, having crawled up on the windowsill and
seen the crowd-darkened street, I asked, "When will they start?" and was
told, "tomorrow." It profoundly impressed me that all these throngs of
people were spending the entire night in the street. Even death first appeared to me in a totally unnatural, elegant, and festive guise. Once I was
walking with Mother and my nurse on the street along the Moyka past the
chocolate building of the Italian Embassy. Suddenly the doors there were
wide open and everyone was freely admitted inside, and there issued forth
a smell of resin, incense, and something sweet and pleasant. Black velvet
was draped over the entrance and the walls, which glistened with silver
and tropical plants. Very high on his bier lay the embalmed Italian ambassador. What had all that to do with me? I do not know, but these impressions were strong and clear and I cherish them to this day.

The ordinary life of the city was poor and monotonous. Every day at
about five o'clock there was promenading on the Bolshaya Morskaya from

Gorokhovaya Street to the General Staff Arch. All the foppish and idle elements of the city then proceeded slowly back and forth along the sidewalks bowing and exchanging smiles: the ring of spurs, the languages of England and France—a living exhibit from the English Store and the Jockey Club. Hither also the nursemaids and governesses, young-looking Frenchwomen, brought the children, in order to sigh and compare it all to the Champs Élysées.

So many French governesses were hired to look after me that all their features have become blurred and resolved into one general patch of portraiture. It is my opinion that the little songs, models of penmanship, anthologies, and conjugations had ended by driving all these French and Swiss women themselves into an infantile state. At the center of their worldview, distorted by anthologies, stood the figure of the great emperor Napoleon and the War of 1812; after that came Joan of Arc (one Swiss girl, however, turned out to be a Calvinist), and no matter how often I tried, curious as I was, to learn something from them about France, I learned nothing at all, save that it was beautiful. The French governesses placed great value upon the art of speaking fast and abundantly and the Swiss upon the learning of little songs, among which the chief favorite was the "Song of Malbrouk." These poor girls were completely imbued with the cult of great men—Hugo, Lamartine, Napoleon, and Molière. On Sundays they had permission to go to mass. They were not allowed to have acquaintances.

Somewhere in the Ile de France: grape barrels, white roads, poplars— and a winegrower has set out with his daughters to go to their grandmother in Rouen. On his return he is to find everything "scellé," the presses and vats under an official seal, the doors and cellars closed with sealing wax. The manager had tried to conceal from the excise tax collectors a few pails of new wine. They had caught him in the act. The family is ruined. Enormous fine. And, as a result, the stern laws of France make me the present of a governess.

But what had I to do with the Guards' festivals, the monotonous prettiness of the host of the infantry and its steeds, the stone-faced battalions flowing with hollow tread down the Millionnaya, gray with marble and granite?

All the elegant mirage of Petersburg was merely a dream, a brilliant covering thrown over the abyss, while round about there sprawled the chaos of Judaism—not a motherland, not a house, not a hearth, but precisely a chaos, the unknown womb world whence I had issued, which I feared, about which I made vague conjectures and fled, always fled.

The chaos of Judaism showed through all the chinks of the stone-clad Petersburg apartment: in the threat of ruin, in the cap hanging in the room of the guest from the provinces, in the spiky script of the unread books of Genesis, thrown into the dust one shelf lower than Goethe and Schiller, in the shreds of the black-and-yellow ritual.

The strong, ruddy, Russian year rolled through the calendar with decorated eggs, Christmas trees, steel skates from Finland, December, gaily bedecked Finnish cabdrivers, and the villa. But mixed up with all this there was a phantom—the new year in September—and the strange, cheerless holidays, grating upon the ear with their harsh names: Rosh Hashanah and Yom Kippur.

IV. *The Bookcase*

As a little bit of musk fills an entire house, so the least influence of Judaism overflows all of one's life. Oh, what a strong smell that is! Could I possibly not have noticed that in real Jewish houses there was a different smell from that in Aryan houses? And it was not only the kitchen that smelled so, but the people, things, and clothing. To this day I remember how that sweetish Jewish smell swaddled me in the wooden house of my grandfather and grandmother on Klyuchevaya Street in German Riga. My father's study at home was itself unlike the granite paradise of my sedate strolls; it led one away into an alien world, and the mixture of its furnishings, the selection of the objects in it were strongly knitted together in my consciousness. First of all, there was the handmade oak armchair bearing the image of a balalaika and a gauntlet and, on its arched back, the motto "Slow but Sure"—a tribute to the pseudo-Russian style of Alexander III. Then there was a Turkish divan completely overwhelmed with ledgers, whose pages of flimsy paper were covered over with the minuscule gothic hand of German commercial correspondence. At first I thought my father's occupation consisted of printing his flimsy letters by cranking the handle of the copying machine. To this day I conceive of the smell of the yoke of labor as the penetrating smell of tanned leather; and the webbed kidskins thrown about the floor, and the pudgy chamois skins with excrescences like living fingers—all this, plus the bourgeois writing table with its little marble calendar, swims in a tobacco haze and is seasoned with the smells of leather. And in the drab surroundings of this mercantile room there was a little glass-front bookcase behind a curtain of green taffeta. It is about that bookcase that I should like to speak now. The bookcase of early childhood is a man's companion for life. The arrangement of its shelves, the choice of books, the colors of the spines are for him the color, height, and arrangement of world literature itself. And as for books which were not included in that first bookcase—they were never to force their way into the universe of world literature. Every book in the first bookcase is, willy-nilly, a classic, and not one of them can ever be expelled.

There was nothing haphazard in the way that strange little library had been deposited, like a geological bed, over several decades. The paternal and maternal elements in it were not mixed, but existed separately, and a cross section of the strata showed the history of the spiritual efforts of the entire family, as well as the inoculation of it with alien blood.

I always remember the lower shelf as chaotic: the books were not standing upright side by side but lay like ruins: reddish five-volume works with ragged covers, a Russian history of the Jews written in the clumsy, shy language of a Russian-speaking Talmudist. This was the Judaic chaos thrown into the dust. This was the level to which my Hebrew primer, which I never mastered, quickly fell. In a fit of national contrition they even tried hiring a real Jewish teacher for me. He came from his Torgovaya Street and taught without taking off his cap, which made me feel awkward. His correct Russian sounded false. The Hebrew primer was illustrated with pictures which showed one and the same little boy, wearing a visored cap and with a melancholy adult face, in all sorts of situations—with a cat, a book, a pail, a watering can. I saw nothing of myself in that boy and with all my being revolted against the book and the subject. There was one striking thing in that teacher, although it sounded unnatural: the feeling of national Jewish pride. He talked about Jews as the French governess talked about Hugo and Napoleon. But I knew that he hid his pride when he went out into the street, and therefore did not believe him.

Above these Jewish ruins there began the orderly arrangement of books; those were the Germans—Schiller, Goethe, Kerner, and Shakespeare in German—in the old Leipzig and Tübingen editions, chubby

little butterballs in stamped claret-colored bindings with a fine print cal-
culated for the sharp vision of youth and with soft engravings done in a
rather classical style: women with their hair down wring their hands, the
lamp is always shown as an oil lamp, the horsemen have high foreheads,
and the vignettes are clusters of grapes. All this was my father fighting his
way as an autodidact into the German world out of the Talmudic wilds.

Still higher were my mother's Russian books—Pushkin in Isakov's
1876 edition. I still think that was a splendid edition and like it more than
the one published by the Academy. It contained nothing superfluous, the
type was elegantly arranged, the columns of poetry flowed freely as soldiers in flying battalions, and leading them like generals were the clear
reasonable years of composition, right up to 1837. The color of Pushkin?
Every color is accidental—what color could one choose for the purl of
speech? Oh, that idiotic alphabet of colors by Rimbaud . . . !

My Isakov Pushkin was in a cassock of no color at all, in a binding of
schoolboy calico, in a brownish black, faded cassock with a tinge of earth
and sand; he feared neither spots, nor ink, nor fire, nor kerosene. For a
quarter of a century the black-and-sand cassock had lovingly absorbed
everything into itself—so vividly do I sense the everyday spiritual beauty,
the almost physical charm of my mother's Pushkin. It bore an inscription
in reddish ink: "For her diligence as a pupil of the Third Form." The
Isakov Pushkin is bound up with stories about ideal schoolmasters and
schoolmistresses, ruddy with consumption and shod in ragged boots: the
1880s in Vilno. The word "intellectual" was pronounced by my mother,
and especially by my grandmother, with pride. Lermontov had a greenish
blue binding with something military about it: not for nothing was he a
hussar. He never seemed to me to be the brother or relative of Pushkin.
Goethe and Schiller I regarded as twins, but in Pushkin and Lermontov I
recognized two men alien to each other and consciously kept them apart.
After 1837, blood and poetry both rang differently in the ears.

And how about Turgenev and Dostoevsky? Those were supplements
to *The Field*. In external aspect they were identical, like brothers. They
were bound in boards covered with a thin leather. Prohibition lay upon
Dostoevsky like a gravestone: it was said that he was "heavy." Turgenev
was altogether sanctioned and open, with his Baden-Baden, *Spring Tor-
rents*, and languid conversations. But I knew that the tranquil life in Turgenev had already vanished and was nowhere to be found.

Would you like to know the key to the epoch, the book that had become positively white-hot from handling, the book that would not under any circumstances agree to die, that lay like someone alive in the narrow coffin of the 1890s, the book whose leaves, perhaps from reading or from having been left in the sun on a bench at someone's *dacha*, had yellowed prematurely, whose first page bore the features of a youth with an inspired arrangement of the hair, features that became an icon? Gazing into the face of the young Nadson, I am astonished by the genuine fieriness of those features and at the same time by their total inexpressiveness, their almost wooden simplicity. Does this not describe the whole book? Does it not describe the era? Send him off to Nice, show him the Mediterranean: he will go on singing his ideal and his suffering generation—with the possible addition of a seagull and the crest of a wave. Do not laugh at Nadsonism: it is the enigma of Russian culture and the essentially uncomprehended sound of it, for we do not understand and hear as they understood and heard. Who is he, this wooden monk with the inexpressive features of an eternal youth, this inspired idol of students—especially of students, that is to say, the elite of certain decades—this prophet of school recitals? How many times, knowing already that Nadson was bad, have I still reread his book and, putting away the poetic haughtiness of the present and pity for the ignorance of this youth in the past, tried to hear it as it sounded to his generation. How greatly was I aided in this by the diaries and letters of Nadson: the continual literary drudgery, the candles, applause, the burning faces; the tight ring of his generation and, in the center, the altar—the lecturer's table and its glass of water. Like summer insects above the hot globe of a lamp, an entire generation was carbonized and scorched by the flame of literary celebrations with garlands of allegorical roses, enormous assemblies which bore the character of a cult and expiatory offering for the generation. Hither came those who wished to share the fate of their generation right up to the point of ruin—the haughty ones remained to one side with Tyutchev and Fet. Actually, all that was serious in Russian literature turned away from this consumptive generation with its ideal and its Baal. What was left to it? Paper roses, the candles of the school recitals, and the barcaroles of Rubinstein. The 1880s in Vilno as mother recalled them. It was everywhere the same: sixteen-year-old girls tried to read John Stuart Mill and at public recitals one could see luminous personalities who—with a certain dense admixture of pedal, a fainting away on the *piano* passage, and blank features—played the latest things of the leonine Anton. But what actually happened was that the intelligentsia, with Buckle and Rubinstein and led by the luminous personalities—who in their beatific idiocy had completely lost the way—resolutely turned to the practice of self-burning. Like high tar-coated torches the adherents of the People's Will Party burned for all the people to see, with Sofia Perovskaya and Zhelyabov,[8] and all of them, all of provincial Russia and all of the students, smouldered in sympathy: not one single green leaf was to be left.

What a meager life, what poor letters, what unfunny jokes and parodies! I used to have pointed out to me in the family album a daguerreotype of my uncle Misha, a melancholiac with swollen and unhealthy features, and it was explained that he had not merely gone out of his mind—he had "burnt up," as that generation put it. They said the same of Garshin, and many were the deaths reduced to that single ritual.

Semyon Afanasich Vengerov, a relative of mine on my mother's side (the family in Vilno and school memories), understood nothing in Russian literature and studied Pushkin as a professional task, but "one thing" he understood. His "one thing" was: the heroic character of Russian literature. He was a fine one with his heroic character when he would drag slowly along Zagorodny Prospekt from his apartment to the card catalog, hanging on the elbow of his ageing wife and smirking into his dense ant beard!

V. *Finland*

The little red bookcase with the green curtain and the armchair with the motto "Slow but Sure" often moved from apartment to apartment. They stood on Maximilian Lane—where, at the end of the arrow-straight Voznesensky Prospekt, one could see the galloping statue of Nicholas—and above Eylers's Flower Shop on Ofitserskaya Street not far from *A Life for the Tsar*, and on Zagorodny Prospekt. In the winter, at Christmastime, there was Finland, Vyborg, and in the summer the *dacha* at Terioki. At Terioki there was sand, juniper, little plank walkways, kennel-like bathing houses[9] with carved hearts (and notches to show the number of baths), and our own domestic foreigners, so dear to the heart of the Petersburger, the cold Finns, lovers of the tarred barrels lighted on the Eve of St. John and the trained bears on the lawn of the Narodny Dom,[10] the "unshaven and greeneyed" Finns, as Blok called them. From Vladimir Solovyov to Blok, pre-revolutionary Petersburg was redolent of Finland, sifting its sand from one hand to the other, rubbing its granite forehead with the light Finnish snow, and listening in its deep delirium to the sleighbells of the squat Finnish horses. I always had a troubled intimation of the special meaning that, for a Petersburger, resided in Finland: people drove there in order to think to the end what could not be thought to the end in Petersburg, pulling the low snowy sky down to their very eyebrows and dozing off in small hotels where the water in the pitcher was icy. And I loved the country where all the women are immaculate laundresses and the drivers of the horsecabs resemble senators.

In the summertime at Terioki there were entertainments for the children. How stupiḍ those were, when one thinks of it! Small boys from the Gymnasium and military school in their tight-fitting jackets, bowing and scraping before full-grown maidens, would dance the *pas de quatre* and the *pas de patineur*, the salon dances of the Nineties, with constrained, expressionless movements. Then came games: a sack race with an egg—that is, with the legs tied up in a sack and with a raw egg balanced on a wooden spoon. In the lottery it was always a cow that was raffled off. What a joy that was for the French governesses! This was the only place where they twittered like heavenly birds and grew young again in spirit, but the children were lost and confused in such strange amusements.

We would go to Vyborg to visit the Sharikovs, a family of merchants who had lived there for a long time. They were descended from the Jewish soldiers in the army of Nicholas, a fact that permitted them to reside legally in Finland, otherwise free of Jews. The Sharikovs—Shariki in Finnish—operated a large shop where they sold Finnish wares—*Sekkatawaaran-kauppa*—and where there was an odor of resin, leather, and bread—the special smell of a Finnish shop—and many nails and groats. The Sharikovs lived in a massive wooden house with oak furniture. Our host was especially proud of a sideboard with carvings showing the history of Ivan the Terrible. They ate so much that one could hardly rise from the table. Old Sharikov swam in fat, like Buddha, and spoke with a Finnish accent. One of his daughters—a plain, dark girl—sat behind the counter, and the other three, who were beautiful, ran away in turn with officers of the local garrison. The house smelled of cigars and money. Mme. Sharikov was uneducated and kind, and her guests, army officers, were lovers of punch and good sleighs and all of them card players to the marrow of their bones.

After the thinnish atmosphere of Petersburg I rejoiced in this stable, oaken family. I landed willy-nilly in the very thick of the frosty winter flirtations of the high-bosomed Vyborg beauties. Somewhere in Fazer's pastry shop with its vanilla wafers and its chocolate, and behind the blue windows the crunch of sleigh runners and the mad jingle of the bells: having been shaken right out of a fast, narrow sleigh and into the warm steam of a rich Finnish coffeehouse, I witnessed the immodest argument of a desperate young lady and an army lieutenant over whether or not he was wearing a corset, and I remember how he swore by God and proposed that she feel his ribs through his tunic. Swift sleighs, punch, cards, a Swedish toy fortress of cardboard, the Swedish language, military music—the Vyborg intoxication was dispersed by the little blue flame on the punch. The Hotel Belvedere, where the First Duma later held its meetings, was famed for its cleanliness and for its snow-cold, blindingly white bed linen. Everything was here—a foreign air and Swedish coziness. The stubborn and crafty little town with its coffee mills, rocking chairs, worsted wool carpets, and Bible verses carved in the headboard of every bed bore the yoke of Russian militarism like the scourge of God. But in every house there hung, in a frame of mourning black, a picture of a bareheaded girl named Suomi, above whose head there bristled the angry two-headed eagle while she fiercely clasped to her breast a book with the label LEX—the Law.

VI. *The Judaic Chaos*

There once arrived at our house a person completely unknown to us, an unmarried lady of about forty, in a little red hat and with a sharp chin and angry dark eyes. On the strength of her having come from the small town of Shavli, she demanded that we find her a husband in Petersburg. She spent a week in the house before we managed to send her packing. From time to time wandering authors would turn up—bearded and long-skirted people, Talmudic philosophers, peddlers of their own printed aphorisms and dicta. They would leave us autographed copies and complain of being tormented by their evil wives. Once or twice in my life I was taken to a synagogue as if to a concert. There was a long wait to get in—one practically had to buy tickets from scalpers—and all that I saw and heard there caused me to return home in a heavy stupor. There is a Jewish quarter[11] in Petersburg: it begins just behind the Mariinsky Theater, where the ticket scalpers freeze, beyond the prison angel of the Litovsky Castle, which was burned down in the Revolution. There on Torgovaya Street one sees Jewish shop signs with pictures of a bull and a cow, women with an abundance of false hair showing under their kerchiefs, and, mincing along in overcoats reaching down to the ground, old men full of experience and philoprogeneity. The synagogue with its conical caps and onion domes loses itself like some elegant exotic fig tree amongst the shabby buildings. Velveteen berets with pompoms, attendants and choristers on the point of physical exhaustion, clusters of seven-branched candelabra, tall velvet headdresses. The Jewish ship, with its sonorous alto choirs and the astonishing voices of its children, lays on all sail, split as it is by some ancient storm into male and female halves. Having blundered into the women's balcony, I edged along stealthily as a thief, hiding behind rafters. The Cantor, like Samson, collapsed the leonine building, he was answered by the velvet headdress, and the awesome equilibrium of vowels and consonants in the impeccably enunciated words imparted to the chants an invincible power. But how offensive was the crude speech of the rabbi—though it was not ungrammatical; how vulgar when he uttered the words "His Imperial Highness," how utterly vulgar all that he said! And all of a sudden two top-hatted gentlemen, splendidly dressed and glossy with wealth, with the refined movements of men of the world, touch the heavy book, step out of the circle and on behalf of everyone, with the authorization and commission of everyone, perform some honorary ritual, the principal thing in the ceremony. Who is that? Baron Ginzberg. And that? Varshavsky.

In my childhood I absolutely never heard Yiddish; only later did I hear an abundance of that melodious, always surprised and disappointed, interrogative language with its sharp accents on the weakly stressed syllables. The speech of the father and the speech of the mother—does not our language feed throughout all its long life on the confluence of these two, do they not compose its character? The speech of my mother was clear and sonorous without the least foreign admixture, with rather wide and too open vowels—the literary Great Russian language. Her vocabulary was poor and restricted, the locutions were trite, but it was a language, it had roots and confidence. Mother loved to speak and took joy in the roots and sounds of her Great Russian speech, impoverished by intellectual clichés. Was she not the first of her whole family to achieve pure and clear Russian sounds? My father had absolutely no language; his speech was tongue-tie and languagelessness. The Russian speech of a Polish Jew? No. The speech of a German Jew? No again. Perhaps a special Courland accent? I never heard such. A completely abstract, counterfeit language, the ornate and twisted speech of an autodidact, where normal words are intertwined with the ancient philosophical terms of Herder, Leibniz, and Spinoza, the capricious syntax of a Talmudist, the artificial, not always finished sentence: it was anything in the world, but not a language, neither Russian nor German.

In essence, my father transferred me to a totally alien century and distant, although completely un-Jewish, atmosphere. It was, if you will, the purest eighteenth or even seventeenth century of an enlightened ghetto somewhere in Hamburg. Religious interests had been eliminated completely. The philosophy of the Enlightenment was transformed into intricate Talmudist pantheism. Somewhere in the vicinity Spinoza is breeding his spiders in a jar. One has a presentiment of Rousseau and his natural man. Everything fantastically abstract, intricate, and schematic. A fourteen-year-old boy, whom they had been training as a rabbi and had forbidden to read worldly books, runs off to Berlin and ends up in a higher Talmudic school, where there had gathered a number of such stubborn, rational youths, who had aspired in godforsaken backwaters to be geniuses. Instead of the Talmud, he reads Schiller—and mark you, he reads it as a new book. Having held out here for a while, he falls out of this strange university back into the seething world of the seventies in order to remember the conspiratorial dairy shop on Karavannaya whence a bomb was tossed under Alexander, and in a glove-making shop and in a leather factory he expounds to the paunchy and astonished customers the philosophical ideals of the eighteenth century.

When I was taken to Riga, to my Riga grandparents, I resisted and nearly cried. It seemed to me that I was being taken to the native country of my father's incomprehensible philosophy. The artillery of band boxes, baskets with padlocks, and all the chubby, awkward family baggage started upon its journey. The winter things were salted with coarse grains of naphthalene. The armchairs stood about like white horses in their stable blankets of slipcovers. The preparations for the trip to the Riga coast seemed to me no fun. I used to collect nails at that time—the absurdest of collecting whimsies. I would run my hands through piles of nails like the Covetous Knight[12] and rejoice at the growth of my spiky wealth. Then they would take my nails away to be used in packing.

The trip was alarming. At night in Dorpat some sort of *Vereins* returning from a large songfest would storm the dimly lit carriage with their loud Estonian songs. The Estonians would stamp their feet and throw themselves against the door. It was very frightening.

My grandfather, a blue-eyed old man in a skullcap which covered half his forehead and with the serious and rather dignified features to be seen in very respected Jews, would smile, rejoice, and try to be affectionate—but did not know how. Then his dense eyebrows would draw together. When he wanted to take me in his arms I almost burst into tears. My kindly grandmother, wearing a black wig over her gray hair and a housecoat with little yellow flowers, walked with tiny little steps over the creaking floorboards and was forever wanting people to eat something.

She kept asking, "Pokushali? Pokushali?" (Have you eaten?)—the only Russian word that she knew. But I did not like the old people's spicy dainties, with their bitter almond taste. My parents left to go to the city. My somber grandfather and sad, bustling grandmother made an effort to distract me with conversation and ruffled their feathers like offended old birds. I tried to explain to them that I wanted to go to mama—they didn't understand. Then I represented my desire to leave by putting my index and middle figures through the motions of walking on the table.

Suddenly my grandfather drew from a drawer of a chest a black-and-yellow silk cloth, put it around my shoulders, and made me repeat after him words composed of unknown sounds; but, dissatisfied with my babble, he grew angry and shook his head in disapproval. I felt stifled and afraid. How my mother arrived just in time to save me I don't remember.

My father often spoke of my grandfather's honesty as of some lofty spiritual quality. For a Jew, honesty is wisdom and almost holiness. The farther one went back amongst the generations of these stern, blue-eyed old men, the more honesty and sternness one found. Great-grandfather Veniamin once said, "I am closing down the business—I need no more money." He had just exactly enough to last him till the day of his death, since he did not leave a kopeck behind.

The Riga seaside is an entire country in itself. It is famed for its oozy, pure yellow, and astonishingly fine sand (even in an hourglass one could hardly find such sand!) and also for the little boardwalks consisting of one or two hole-riddled planks that had been thrown down across the twenty versts of the villa-dotted Sahara.

There are no watering places anywhere that can compare with the swing and scope of the *dacha* life along the Riga coast. The boardwalks, flower beds, enclosed front gardens, and decorative glass balls stretch out in a huge, endless city, all on a yellow, finely milled, canary sand, such as children play with.

In the backyards Latvians dry and cure flounder, a one-eyed, bony fish, flat as a broad palm. The wailing of children, piano scales, the groans of patients from the innumerable dentists' offices, the clatter of crockery in the little resort pensions, the roulades of singers and the shouts of the peddlers—these noises are never silenced in the labyrinth of kitchen gardens, bakeries and barbed wire, and as far as the eye can see along the sand embankment run little toy trains, shod with rails and filled to overflowing with "hares"[13] who leap about during the trip from prim German Bilderlingshof to congested Jewish Dubbeln, which smelled of swaddling clothes.[14] Wandering musicians strolled about among the sparse pine groves: two convoluted trumpets, a clarinet, and a trombone. Forever being chased away, they blow out their mercilessly false brass note and now here, now there, strike up the equestrian march of the splendid Karolina.

The whole region was controlled by a monocled baron named Firks. He divided his land into two parts: that which had been cleansed of Jews and that which had not. In the clean half, German students sat scraping their beer steins about on small tables. In the Jewish section babies' diapers hung from lines, and piano scales would gasp for breath. In the Germans' Majorenhof there were concerts: Strauss's *Death and Transfiguration* played by a symphony orchestra in the shell in the park. Elderly German women, their cheeks glowing and their mourning freshly donned, found it consoling.

In Jewish Dubbeln the orchestra strained at Tchaikovsky's *Symphonie Pathétique*, and one could hear the two nests of strings calling back and forth to each other.

At this time I conceived for Tchaikovsky a painfully nervous and tense love that recalled the desire of Dostoevsky's Netochka Nezvanova to hear the violin concerto behind the red flame of the silk curtains. The broad, flowing, purely violin passages in Tchaikovsky I heard from behind a barbed-wire fence and more than once tore my clothes and covered my

hands with scratches as I made my way gratis to the orchestra shell. From
the wild discordant gramophone of music emanating from the *dachas* I
would pick out the strong violin passages. I do not remember how this
veneration of mine for the symphony orchestra was developed, but I think
that I correctly understood Tchaikovsky, having guessed in him a special
sense for the concertante.

What conviction sounded in those violin voices, softened by Italian
docility but still Russian, in the dirty Jewish sewer! What a thread it is that
runs from these first wretched concerts to the silk flame of the Nobility
Hall and frail Scriabin, whom one expected to see crushed at any moment
by the still mute semicircle of singers about him and the string forest of
Prometheus, above which there hung like a shield a sound recording device, a strange glass apparatus.[15]

VII. *The Concerts of Hofmann and Kubelik*

In the season of 1903–04 Petersburg witnessed concerts in the grand manner. I am speaking of the strange, never-to-be-surpassed madness of the
concerts of Hofmann and Kubelik in the Nobility Hall during Lent.[16] I
can recall no other musical experiences, not even the premiere of Scriabin's *Prometheus*, that might be compared with these Lenten orgies in the
white-columned hall. The concerts would reach a kind of rage, a fury. This
was no musical dilettantism: there was something threatening and even
dangerous that rose up out of enormous depths, a kind of craving for movement; a mute prehistorical malaise was exuded by the peculiar, the almost
flagellant zeal of the halberdiers in Mikhaylovsky Square, and it whetted
the Petersburg of that day (the year 1905 had not yet struck) like a knife. In
the dim light of the gas lamps the many entrances of the Nobility Hall were
beset by a veritable siege. Gendarmes on prancing horses, lending to the
atmosphere of the square the mood of a civil disturbance, made clicking
noises with their tongues and shouted as they closed ranks to guard the
main entry. The sprung carriages with dim lanterns slipped into the glis-

tening circle and arranged themselves in an impressive black gypsy camp. The cabbies dared not deliver their fares right to the door; one paid them while approaching, and then they made off rapidly to escape the wrath of the police. Through the triple chains the Petersburger made his way like a feverish little trout to the marble ice-hole of the vestibule, whence he disappeared into the luminous frosty building, draped with silk and velvet. The orchestra seats and the places behind them were filled in the customary order, but the spacious balconies to which the side entrances gave access were filled in bunches, like baskets, with clusters of humanity. The Nobility Hall inside is wide, stocky, and almost square. The stage itself takes up very nearly half the area. The gallery swelters in a July heat. The air is filled with a ceaseless humming like that of cicadas over the steppe.

Who were Hofmann and Kubelik? To begin with, in the consciousness of the Petersburg populace of that time, they had become amalgamated into one image. Like twins, they were identical in height and in the color of their hair. Smaller than the average, almost dwarfish, they had hair blacker than a raven's wing. Each had a very low forehead and very small hands. As I recall them now, they both seem to have been something like leading men in some troupe of Lilliputians. I was taken to the Hôtel d'Europe[17] to pay my respects to Kubelik, although I did not play the violin. He lived like a real prince. Fearing that the boy might play the violin, he waved his little hand in alarm, but was immediately reassured and gave his autograph as he was requested to do.

Now when these two little musical demigods, these two *jeunes premiers* of the Lilliputian theater, had to make their way across the stage, sagging under the pressure of the crowd, I would be terrified for them. It would begin as with an electric spark, like the first gust of an approaching thunderstorm. Then the attendants would with difficulty clear a path through the throng, and to the accompaniment of an indescribable roar from all sides of the hot shoving human mass—neither bowing nor smiling, almost trembling, and with a kind of angry expression on their faces—they would make their way to the music stand and the piano. To this day that passage strikes me as perilous: I cannot get rid of the thought that the crowd, simply from not knowing what to do, was ready to tear its darlings to pieces. In what followed, these little geniuses, holding sway over the stunned musical mob of maids of honor and girl students, fat art patrons and shock-headed singing coaches, would try with all the means of their art, with all the logic and splendor of their sound, to chain and cool the

unbridled Dionysian element. I have never heard from anyone such a
pure, primordially clear and transparent sound, in the piano sober as
spring water, and producing in the violin a voice of the utmost simplicity,
indivisible into its component filaments; and I have never again heard such
a virtuoso, such an alpine cold, as in the frugality, sobriety, and formal
clarity of these two legalists of the violin and the pianoforte. But what in
their performance was clear and sober served only to enrage and incite to
new frenzies the crowd that clung to the marble columns, hung in clusters
from the gallery, sprouted from the flower beds of the orchestra, and thickened hotly on the stage. Such was the power in the rational and pure playing of these two virtuosi.

VIII. *The Tenishev School*

On Zagorodny Prospekt, in the courtyard of a huge apartment house,
one side of which was a blank wall that could be seen from a great distance
and which bore an advertisement for Shustov cognac, about thirty boys
dressed in shorts, wool socks, and English blouses played soccer to the
accompaniment of horrendous shouting. They all looked as if they had
been transported to England or Switzerland and there fitted out in a way
that was not Russian or that of a Gymnasium student, but somehow rather
Cambridge in style.

I recall a solemn occasion: an unctuous priest in a violet cassock, the
excited audience attending the opening day exercises, and suddenly all
make way amidst a fluster of whispers: Witte had arrived.[18] It was commonly said of Witte that he had a golden nose, and the children, who
blindly believed this, looked at nothing but his nose. The nose, however,
was ordinary and appeared fleshy.

What was said then I do not remember; but on Mokhovaya Street in our
own amphitheater, with its comfortable deputy's seats à la parliament
there took place a rather elaborate ritual, and in the early days of September there would be formal exercises to celebrate the good fortune of our
exemplary school. At these meetings, which resembled a juvenile House
of Lords, an elderly doctor of hygiene named Virenius would inevitably

say a few words. He was a rosy-cheeked old man, like the child on a can of Nestlé's. Every year he gave one and the same talk: on the beneficial effects of swimming. Since all this would take place in the fall, with the next swimming season about ten months away, there was something malapropos about his maneuvers and demonstrations, but this apostle of swimming regularly delivered his sermon every year on the very threshold of winter. Another professor of hygiene was Prince Tarkhanov, an Oriental gentleman with an Assyrian beard, who used to go from desk to desk during the physiology lesson and make the students listen to his heart through his thick vest. One could not be sure whether it was a heart ticking or a gold watch, but the vest was indispensable.

The amphitheater, with its collapsible desks, its capacious aisles dividing it into sections, and its strong overhead light, would be taken by storm on such grand occasions, and all Mokhovaya Street would seethe, inundated by the police and the massed intelligentsia.

This was all at the beginning of the 1900s.

The Tenishev auditorium was most often engaged by that citadel of radicalism the Literary Fund, which held the copyright on the works of Nadson. The Literary Fund was by its nature a commemorative organization: it revered. It had a meticulously worked out annual program, something like a calendar of saints, in accordance with which it celebrated the anniversaries of birth and death of, if I am not mistaken, Nekrasov, Nadson, Pleshcheev, Garshin, Turgenev, Gogol, Pushkin, Apukhtin, Nikitin, and others. These literary requiems were all alike, and in the choice of things to be read little attention was given to the question whether the deceased had actually written it.

It usually began with the aged Pyotr Isaevich Weinberg,[19] a kind of goat in a plaid lap robe, reading one invariable selection: "In front of me the sea, my old friend, unfolded like an endless shroud. . . ."

Then there would appear Samoylov, the actor from the Aleksandrinsky Theater, to read Nikitin's poem "The Master" in a heart rending voice, striking himself on the breast and delivering himself of staggering shouts which subsided into sinister whispering.

Next would follow the conversation of the ladies, delightful in every respect, from *Dead Souls*. Then Nekrasov's "Grandfather Mazay and the Hares" or "Reflections at the Main Entrance." Vedrinskaya would twitter Fet's poem "I come to you with greetings . . ." and the conclusion would be the playing of Chopin's *Funeral March*.

So much for literature. Now the performances of a civic nature. There were first of all the sessions of the Juridical Society, led by Maksim Kovalevsky and Petrunkevich,[20] where amidst a low hissing and buzzing they decanted the poison of constitutionalism. Maksim Kovalevsky, carrying all before him by virture of his imposing figure, would preach an Oxfordian legality. While all about him heads were being chopped off, he delivered an immensely long and erudite speech on the right of perlustration, i.e., the censoring of private correspondence, in the course of which he cited the English example, admitted such a right, then qualified it, and finally curtailed it. The celebrants of these civic services were M. Kovalevsky, Rodichev, Nikolay Fyodorovich Annensky, Batyushkov, and Ovsyaniko-Kulikovsky.[21]

It was in the near proximity of such a domestic forum as this that we received our education in the high glass boxes with steam-heated window-sills that were our huge classrooms, seating twenty-five students. And our corridors were not corridors but riding halls with tall ceilings and parqueted floors, the atmosphere of which, crossed by slanting columns of dust-laden sunlight, generally smelled of gas from the physics laboratories. The practical demonstrations consisted of cruel and needless vivisections, the expulsion of all the air from a glass bell in order to observe a poor mouse die of suffocation on its back, the torturing of frogs, the scientific boiling of water, with a description of this process, and the melting of little glass rods on the gas burners.

The heavy, sweetish smell of gas in the laboratories gave one a headache, but the real hell for the majority of the awkward, nervous, and not unduly healthy children was the class of manual crafts. Towards the end of the day, heavy with lessons and sated with conversations and demonstrations, we would gasp with fatigue among the wood shavings and sawdust, unable to saw a board in half. The saw would get bent, the plane would go crooked, the chisel would strike against fingers: nothing came out right. The instructor would busy himself with two or three of the skillful boys, and the others would damn all handicrafts.

At our German lessons we would sing "O Tannenbaum, O Tannenbaum!" under the direction of the Fräulein, who also used to bring to class pictures of milky alpine landscapes with dairy cows and little tile-roofed houses.

There was in the school a military, privileged, almost aristocratic undercurrent that was forever threatening to break through: this was composed of the children of certain ruling families who had landed here by some strange parental caprice and now lorded it over the flabby intellectuals.[22] A certain Voevodsky, the son of a court official and a strikingly handsome boy with a classical profile in the style of Nicholas I, proclaimed himself "commander" and compelled everyone to take an oath of fealty to him, kissing the cross and Bible.

Here is a short portrait gallery of my class.

Vanyusha Korsakov. Nicknamed "Porkchop." Flaccid boy from a family with ties to the *zemstvo* tradition (Petrunkevich, Rodichev). Wore his hair in a bowl cut. A Russian shirt with a silk belt.

Barats. His family intimate with Stasyulevich[23] (*Messenger of Europe*). A passionate mineralogist, mute as a fish, talked only of quartz and mica.

Leonid Zarubin. Large coal-mining industry in the Don Basin. To begin with, dynamos and batteries; later on, nothing but Wagner.

Przesiecki. Poor Polish gentry. Specialist at spitting.

Slobodzinski. Top student. A person from the second part of *Dead Souls*, burned by Gogol. Positive type of the Russian *intelligent*. Moderate mystic. Truth lover. Good mathematician. Well read in Dostoevsky. Later on he ran a radio station.

Nadezhdin. A classless intellectual. Sour odor from the apartment of a minor clerk. Gaiety and insouciance, since there was nothing to lose.

The Krupenskys. Twins. Landed gentry from Bessarabia. Connoisseurs of wine and Jews.

And finally, Boris Sinani. Belonged to the generation that is now active, having ripened for great events and historical work. He had hardly graduated before he died. How he would have shone during the years of the revolution!

There are still today various old ladies and good provincial people who, when they wish to praise someone, say that he is "a luminous personality."[24] And I understand what they mean. There is no other way to speak of our Ostrogorsky except in the language of that period, and the old-fashioned pompousness of that absurd expression no longer strikes one as comical. It was only during the first few years of the century that the coattails of Ostrogorsky could be seen flitting about the corridors of the Tenishev School. He was nearsighted and squinted, his eyes brilliant with mockery—a great, scrofulous ape in a frock coat, with a beard and hair of golden-red. There was, I am sure, something very Chekhovian about his incredible smile. He did not take root, somehow, in the twentieth century, though he wanted to. He loved Blok (and at what an early date!), and published his poems in his journal *Education*.

He was no administrator—he just squinted and smiled and was terribly absentminded. It was rare to have a talk with him. He shrugged everything off with a joke, even when there was no call to do so.

"What class do you have now?"

"Geology."

"Geology yourself."

The whole school, with all its humanistic twaddle and nonsense, was held together by his smile.

Still, there were some good boys in the Tenishev School. The same flesh and blood as the children in the portraits of Serov. Little ascetics, monks in their children's monastery, where the notebooks, equipment, glass retorts, and German books contained more spirituality and inner harmony than can be found in the grown-up world.

IX. *Sergey Ivanych*

The year 1905 was the chimera of the Russian Revolution with the little lynx eyes of a policeman and wearing a student's blue beret, flat as a pancake! The Petersburgers could sense your coming from a great distance, they could catch the sound of your horses' hooves, and they shivered in your drafts in the alcohol-preserved auditoriums of the Military Medical College or in the immensely long *jeu de paume* of the Menshikov University, where the future orator of the Armenians would roar like an enraged lion at some feeble SR or SD,[25] and those whose job it was to listen would stretch out their avine necks. Memory loves to go hunting in the dark, and it was in the densest possible murk that you were born, O moment, when—one, two, three—the Nevsky blinked shut its long electric lashes to bury itself in the blackness of outer night and from the far end of the boulevard there appeared out of the dense shaggy dark the chimera with its little lynx policeman eyes and flattened student's cap.

For me the year 1905 is in Sergey Ivanych. There were many of them—the tutors of the revolution! One of my friends, a rather haughty person, used to say, not without some justice, "Some men are books, others—

newspapers." Poor Sergey Ivanych would not have found a place in such
an analysis; for him it would have been necessary to establish a third cate-
gory: some men are interlinear translations. Interlinear translations of the
revolution poured from him, in his cold-stuffed head their cigarette-paper
pages rustled, he shook from the cuffs of his sea-green cavalry jacket an
ethereally light contraband literature, his Russian cigarette burned with a
forbidden smoke, as if it had been rolled out of illegal paper.

I do not know where and how Sergey Ivanych had learned his trade. I
was too young to know anything about that side of his life. But once he took
me along to his place and I saw the room which served him for study,
bedroom, and laboratory. At that time he and I were engaged in a large and
grandly futile enterprise: writing a paper on the reasons for the fall of the
Roman Empire. In the space of one week Sergey Ivanych dictated to me in
sudden volleys 135 tightly crammed notebook pages. He would speak
without a moment's reflection, without checking any sources, and like a
spider would spin—out of cigarette smoke, I suppose—a fragile web of
learned phraseology, drawing out lengthy periods and making little knots
of the social and economic features. He enjoyed the patronage of our
house, as of many others. Was this not the way Romans hired Greek slaves,
so as to be able to shine at dinner by showing off some learned treatise? At
the height of the work which I mentioned above Sergey Ivanych took me
to his place. He lived somewhere in the 100 block of the Nevsky Prospekt,
beyond the Nicholas Station, where all the houses have renounced any
effort towards chic and are, like cats, gray. I shuddered at the heavy, acrid
smell of Sergey Ivanych's dwelling. The atmosphere of the room, having
been breathed and smoked for years, was by this time no longer air but
some new and unknown substance with a different specific weight and
other chemical properties. And I involuntarily recalled the dog cave of
Naples from my physics course. During all the time that he had lived here
the master of these quarters had never lifted or changed the position of
anything and treated the arrangement of things like a veritable dervish,
throwing permanently onto the floor whatever proved to be superfluous.
At home, Sergey Ivanych recognized only the supine position. While he
dictated, I would steal side glances at his coal-dust-colored linen, and how
astonished I was when Sergey Ivanych called a break and prepared two
glasses of the most magnificent, thick, and aromatic hot chocolate. It
turned out that he had a passion for chocolate. He cooked it with a master's
touch—much stronger than the usual. What conclusion is one to draw
from this? Was Sergey Ivanych a sybaritic voluptuary, or had some choco-

late demon entered his soul, fastening itself upon this ascetic and nihilist? Oh, the gloomy authority of Sergey Ivanych, oh, his subversive depths, his cavalry jacket and trousers of some gendarme material! His walk resembled that of a man who had just been seized by the shoulder and led into the presence of some terrible satrap while trying to appear completely nonchalant. It was an unadulterated pleasure to walk down the street with him, for he would point out all the government spies, of whom he was not in the least afraid.

I think that he was himself something like a spy—perhaps from his constant preoccupation with that subject, or perhaps from the law of protective coloration, which causes birds and butterflies to take their color and plumage from that of the cliff. Yes, there was in Sergey Ivanych something of the gendarme. He was querulous, he was peevish, he would wheeze the kind of anecdotes that generals like, and would utter the first five grades of the military and civil services with both relish and disgust. The sleepy face of Sergey Ivanych, crumpled like a student beret, always wore the expression of a purely gendarme disgust. To push some general or some Actual State Councilor face first into the mud was for him the very summit of happiness—a happiness, I think, rather mathematical and abstract.

Thus an anecdote in his mouth sounded like a theorem. A general runs through all the dishes on a menu, rejects them all, and exclaims: "What filth!" A student who had overheard the general's remark asks him to name the various ranks of the government service and when he has finished, exclaims: "Is that all? What filth!"

Somewhere in Siedlce or in Rovno, Sergey Ivanych, being at the time probably a boy of tender years, had broken away from some official police rock. His family tree included minor provincial governors of the Western Region, and he himself—this was after he had already become a tutor of the revolution and a slave to the chocolate demon—sought to marry some governor's daughter who had also, apparently, broken away for good. Of course, Sergey Ivanych was not a revolutionary. Let his epithet stick: a tutor of the revolution. Like a chimera he dissolved at the first light of the historic day. As the year 1905 and the fatal hour drew closer, his secrecy thickened and his gloomy authority increased. He should have shown himself at last, he should have taken some kind of decisive action, should have at least—well—brandished a revolver from the midst of an armed squad or given some other concrete proof of his consecration to the revolution.

But then, at the very height of the alarm in 1905, Sergey Ivanych became the guardian of the pleasantly and harmlessly frightened burghers, and, grinning with satisfaction like a cat, he brought reliable news that on such and such a day there would inevitably occur a pogrom of the Petersburg intelligentsia. As a member of one of the armed squads he promised to come with his Browning, guaranteeing everyone's complete safety.

I chanced to meet him many years after 1905. He was totally faded. He had absolutely no face, so erased and bleached were his features. A faint shadow of his former disgust and authority. It turned out that he had found a place and served as an assistant in the astronomical observatory at Pulkovo.

If Sergey Ivanych had been transformed into a pure logarithm of stellar velocities or a function of space it would not have surprised me. He had to depart this life, such a chimera was he.

X. Yuly Matveich

In the time it took Yuly Matveich to climb up to the fifth floor one could have run down to the doorman and back several times. He had to be supported under the arms and allowed to stop for breath at each landing. In the entrance hall he would stop and wait while they took off his fur coat. A little man with short legs, wearing an old man's fur coat that reached to his heels and a heavy fur cap, he would puff and wheeze until he had been freed from the hot beaver fur, and then he would sit down on the divan with his legs sticking out like a child's. His appearance in the house signalled either a family council or the pacification of some domestic row. Every family is, when all is said and done, a government. He loved family fallings-out the way a government official loves political difficulties. He had no family of his own and had chosen to work on ours as being extraordinarily difficult and complex.

We children were seized by stormy joy the moment we caught sight of his ministerial head (so much like Bismarck's that it was funny), tender and bald as a baby's, not counting the three hairs on the very top.

In answer to a question Yuly Matveich would make some indistinct

sound with a strange chesty timbre, like something produced on a trumpet
by an unskillful musician, and only after having made this preliminary
noise would he commence his statement with the invariable phrase:
"Didn't I tell you . . ." or "I always told you. . . ."

Childless, helplessly walrus-footed, the Bismarck of someone else's
family, Yuly Matveich inspired in me a profound sympathy.

He had grown up amongst enterprising southern landowners, somewhere between Bessarabia, Odessa, and Rostov.

How many contracts had been fulfilled, how many vineyard estates and
stud farms sold with the aid of a Greek notary in the lousy hotel rooms of
Kishinyov and Rostov!

All of them—the Greek notary, the sharp-dealing landowner, and the
gubernia secretary, a Moldavian—put on their white dusters and, in the
choleraic heat, jolted along the highways and paved roads of the gubernia
in a canopied *brichka*. It was there that his experience had multiplied and
his capital rounded out, and together with this grew his epicureanism. His
little arms and legs had already begun to refuse their function and were
turning into short little flippers, and Yuly Matveich, dining with the mar-
shal of nobility and a contractor in the hotels of Kishinyov and Rostov,
would summon the waiter with that same indistinct trumpet sound which
I mentioned above. He was gradually transformed into a real Jewish general. Cast in iron, he might have served as a monument—but where and
when could iron give a true notion of the three Bismarckian hairs? The
worldview of Yuly Matveich grew to be something wise and cogent. His
favorite reading was Menshikov and Renan. A strange combination at first
glance, but, when one thinks of it, even for a member of the government
council it would have been impossible to choose better reading. About
Menshikov he said, raising his little senatorial hand, that he had an "intelligent head," and as for Renan, he agreed with him in absolutely everything concerning Christianity. Yuly Matveich was contemptuous of death,
hated doctors, and, as an edifying instance, loved to tell of how he had
escaped unharmed from the cholera. In his youth he had made a trip to
Paris, and when, thirty years after the first trip, he found himself once
more in Paris he refused to enter a single restaurant and kept looking for
some "Coq d'Or" where he had once had a good meal. But the Coq d'Or no
longer existed. A "Coq" did turn up, but it was the wrong one, and even
that was practically impossible to locate. Yuly Matveich went about the
business of choosing dishes from the menu with the air of a gourmet, the

garçon was breathless in anticipation of some complicated and subtle order, and then Yuly Matveich would settle on a cup of bouillon. It was no easy matter to get ten or fifteen rubles out of Yuly Matveich: He would expatiate for over an hour on sagacity, epicureanism, and—"Didn't I tell you." Then he would shuffle about the room for a long time looking for the keys, wheeze, and root about in concealed drawers.

The death of Yuly Matveich was terrible. He died like the old man in Balzac, practically thrown out on the street by a shrewd and powerful family of shopkeepers, to whom he had in his old age transferred his services as a domestic Bismarck and whom he had permitted to take over his life.

They drove the dying Yuly Matveich out of their commercial quarters on Razezzhaya Street and rented a room for him in a small *dacha* in the Lesnoy section.

Unshaven and in a frightful condition, he sat with his spittoon and a copy of the *New Times*. His deadly blue cheeks were covered with a dirty bristle. In his trembling hand he held a magnifying glass and moved it along the lines of the paper. In the dark pupils of his eyes, afflicted with cataract, there lay the fear of death. The servant would place a dish before him and immediately disappear without asking whether he needed anything.

To the funeral of Yuly Matveich there came an extraordinary number of relatives, respectable and unknown to each other, and his nephew from the Azov-Don Bank shuffled about on his little short legs and kept shaking his heavy Bismarckian head.

XI. *The Erfurt Program*

"Why do you read pamphlets? What kind of sense is there in them?"—the voice of the extremely intelligent V. V. G.[26] sounds right above my ear. "You want to learn something about Marxism? Get Marx's *Kapital*." So I got it, got burnt by it, and threw it away: back again to the pamphlets. Och . . . wasn't my splendid Tenishev mentor playing a trick on me? Marx's *Kapital* is the same as Kraevich's *Physics*. Surely no one can think that

Kraevich leads to any new ideas. But a pamphlet plants a little larva—that
is just its function. And the larva gives birth to thought.

What a hodgepodge, what true historical dissonance lived in our
school, where geography, puffing away at a pipeful of "Capstan" tobacco,
was transformed into anecdotes about American trusts, what a lot of history knocked and fluttered alongside the Tenishev hothouse on its chicken
legs[27] and beside the troglodytic soccer games.

No, Russian boys are not English. You won't catch them with sport or
with the boiled water of political amateurism. Life, with all its unexpected
interests and its passionate intellectual diversions, life will burst in upon
the most hothouse-like, the most completely sterilized Russian school, as
it once burst into Pushkin's lycée.

A copy of *The Scales* under the desk, and next to it the slag and metal
shavings from the Obukhov factory, and not a word, not a sound, as though
by some conspiracy, about Belinsky, Dobrolyubov, or Pisarev; Balmont,
however, was held in high regard and his imitators weren't bad; and the
Social Democrat is at the throat of the Populist, drinking his SR blood,
and the latter calls in vain upon the princes of his church—Chernov, Mikhaylovsky, and even—the *Historical Letters* of Lavrov.[28] Everything that
represented an attitude toward life was greedily devoured. I repeat: my
schoolmates could not endure Belinsky on account of the diffuseness of his
attitude toward life, but Kautsky was respected, and so was Protopop Avvakum, whose autobiography, in the Pavlenkov edition, was made a part
of our study of Russian literature.

Of course, none of this could have been without V. V. G., the molder of
souls and teacher for remarkable people (only it turned out that there were
none on hand). But about him more later; for now, hail and farewell to
Kautsky, the thin red band of light in the east of the Marxist dawn!

Early, O Erfurt Program, you Marxist propylaea, too early did you train
our spirits to a sense of harmoniousness, but to me and to many others you
gave a sense of life in those prehistoric years when thought hungered after
unity and harmoniousness, when the backbone of the age was becoming
erect, when the heart needed more than anything the red blood of the
aorta! Is Kautsky Tyutchev? Surely he was not gifted with the power to
evoke cosmic sensations ("And the thin thread of the spider's web trembles
on the empty furrow")? But just imagine—for a person at a certain age and
at a certain moment Kautsky (I say Kautsky, of course, just as an example
and might with even greater justice have said Marx, Plekhanov) *is*
Tyutchev, that is, the source of a cosmic joy, the bearer of a strong and

harmonious attitude toward life, the thinking reed, and a cover thrown over the abyss.

That year, in Segewold, on the Courland river Aa, there was a radiant autumn with spiderwebs in the fields of barley. The estates of the barons had just been burned down, and after the pacification there arose out of the charred brick outbuildings a grim cruel silence. From time to time there would come clattering along the hard German road a two-wheeled cart with the bailiff and a constable and some oaf of a Latvian would doff his cap. In its brick-red, layered, cave-riddled banks the romantic little river flowed along like a German water nymph and the towns were sunk up to their ears in green foliage. The inhabitants kept a dim memory of Konevskoy,[29] who had recently drowned in the river. That was a young man who had reached maturity too early and was thus not read by Russian youth: his lines had a difficult sound like the rustling of the roots of a forest. And so, in Segewold with the Erfurt Program in my hands, I was closer in spirit to Konevskoy than if I had poeticized à la Zhukovsky and the Romantics, because I was able to populate, to socialize the visible world with its barley, dirt roads, castles, and sunlit spiderwebs, breaking it down into diagrams and setting up under the pale blue firmament ladders, far from biblical, upon which not the angels of Jacob but small and large property holders ascended and descended, passing through the stages of capitalist economy.

What could be stronger, what could be more organic: I perceived the entire world as an economy, a human economy—and the shuttles of English cottage industry that had fallen silent a hundred years ago sounded once more in the ringing autumn air! Yes, I heard with the sharpness of ears caught by the sound of a distant threshing machine in the field the burgeoning and increase, not of the barley in its ear, not of the northern apple, but of the world, the capitalist world, that was ripening in order to fall!

XII. The Sinani Family

When I arrived in class a completely prepared and finished Marxist, a very serious opponent was waiting for me. When he had listened intently to my self-assured speeches, there came up to me a boy wearing a thin belt around his waist, his hair almost red, and somehow narrow all over—narrow in the shoulders, with a narrow face, gentle and manly, narrow hands, and small feet. Above his lip he had a red splotch, like a fiery sign. There was little in his dress to recall the Anglo-Saxon style of the Tenishev School. It was as if they had taken an old, old pair of trousers and a shirt, scrubbed them very hard with soap in a cold stream, dried them in the sun, and given them to him, unironed, to put on. Anyone looking at him would have said, What frail bones! But anyone glancing at his high, modest forehead would have been astonished at his almost slanted eyes, which had a greenish cast to their smile, and would have been stopped by the expression of his small mouth, bitterly proud. His movements, when necessary, could be large and bold, like the gesture of the boy playing jacks in Fyodor Tolstoy's sculpture, but he generally avoided sharp movements, saving his accuracy and lightness for play. His walk was astonishingly light—a barefoot walk. It would have suited him to have a sheepdog at his legs and a long staff in his hands. His cheeks and chin were covered with a golden, animal down. He was something between a Russian boy playing a Russian game and an Italian John the Baptist with a barely noticeable hook in his sharp nose.

He volunteered to be my teacher, and I did not leave him for as long as he lived, but followed after him, rapt by the clarity of his mind, by his courage, by the presence of his spirit. He died on the eve of the arrival of the historic days for which he had prepared himself, for which nature had prepared him, just at the moment when the sheepdog was ready to lie down calmly at his feet and the slender staff of the Baptist was to have been exchanged for the rod of the shepherd. His name was Boris Sinani. I utter that name with tenderness and respect. He was the son of the famous Petersburg doctor who treated people by means of suggestion, Boris Naumovich Sinani. His mother was Russian, but his father stemmed from the Karaite Jews of the Crimea. Could this not account for the duality of his appearance? A Russian boy from Novgorod, but with an un-Russian aquiline nose and on his skin the golden down of a Crimean shepherd from the Yaila Mountains. From the earliest moment of his conscious existence Boris Sinani, by a tradition of his strong and extraordinarily interesting family, regarded himself as the chosen vessel of Russian Populism. It seems to me that what attracted him in Populism was not its theory but rather the quality of its spirit. One felt in him a realist ready to abandon all arguments, when necessary, for the sake of action, but for the time being his youthful realism, free of anything that was trivial and deadening, was charming and breathed with an innate spirituality and nobility. With a deft hand Boris Sinani removed from my eyes the cataract which, he believed, had prevented my seeing the agrarian question. The Sinanis lived on Pushkin Street, opposite the hotel Palais Royal. They were a powerful family in the strength of their intellectual character, which sometimes took the form of an eloquent primitiveness. Dr. Boris Naumovich Sinani had evidently lived on Pushkin Street for a long time. The gray-haired doorman had a boundless respect for the entire family, from the ferocious psychiatrist Boris Naumovich all the way to the little hunchback Lenochka. No one crossed that threshold without trepidation, since Boris Naumovich reserved the right to eject anyone to whom he took a dislike, whether it was a patient or simply a guest who had said something stupid. Boris Naumovich Sinani was the physician and executor of Gleb Uspensky, the friend of Nikolay Konstantinovich Mikhaylovsky—by whose personality, incidentally, he was far from being always blinded—and the advisor and confidant of the leading SR's of that day.

His appearance was that of a stocky Karaite Jew—he even kept the Karaite cap—with a hard and unusually heavy face. Not everyone could endure the savage, intelligent gaze through his eyeglasses; when he smiled, though, into his curly, sparse beard, his smile was that of a child and altogether charming. Entrance into the study of Boris Naumovich was strictly forbidden. There, by the way, hung his emblem and the emblem of the whole house, the portrait of Shchedrin, glowering from beneath his dense gubernatorial brows and menacing the children with the frightful spade of his shaggy beard. This Shchedrin looked like something between the demon in Gogol's *Viy* and a governor, and he was terrifying, especially in the dark. Boris Naumovich was a widower, and about his widowerhood there was something stubborn and wolfish. He lived with his son and two daughters, Zhenya, the elder, slant-eyed as a Japanese and very miniature and elegant, and the little hunchback Lena. He had few patients, but those whom he had he held in servile terror, especially the women. In spite of the rudeness of his manner, they would present him with little embroidered shoes and slippers. In his leather study under the beard of Shchedrin he lived like a forester in his lodge, and on all sides he was surrounded by enemies: mysticism, stupidity, hysteria, and boorishness. If you must live with wolves, then howl like a wolf.

Even among the most outstanding men of that time the authority of
Mikhaylovsky was obviously enormous, and it is not likely that Boris Naumovich found this easy to accept. By virtue of some fatal contradiction, he
himself, an ardent rationalist, needed authority and revered authority and
this tortured him. Whenever some abrupt changes occurred unexpectedly
in the political or social sphere, the question was instantly raised in the
house, What would Nikolay Konstantinovich say? In a short while the
senate of the Populist journal Russian Wealth would actually be called into
session at Mikhaylovsky's and Nikolay Konstantinovich would deliver
himself of his opinions. It was precisely these pronouncements that the
elder Sinani valued in Mikhaylovsky. The scale of his reverence for the
leaders of Populism was constituted thus: Mikhaylovsky was good as an
oracle, but his journalistic writing was pure water, and as a man he was not
respectable. When all was said and done, he did not like Mikhaylovsky. He
conceded that Chernov had gumption and a peasant, agrarian intellect.
Peshekhonov he regarded as a dishcloth. He felt some tenderness for Mya-
kotin as the Benjamin of the lot. Not one of them did he take seriously. He
genuinely respected the elderly Natanson, a member of the central committee of the SR party.[30] Gray, bald, looking like an old doctor, Natanson
came to the house two or three times to talk with Boris Naumovich, and his
visits were not kept secret from us children. There was no limit to the
excited flutter and proud joy: the house contained a member of the Central
Committee.

The domestic order of the house, in spite of its lack of a mistress, was
strict and simple, as in the family of a merchant. The little hunchbacked
girl, Lena, very nearly ran the house, but such was the harmony of the will
which ruled here that the house kept itself.

I knew what Boris Naumovich was doing in his study. He kept reading
and reading harmful, foolish books filled with mysticism, hysteria, and all
manner of pathology; he struggled with them, he settled accounts with
them, but he could not tear himself away from them and kept forever
coming back to them. Set him a diet of pure positivism and old Sinani
would have immediately shriveled up. Positivism is good for a share-
holder, it brings in its five percent of progress annually. Boris Naumovich
required sacrifices for the glory of positivism. He was the Abraham of
positivism, and would not have hesitated to sacrifice his own son to it.

Once, at tea, there was a mention of life after death, and Boris Naumovich raised his eyes in astonishment. "What is that? Do I remember what

was before my birth? I remember nothing. There was nothing. And after death there won't be anything."

His Bazarovism had finally a classical Greek simplicity. Even the one-eyed cook became infected with the general atmosphere.

The central feature of the Sinani household was what I should call an aesthetic of the intellect. Positivism is usually hostile to aesthetic contemplation, the disinterested pride and joy of the movements of the mind. But for these people the intellect was joy, health, sport, and almost religion, all at once. The circle of their intellectual interests was, however, extremely limited, their field of vision was narrow, and the fact is that their avid minds had to gnaw on scanty nourishment: the eternal quarrels of the SR's and SD's, the role of personality in history, the notorious harmonious personality of Mikhaylovsky, the agrarian badgering of the SD's—that was the poor extent of it. Bored by the thought he found at home, Boris lost himself in reading the legal speeches of Lassalle—marvelously constructed, fascinating and full of life. That was in truth pure intellectual aesthetics and real sport. And in imitating Lassalle we were carried away by the sport of eloquence, oratorical improvisation. Much in vogue were agrarian philippics directed against an assumed target from among the SD's. Some of these speeches offered to the void were positively brilliant. I still recall how at one meeting Boris, still a boy at the time, hounded an experienced old Menshevik named Kleinbort,[31] a contributor to the learned quarterlies, and caused him to break into a sweat. Kleinbort simply panted and looked around in confusion: the mental elegance of his opponent apparently struck him as a new and unexpected weapon of argument. All this, to be sure, was nothing more than the pebbles that Demosthenes carried about in his mouth, but God save any youthful orators from such teachers as N. K. Mikhaylovsky! What a windbag that was! What Manilovism!! Dressed out with truisms and arithmetical computations, that empty blather about the harmonious personality crept out like a weed from everywhere and occupied the place of living, fruitful thought.

According to the constitution of the house the severe old man Sinani dared not so much as glance into the young people's room, called the pink room. The pink room corresponded to the divan room in *War and Peace*. Of the visitors to the pink room, of whom there were not many, I recall one, a certain Natasha, a nice, nonsensical creature. Boris Naumovich tolerated her as a kind of household fool. Natasha was in turn an SD, an SR, a Russian Orthodox, a Roman Catholic, a Hellenist, and a Theosophist, with various intermissions for breath. This frequent change of her convictions caused her to turn prematurely gray. While she was a Hellenist she published a novel based on the life of Julius Caesar at the Roman spa in Baiae, Baiae having assumed a striking resemblance to Sestroretsk (Natasha was terribly wealthy).

In the pink room as in every divan room confusion reigned. And what constituted the confusion that reigned in the aforesaid divan room at the beginning of this current century? Wretched postcards with allegories of Stuck and Zhukov,[32] the "fairytale postcard" (something straight out of Nadson), a bareheaded girl with her arms tied, a charcoal enlargement printed on an oversized card. The terrible publication called *The Reader and Declaimer*, and all sorts of *Russian Muses* with P. Ya., Mikhaylov, and Tarasov,[33] where we made a conscientious search for poetry but were, anyway, sometimes embarrassed. Much attention was devoted to Mark Twain and Jerome K. Jerome (the best and most wholesome of all our reading). A rubbish heap of various *Anathemas, Sweetbriers*, and the miscellanies put out by the Znanie publishing house. Our evenings were grounded in the vague recollections of the estate in Luga where the guests would sleep on the little semicircular sofas in the parlor and the six poor aunts would all run everything at once. Then there were diaries and autobiographical novels in the bargain: was there not enough confusion?

One person who was practically a member of the family in the Sinani house was Semyon Akimych Ansky, who would drop out of sight occasionally on some Jewish business in Mogilyov and then turn up again in Petersburg to spend the night beneath Shchedrin, though without the right of domicile. Semyon Akimych Ansky combined in himself a Jewish folklorist with Gleb Uspensky and Chekhov. In his single person he contained a thousand provincial rabbis, if one reckons by the amount of his advice and consolations, conveyed in the guise of parables, anecdotes, and so on. All that Semyon Akimych needed in life was a place to spend the night and strong tea. People ran after him to hear his stories. The Russian-Jewish folklore of Semyon Akimych flowed out like a thick stream of honey in marvelous unhurried stories. Semyon Akimych was not yet old but he had an aged grandfatherly appearance and was stooped over from the excess of Jewishness and Populism: governors, pogroms, human misfortunes, encounters, the most cunning patterns of public life in the improbable circumstances of the Minsk and Mogilyov satrapies, etched as though with a fine engraving needle. Semyon Akimych preserved everything, remembered everything—a Gleb Uspensky out of the Talmud-Torah. Behind the modest tea table he sat with his gentle biblical gestures, his head inclined to one side, like the Jewish apostle Peter at the Last Supper. In a house where everyone was knocking against the graven image of Mikhaylovsky and cracking the tough agrarian nut, Semyon Akimych gave the impression of a gentle Psyche afflicted with hemorrhoids.

At that time Modernism and Symbolism somehow managed to live together in my head with the most desperate Nadsonism and the poesy from the journal *Russian Wealth*. I had already read all of Blok, including *The Puppet Show*, and he got on splendidly with the civic themes and all that gibberish verse. He was not ill disposed toward it; in fact, it was from there that he himself issued. The "thick reviews"[34] bred a kind of poetry to wilt the ears, but it was there that the most attractive little loopholes were kept for the eccentric failures, young suicides, and poetic underground men, who in fact differed little from the homey lyricists of *Russian Wealth* and *The Messenger of Europe*.

On Pushkin Street, in a very decent apartment, there lived a former German banker by the name of Goldberg, the editor and publisher of a little magazine called *The Poet*.

Goldberg, a fat bourgeois, considered himself a German poet, and he entered into the following agreement with his clients: he would print their verses gratis in the magazine *Poet*, and in return they would undertake to listen to his, Goldberg's, composition, a lengthy German philosophical poem with the title *The Parliament of the Insects*—in German, or in the case of someone's not knowing German, then in Russian translation.

To all his clients Goldberg would say, "Young man, your writing is going to become better and better."[35] He especially prized one gloomy poet whom he considered to have suicidal tendencies. Goldberg had hired a youth of the most heavenly poetic appearance to help him put the issues together. The old chronic failure of a banker and his Schilleresque assistant—who was, by the way, the translator of the *Parliament of Insects* into Russian—labored selflessly over that dear misshapen magazine. Some strange banker's muse guided the pudgy fingers of Goldberg. The Schiller in his employ was evidently pulling his leg. In Germany, though, when times were good, Goldberg had printed a collected edition of his works, which he himself showed to me.

How profoundly Boris Sinani understood the essence of the Socialist Revolutionary doctrine and how far, even as a boy, he had spiritually outgrown it can be seen in a nickname which he invented; we used to call a certain type of person of the SR persuasion a "Christling"—very wicked irony, you must admit. The "Christlings" were those infinitely Russian people with gentle faces, the bearers of "the idea of personality in history," who in fact, many of them, really did look like Nesterov's paintings of Jesus. Women were very fond of them, and they themselves were easily inflamed. At the polytechnical balls held in the Lesnoy quarter such a "Christling" would serve as a Childe Harold, an Onegin, or a Pechorin. In general, the revolutionary rabble of the days of my youth, the innocent "periphery," seethed with novels. In 1905, boys went into the revolution with the same feelings as Nikolenka Rostov had on going into the Hussars: it was a question of love and honor. To both, life seemed impossible unless it were warmed by the glory of one's age; both thought it impossible to breathe without valor. War and Peace lived on—only the glory had moved elsewhere. Glory was not, after all, with Colonel Min of the Semyonovsky Regiment and it was not with the general in polished boots who rode in the Emperor's retinue. Glory was in the Central Committee, glory was in the "fighting organization,"[36] and feats of valor began with a novitiate as a propagandist.

Late autumn in Finland, a remote *dacha* in Raivola. Everything boarded up, the wickets barred, the wolfhounds snarling beside empty summer houses. Fall overcoats and old lap robes. The warmth of a kerosene lamp on a cold balcony. The fox snout of young T., living in the reflected glory of his father, a member of the Central Committee. No mistress of the house, but a timid consumptive creature who was not even allowed to look the guests in the face. One by one out of the darkness of the *dachas* they approach in English greatcoats and bowler hats. Sit quietly, do not go upstairs. Passing through the kitchen, I noticed the large, closely cropped head of Gershuni.[37]

War and Peace goes on. The wet wings of glory strike at the window: both ambition and the same craving for honor! The midnight sun in a Finland blind with rain, the conspiratorial sun of the new Austerlitz! Boris, dying, had hallucinations of Finland and raved of the move to Raivola and of some sort of cords for packing the baggage. We used to play skittles here, and Boris, lying in a Finnish meadow, loved to gaze into the blank sky with the cold astonished eyes of Prince Andrew.

I was troubled and anxious. All the agitation of the times communicated itself to me. There were strange currents loosed about me—from the longing for suicide to the expectation of the end of the world. The literature of problems and idiotic universal questions had just taken its gloomy malodorous leave, and the grimy hairy hands of the traffickers in life and death were rendering the very words life and death repugnant. That was in very truth the night of ignorance! Literati in Russian blouses and black shirts traded, like grain dealers, in God and the Devil, and there was not a single house where the dull polka from *The Life of Man*, which had become a symbol of vulgar tawdry symbolism, was not picked out with one finger on the piano. For too long the intelligentsia had been fed on student songs. Now it was nauseated by its universal questions. The same philosophy from a beer bottle!

That was all the vilest scum when compared to the world of the Erfurt Program, the Communist Manifestoes, and agrarian debates. They had their own Protopop Avvakum and their own dispute over whether the sign of the cross was to be made with two fingers or three (for example, the question of horseless peasants). Here in the deep and passionate strife of the SR's and SD's one could sense the continuation of the ancient feud of the Slavophiles and the Westerners.

This life, this struggle, received the distant blessings of men so far apart as Khomyakov and Kireevsky, on the one hand, and on the other the passionately Western Herzen, whose stormy political thought will always sound like a Beethoven sonata.

These men did not traffic in the sense of life, but they had spirituality, and in their spare partisan polemics there was more life and more music than in all the writings of Leonid Andreev.

XIII. *Komissarzhevskaya*

My desire is not to speak about myself but to track down the age, the noise and the germination of time. My memory is inimical to all that is personal. If it depended on me, I should only make a wry face in remembering the past. I was never able to understand the Tolstoys and Aksakovs, all those grandson Bagrovs, enamored of family archives with their epic domestic memoirs. I repeat—my memory is not loving but inimical, and it labors not to reproduce but to distance the past. A *raznochinets*[38] needs no memory—it is enough for him to tell of the books he has read, and his biography is done. Where for happy generations the epic speaks in hexameters and chronicles I have merely the sign of the hiatus, and between me and the age there lies a pit, a moat, filled with clamorous time, the place where a family and reminiscences of a family ought to have been. What was it my family wished to say? I do not know. It was tongue-tied from birth— but it had, nevertheless, something that it might have said. Over my head and over the head of many of my contemporaries there hangs congenital tongue-tie. We were not taught to speak but to babble—and only by listening to the swelling noise of the age and bleached by the foam on the crest of its wave did we acquire a language.

A revolution is itself life and death and cannot endure idle chatter about life and death in its presence. Its throat is parched with thirst, but it would not accept a single drop of moisture from alien hands. Nature—revolution—is an eternal thirst, an inflammation (perhaps it envies those ages when thirst was quenched in a quiet homelike way by simply going off to the place where the sheep were watered. This apprehensiveness is characteristic of revolution, this dread of receiving anything at all from the hands of others; it dares not, it is afraid to approach the sources of existence).

But what did these "sources of existence" ever do for the revolution? Very indifferent was the flow of their rounded waves! For themselves they flowed, for themselves they joined together to form a current, for themselves they boiled and spouted! ("For me, for me, for me," says the revolution. "On your own, on your own, on your own," answers the world.)

Komissarzhevskaya had the straight back of a girl student, a small head, and a little voice that was made for church singing.[39] Bravich played Judge Brack and Komissarzhevskaya was Hedda. She found walking and sitting tedious. The result was that she always stood. She would, for instance, walk up to the blue lantern in the window of Ibsen's professorial parlor and stand there for a long, long time, her flat, slightly stooped back turned to the audience. What was the secret of Komissarzhevskaya's charm? Why was she such a leader, a kind of Joan of Arc? Why, alongside her, did Savina seem to be an expiring *grande dame*, exhausted by a shopping trip?

The truth of the matter is that Komissarzhevskaya expressed the Protestant spirit of the Russian intelligentsia, the peculiar Protestantism of its views on art and the theater. Not for nothing was she drawn to Ibsen and raised to heights of virtuosity in that professorial drama with its Protestant decorum. The intelligentsia never loved the theater and strove to celebrate its cult in the most modest and decorous way possible. Komissarzhevskaya went to meet this Protestantism in the theater halfway, but she went too far and, exceeding the bounds of the Russian, became almost European. To begin with, she discarded all theatrical trumpery: the heat of candles, the red flower beds of the orchestra seats, the satin nests of the loges. A wooden amphitheater, white walls, gray hangings—clean as a yacht and bare as a Lutheran church. Komissarzhevskaya had, nevertheless, all the gifts of a great tragic actress, but they were in embryonic form. Unlike the Russian actors of that day—and also, perhaps, of the present day—Komissarzhevskaya possessed an inner sense of music; she raised and lowered her voice just as the breathing of the verbal sequence required. Her acting was three-quarters verbal and was accompanied only by the most essential, spare gestures, and even of these there were not many—things like wringing the hands above the head. In creating the plays of Ibsen and Maeterlinck, she was groping for the European drama, and she was sincerely convinced that Europe could offer nothing better and greater than that.

The rosy meat pies of the Aleksandrinsky Theater seemed so out of harmony with that incorporeal, spectral little world where it was always Lent. Komissarzhevskaya's small theater itself was exclusively surrounded by an atmosphere of sectarian devotion. I do not think that any perspectives for the future of the theater were opened up here. That chamber drama came to us from little Norway. Photographers. *Privatdocents*. Civil servants. The comical tragedy of a lost manuscript. The apothecary from Christiania was able to lure a storm into a professor's henhouse and to raise to the heights of tragedy the ominously polite squabbling of Hedda and Brack. For Komissarzhevskaya Ibsen was a foreign hotel, nothing more. Komissarzhevskaya broke out of the ordinary run of Russian theatrical life as out of a madhouse. She was free, but the heart of the theater was coming to a stop.

When Blok was leaning down over the deathbed of the Russian theater he recalled the name Carmen—that is to say, that from which Komissarzhevskaya could not have been more distant. The days and hours of her small theater were always numbered. Here they breathed the false and impossible oxygen of a theatrical miracle. Blok laughed maliciously at this theatrical miracle in his *Puppet Show*, and when Komissarzhevskaya produced *The Puppet Show* she mocked herself. Amid the grunting and roaring, the whining and declamation, her voice, kin to the voice of Blok, grew stronger and more mature. The theater has lived and will live by the human voice. Petrushka presses to the roof of his mouth a leaf of copper in order to alter his voice. Better Petrushka than Carmen and Aïda, than the pig snout of declamation.

XIV. *In a Fur Coat above One's Station*

Towards midnight the waves of a snowstorm were raging along the streets of Vasily Island. Blue house lamps in their mica boxes glowed at the corners of gateways. The bakery shops, unconstrained by regular hours of trade, exhaled a rich steam onto the street, but the watchmakers had long ago closed their shops, filled with a feverish muttering and the murmur of cicadas.

Clumsy doormen, bears with badges, dozed at their gates.

That is how it was a quarter of a century ago. Even now, the raspberry globes of pharmacies burn there in the winter.

My companion, emerging from his literary lair of an apartment, from his crypt-apartment with its green myopic lamp and its trough of an ottoman, with its study where the miserly hoard of books threatened to avalanche like the crumbling walls of a ravine, emerging from an apartment where the tobacco seemed to smell of wounded pride—my companion became downright cheerful and, wrapping himself in a fur coat that was above his station in life, turned upon me his ruddy, prickly, Russo-Mongolian face.

He did not summon a cabby. He bellowed for a cabby with such an imperious and chilling stentorian blast that one would have thought such a cry intended for an entire kennel of huskies plus several troikas, not the quilted little nag of a cabby.

Night. The *raznochinets littérateur* in the fur coat above his station in life is angry. Oho! But that is an old acquaintance of mine! Under the film of waxed paper in the works of Leontev there is a portrait of some spiny beast in a tall fur cap like a mitre—the high priest of frost and the state. Theory scrapes on the frost like the runners of the cabby's sleigh. Are you cold, Byzantium? Shivering and raging is the *raznochinets* author in the fur coat above his station in life.

That was just the way the Novgorodians and Pskovians used to be depicted as raging on their ikons; in tiers on each other's heads stood the laity, to the right and left, disputing and scolding, in astonishment turning their wise peasant heads on short necks toward the event. The beefy faces and hard beards of the disputants were turned toward the event with malign amazement. I think I can discern in them the archetype of literary spite.

As the Novgorodians voted spitefully with their beards on the ikon of the Last Judgment, so literature rages for a century and glowers at the event with the ardent slant-eyed gaze of a *raznochinets* and chronic failure, with the spite of a lay brother who had been awakened too late, summoned, or better to say dragged by the hair, to be a witness in the Byzantine court of history.

Literary spite! Were it not for you, what should I have to eat the salt of the earth with?

You are the seasoning for the unleavened bread of understanding, you are the joyful consciousness of injustice, you are the conspiratorial salt which is transmitted with a malicious bow from decade to decade, in a cut-glass salt cellar, with a serving cloth! That is why I so love to extinguish the heat of literature with frost and the barbed stars. Will it crunch like the crust of snow? Will it brighten up in the frosty weather of the Nekrasovian street? If it is genuine, the answer is yes.

To remember not living people but the plaster casts struck from their voices. To go blind. To feel and recognize by hearing. Sad fate! Thus does one penetrate into the present, into the modern age, as via the bed of a dried-up river.

And, you know, those were not friends, not near ones, but alien, distant people! Still, it is only with the masks of other men's voices that the bare walls of my house are decorated. To remember is to make one's way alone back up the dried riverbed!

The first literary encounter is irremediable. That was a man with a parched throat. The nightingales of Fet have long ago boiled away: an

alien, patrician pastime. A subject of envy. Lyric. "Mounted or afoot" . . .
"The grand piano was fully open." . . . "And by the burning salt of imperishable words."

The painful, inflamed eyelids of Fet drove away sleep. Tyutchev entered the veins like an early sclerosis, like a layer of lime. The five or six last Symbolist words, like the five fish of the gospel, were heavy in the basket, and among them was the big fish: Existence.

But one could not feed the hungry time with them and it was necessary to throw all five out of the basket, including the large dead fish Existence.

At the end of an historic era abstract concepts always stink like rotten fish. Better the wicked and gay sibilance of Russian verse.

The person who had bellowed for a cabby was V. V. Gippius,[40] a teacher of literature, who taught children not literature but the far more interesting science of literary spite. Why did he puff himself up in front of the children? Surely children have no need of the sting of pride, the reptilian hiss of the literary anecdote?

Even then I knew that there gather around literature its witnesses, the members, so to speak, of its household—take, just for example, the Pushkinists and so on. Later I got to know some of them. How vapid they were in comparison with V. V.!

He differed from the other witnesses of literature precisely in this malign astonishment. He had a kind of feral relationship to literature, as if it were the only source of animal warmth. He warmed himself against literature, he rubbed against it with his fur, the ruddy bristle of his hair and his unshaven cheeks. He was a Romulus who hated his wolf mother and, hating her, taught others to love her.

To arrive at V. V.'s place almost inevitably meant to wake him up. Crushing an old copy of *The Scales* or *Northern Flowers* or *The Scorpion*, he would sleep on the hard divan in his study, poisoned by Sologub, wounded by Bryusov, recalling in his sleep Sluchevsky's savage poetry, his poem "Execution in Geneva," the comrade of Konevskoy and Dobrolyubov,[41] those belligerent young monks of early Symbolism.

The hibernation of V. V. was a literary protest, something like a continuation of the policy of the old *Scales* and *Scorpion*. Awakened, he would puff himself up and begin asking about this and that with a malign little smile. But his real conversation consisted of a simple picking over of literary names and books with a kind of animal greed, with a mad but noble envy.

He was inclined to worry about his health and of all diseases he most feared tonsillitis, which prevents one from talking.

It was, nevertheless, in the energy and articulation of his speech that one found all the strength of his personality. He was unconsciously attracted to the sibilant and hissing sounds and to "t" in word endings. To put it in learned terms: a predilection for the dentals and palatals.

Inspired by the happy example of V. V. I still conceive of early Symbolism as a dense thicket of these *shch* sounds. "Nado mnoj orly, orly govorjashchie" (Above my head eagles, eagles speaking). Thus my teacher gave his preference to the patriarchal and warlike consonants of pain and attack, insult and self-defense. For the first time I felt the joy of the outward disharmony of Russian speech when V. V. took it into his head to read to us children the *Firebird* of Fet. "Na suku izvilistom i chudnom" (On the sinuous, miraculous branch): it was as if snakes were hanging above the school desks, a whole forest of sibilant snakes.* The hibernation of V. V. frightened and attracted me.

But surely literature is not a bear sucking its paws, not a heavy sleep on the study sofa after work? I would come to him to wake up the beast of literature. To listen to him growl, to watch him toss and turn. I would come to my teacher of "Russian" at home. The whole savor of the thing lay in that coming to him "at home." Even now it is difficult for me to free myself from the notion that I was then at literature's own house. Never again was literature to be a house, an apartment, a family, where red-haired little boys slept side by side in their netted cribs.

Beginning as early as Radishchev and Novikov, V. V. had established personal relations with Russian writers, splenetic and loving liaisons filled with noble enviousness, jealousy, with jocular disrespect, grievous unfairness—as is customary between the members of one family.

An intellectual builds the temple of literature with immovable idols. Korolenko, for example, who wrote so much about the Komi, seems to me

*It would be appropriate here to recall another of the intimates of literature's house and a declaimer of poetry whose personality was reflected with extraordinary force in the peculiarities of the pronunciation—N. V. Nedobrovo.

A mordantly polite Petersburger, loquacious frequenter of the salons of late Symbolism, impenetrable as a young clerk guarding a state secret, Nedobrovo turned up everywhere to recite Tyutchev—almost, as it were, to intercede for him. His speech, which was, anyway, most extraordinarily clear, with wide open vowels, as if it were inscribed on silver phonograph records, became astonishingly brilliant when he read Tyutchev, especially the alpine lines of "A kotoryj god beleet" and "A zarja i nynche seet." Then began a veritable flood of open *a*'s—it seemed as though the speaker had just washed his throat with a draught of cold alpine water.

to have turned himself into a little tin god of the Komi. V. V. taught that one should build literature not as a temple but as a gens. What he prized in literature was the patriarchal, paternal principle of culture.

How good it is that I managed to love not the priestly flame of the ikon lamp but the ruddy little flame of literary (V. V. G.) spite!

The judgments of V. V. continue to hold me in their power down to the present day. The grand tour which I made with him through the patriarchate of Russian literature from the Novikov-Radishchev period all the way to the Konevits[42] of early Symbolism, has remained the only one. After that, I merely "read a bit."

In place of a necktie there dangled a piece of string. His short neck, subject to tonsillitis, moved nervously in the colored, unstarched collar. From his larynx were torn sibilant, gurgling sounds: the belligerent *shch* and *t*.

It seemed as though this person was forever suffering the final agony, belligerent and passionate. Something of the death agony was in his very nature, and this tortured and agitated him, nourishing the drying roots of his spiritual being.

By the way, something like the following conversation was a commonplace in the Symbolist milieu:

"How do you do, Ivan Ivanovich?"

"Oh, all right, Pyotr Petrovich. I live in the hour of my death."

V. V. loved poems in which there were such energetic and happy rhymes as *plamen'* (flame)—*kamen'* (stone), *ljubov'* (love)—*krov'* (blood), *plot'* (flesh)—*Gospod'* (Lord).

His vocabulary was, without his being conscious of it, controlled by two words: *bytie* (existence) and *plamen'* (flame). If the entire Russian language were given over to his keeping, I seriously think that he would, out of carelessness, burn it up, destroy the whole Russian lexicon to the glory of *bytie* and *plamen'*.

The literature of the century was well born. Its house was a full cup.[43] At the broad open table the guests sat with Walsingham.[44] New guests, throwing off their fur coats, came in out of the cold. The little blue flames on the punch reminded the new arrivals of pride, friendship, and death. Around the table flew the request which, it seemed, was always being uttered for the last time—"Sing, Mary"—the anguished request of the last banquet.

But not less dear to me than the beautiful girl who sang that shrill Scottish song was the one who, in a hoarse voice worn out with talk, asked her for the song.

If I had a vision of Konstantin Leontev yelling for a cabby on that snow-covered street of Vasily Island it was only because he of all Russian writers is most given to handling time in lumps. He feels centuries as he feels the weather, and he shouts at them.

He might have shouted, "Oh, fine, what a splendid century we have!"—something like "A nice dry day it turned out!" Only it didn't turn out that way! He was struck dumb. The hard frost burned his throat, and the peremptory shout at the century froze like a column of mercury.

Looking back at the entire nineteenth century of Russian culture—shattered, finished, unrepeatable, which no one must repeat, which no one dares repeat—I wish to hail the century, as one would hail settled weather, and I see in it the unity lent it by the measureless cold which welded decades together into one day, one night, one profound winter, within which the terrible State glowed, like a stove, with ice.

And in this wintry period of Russian history, literature, taken at large, strikes me as something patrician, which puts me out of countenance: with trembling I lift the film of waxed paper above the winter cap of the writer. No one is to blame in this and there is nothing to be ashamed of. A beast must not be ashamed of its furry hide. Night furred him. Winter clothed him. Literature is a beast. The furriers—night and winter.

Theodosia

I. *The Harbor Master*

The starched white tunic inherited from the old regime made him look miraculously younger and reconciled him with himself: the freshness of a gymnasium student and the brisk cheerfulness of an executive—a combination of qualities which he prized in himself and feared to lóse. He conceived of the entire Crimea as one blinding, stiffly starched geographical tunic. On the other side of Perekop was night. There beyond the salt marshes there was no longer any starch, there were no washerwomen, no glad subordination, and it would be impossible there to have that springy step, as after a swim, that permanent excitement: the blended sense of well-bought currency, of clear government service, and, at the age of forty, the feeling of having passed one's exams.

Conditions were only too favorable. The businesslike briefcase was arranged with the easy domestic elegance of a traveling case, with little recesses for razor, soap dish, and brushes of various kinds. Without him, that is without the harbor master, there passed not one single ton for the barley men and the wheat men, not one ton for the grain shippers, not even for Rosh himself, the commissioner of yesterday, today an upstart, nor for the legendary Kanitfershtan, lazy and languid in the Italian manner, who shipped barley to Marseilles, nor for the wheaty Lifschitz, a scrawny turkey, the minister of the public garden of Ayvazovsky, nor to the Tsentrosoyuz,[1] nor to the Reisners, whose affairs were going so well that instead of their silver they celebrated their golden wedding anniversary, and the father, out of happiness, fraternized with the son.

Each of the filthy steamers, smelling of the kitchen and soya, with a crew of mulattoes, and with a captain's cabin that was thoroughly heated, like the international sleeper, but more like the garret of a well-to-do doorman, carried away his tons, too, indistinguishably mixed with the others.

People knew perfectly well that they were selling, along with the grain, the land on which they walked, but they went on selling that land, observing how it crumbled into the sea, and counting on leaving when they should feel under their feet the last slip of the sinking earth.

Whenever the harbor master walked along the densely shaded Italian

Street, beloved by its old residents, he was stopped every minute, taken by the arm, and led aside—which was, by the way, one of the customs of the city, where all matters were decided on the street and no one knew on leaving home when he would reach or even whether he would reach the place he had set out for. And he had developed the habit of talking with everyone just about as he would have talked with the wife of a superior—inclining his ovoid head to one side, keeping always to the left—so that the person to whom he was talking was from the outset grateful and embarrassed.

He would greet certain of the elect as if they were old friends returning from a long voyage, and would award them juicy kisses. He carried these kisses about with him like a box of fresh peppermints.

At nightfall, since I did not belong to the respected citizenry of Theodosia, I would knock at various doors in search of a place to bed down. The northeast wind was raging in the toy streets. The Ginsbergs, the Landsbergs, et al. drank their tea with white Jewish *chale* bread. The Tartar nightwatchmen walked about under the windows of money-changing shops and secondhand stores, where chibouks and guitars were draped in the silk dressing-gown of a colonel. Occasionally, too, there would pass by a belated company of cadets thundering with the soles of their English boots and rending the air with a certain paean containing several indecent expressions, which were omitted during the day at the insistence of the local rabbi.

It was then that I would rush about, in the fever familiar to every vagrant, searching for a place to sleep. And Aleksandr Aleksandrovich would open to me as a nightly asylum the harbor administration office.

I think there never was a stranger lodging. At the sound of the electric bell the door was opened by a drowsy, secretly hostile servant, made of canvas. The bright light bulbs, white as sugar, flashed on, lighting up vast maps of the Crimea, tables of ocean depths and currents, diagrams and chronometric clocks. I would carefully remove the bronze inkstand from the conference table, covered with a green cloth. Here it was warm and clean, as in a surgical ward. All the English and Italian ships that had ever awakened Aleksandr Aleksandrovich were registered in journals and lay sleeping like bibles on the shelves.

In order to understand what Theodosia was like under Denikin and Wrangel, one must know what it was like before. It was the particular quirk of this city to pretend that nothing had changed, that everything remained just exactly as it had always been. And in old times the city resembled not Genoa, that nest of military and mercantile predators, but gentle Florence. In the observatory at Harbor Master Sarandinaki's, the recording of the weather and plotting of isotherms were not the only activities: there were also weekly gatherings to hear plays and poetry, both by Sarandinaki himself and by other inhabitants of the city. The Chief of Police himself once wrote a play. Mabo,[2] the director of the Azov Bank, was better known as a poet. And when Voloshin used to appear in the pockmarked roadways of Theodosia in his town outfit—woolen stockings, velveteen trousers, and velvet jacket—the city was seized by a sort of classical melting mood, and merchants ran out of their shops.

There's no disputing it: we should be grateful to Wrangel for letting us breathe the pure air of a lawless sixteenth-century Mediterranean republic. But it was not easy for Attic Theodosia to adjust herself to the severe rule of the Crimean pirates.

That is why she cherished her kindly patron, Aleksandr Aleksandrovich, that sea-kitten in a tropical cork helmet, a man who, blinking sweetly, looked history in the face and answered its insolent tricks with a gentle meow. He was, however, the sea-god of the city—in his own way, Neptune. The more powerful the man, the more significant his manner of getting up. The French kings did not even get up, but *rose*, like the sun, and that not once but twice: the "small" and "great" rising. Aleksandr Aleksandrovich awoke together with the sea. But how did he keep in touch with the sea? He kept in touch with the sea by telephone. In the half-light of his office there was a gleam of English razors and the smell of fresh linen and strong eau de Cologne and of a sweetish imported tobacco. These splendid masculine sleeping quarters, which would have been the envy of any American, were nevertheless a captain's deckhouse and the hub of maritime communications.

Aleksandr Aleksandrovich would awake with the first steamer. Two aides, orderlies in white sailcloth, as schooled in their work as hospital attendants, would burst into headlong action at the first telephone bell and whisper to the chief, who at that moment resembled a drowsy kitten, that there had arrived and was anchored in the roads some English, Turkish, or even Serbian steamer. Aleksandr Aleksandrovich opened tiny little eyes and, though he was powerless to change anything about the arrival of the ship, said, "Ah! Good! Very good!" Then the ship became a citizen of the roads, the civic day of the sea got under way, and the harbor master changed from a sleeping kitten into the protector of merchants, into the inspirer of the customs house and of the fountain of the stock exchange, into the cognac god, the thread god, the currency god—in short, into the civic god of the sea. There was in him something of the swallow, fretting with housewifely concern over her nest—for the time being. And you would not notice that she was training with her little ones for a flight over the Atlantic. For him evacuation was not a catastophe nor a chance occurrence, but a joyous flight across the Atlantic (according to his instinct as a father and family man); it was, so to speak, the triumph of his lifelong resiliency. He never said anything about it, but he prepared for it, perhaps unconsciously, from the first moment.

II. *The Old Woman's Bird*

At the farther end of Italian Street, beyond the last secondhand store, past the abandoned gallery of the Gostinny Dvor, where there was formerly a carpet auction, behind the little French house, ivy-covered and with jalousies, where the theosophist Anna Mikhaylovna starved to death in the upholstered parlor, the road takes an upward turn toward the quarantine quarter.

From January on, the winter became extraordinarily harsh. Heavy artillery was transported along the ice at frozen Perekop. In the coffeehouse next door to the Astoria, English soldiers—"bobbies"[3]—set up a warming station. They sat in a circle around the brazier, warmed their large red hands, sang Scottish songs, and so crowded the delicate proprietors that they were prevented from cooking coffee and frying eggs. Warm and gentle, the sheep-spirited city was turned into hell. The honorary village idiot, a merry, black-bearded Karaite, no longer ran about the streets with his retinue of urchins.

The quarantine quarter: a labyrinth of little low-lying clay-walled houses with tiny windows, zigzag lanes with clay fences as tall as a man, where one stumbled over ice-covered rope or into cornel bushes. A pitiful clay Herculaneum just dug out of the earth and guarded by ill-tempered dogs. During the day you walked through this little city as though following the plan of dead Rome, and at night, in the impenetrable gloom, you were ready to knock at the door of any *petite bourgeoise* if only she would shelter you from the vicious dogs and let you in where the samovar was. The life of the quarantine district was centered about the concern for water. It guarded as the apple of its eye its ice-covered pumphouse. The noise of a clamorous female assembly never subsided on the steep hillock where the jets of pumped water had no time to freeze, and where, to keep the buckets from overflowing when they were raised, filled to the brim, the old women sealed their icy burden with floats of fagots.

The idyl of quarantine lasted several days. In one of the clay huts I rented a room from an old woman for the price of a hen's egg. Like all the housewives of the quarantine quarter, the old woman lived in the festive cleanliness of one about to die. She did not simply tidy her little house, she purified it. In the hallway there was a tiny washbowl, but so miserly was the flow of water that there was not the faintest possibility of milking it to the end. There was the smell of bread, of the burnt kerosene in a dull nursery lamp, and of the pure breath of old people. The clock ticked ponderously. Like large grains of salt, the winter stars were sprinkled about the court. And I was glad that the room was warm with breath, that someone was pottering about behind the wall, preparing a meal of potatoes, onions, and a handful of rice. The old woman kept her tenant like a bird: she thought it necessary to change his water, clean out his cage, and scatter some grain. At that time it was better to be a bird than a man, and the temptation to become the old woman's bird was enormous.

When Denikin was retreating from Kursk, the military authorities herded the railroad workers and their families together, put them into heated cars, and before they realized what was going on they were rolling off to the Black Sea. Now these railroad birds[4] from Kursk, taken from their comfortable roost, had settled in the quarantine, made themselves at home, cleaned their pots with bricks, but had still not recovered from their astonishment. The old woman could not talk without a superstitious horror of how they had been "taken down from Kursk," but as for talk about being taken back, there was none, since it was irreversibly supposed that they had been brought here to die.

If one went outside on one of those icy Crimean nights and listened to the noise of footsteps on the snowless clayey earth, frozen solid like our northern wheel tracks in October, if in the darkness one groped with the eyes among the city's hills—populated sepulchres, but with extinguished lights—if one swallowed that gruel of smothered life, thickened with dense barking of dogs and salted with stars, one began to sense with physical clarity the plague that had descended upon the world, a Thirty Years' War, with pestilence, darkened lamps, barking of dogs, and, in the houses of little people, appalling silence.

III. *The Royal Mantle of the Law*

Breath, condensed in droplets, settled on the yellow walls of the bathhouse. Tiny black cups, guarded by sweating glasses of ferriferous Crimean water, were arranged as bait for the red snoutlike lips of Karaites and Greeks. There where two were sitting a third immediately planted himself, and behind the third, suspiciously and as if for no reason at all, there stood two more. The little groups scattered and resolved like tumors, governed by the peculiar law of the gravitation of flies: people clung round the unseen center, buzzing and hanging above a piece of invisible sugar, and dashed away with malicious whining from some deal that had fallen through.

The dirty little newspaper of the OSVAG,[5] printed on gray pulp that always looked like proof sheets, called up impressions of Russian autumn in the shop of a petty merchant.

Meanwhile, above the fly-weddings and braziers, the life of the city proceeded along large, clean lines. From the Mithradates—the ancient Persian fortress on a stone mountain resembling a cardboard stage-setting—to the long arrow of the breakwater and the strictly genuine backdrop of highway, prison, and bazaar, the city described the aerial flanks of a triangle formation of cranes and offered to negotiate peace between the earth, sky, and sea. As in most of the amphitheatrical cities of the southern coast, its light blue and gray flocks of gleefully stupid houses ran down from the mountain like a consignment of sheep.

The city was older, better, and cleaner than anything that was going on in it. No dirt stuck to it. Into its splendid body bit the pincers of prison and barracks, along its streets walked cyclopes in black felt cloaks, *sotniks*,[6] smelling of dog and wolf, guardsmen of the defeated army, wearing service caps and charged to the soles of their shoes with the foxy electricity of health and youth. On some people the possibility of committing murder with impunity acts like a fresh mineral bath, and for such people, with their childishly impudent and dangerously empty brown eyes, the Crimea was simply a spa where they were following a course of treatment, keeping to a stimulating and salutary regime, suited to the requirements of their nature.

Colonel Tsygalsky played nursemaid to his sister, feebleminded and lachrymose, and to the eagle—the sick, pitiful, blind, broken-clawed eagle of the Volunteer Army. In one corner of his quarters the emblematic eagle, as it were, pottered about invisibly to the tune of the hissing primus stove, and in the other, wrapped in an overcoat or a down shawl, huddled his sister, looking like a mad clairvoyant. His extra pair of patent leather boots cried out to go—not, like seven-league boots, to Moscow—but to be sold at the bazaar. Tsygalsky was born to nurse someone and especially to guard someone's sleep. Both he and his sister looked like blind people, but in the colonel's eyes, bright with agate blackness and feminine kindness, there stagnated the dark resolve of a leader, while his sister's contained only bovine terror. He gave his sister grapes and rice to eat and would sometimes bring home from the cadet academy certain modest ration packets, which reminded one of the food rations given out to intellectuals and those who lived in the House of Scholars.

It is difficult to imagine why such people are necessary in any army at all. Such a man would be capable, I think, of throwing his arms around a general at some critical moment and saying, "Forget it, my dear fellow— let's rather go to my place and have a talk." Tsygalsky used to go to the cadets to lecture on gunnery like a student going to his lesson.

Once—embarrassed by his voice, the primus stove, his sister, the unsold patent leather boots and the bad tobacco—he read some verses aloud. There was the awkward expression, "I care not: without the throne or with the czar . . ." and some further wishes about the kind of Russia he needed—"crowned with the royal mantle of the Law"—and so on, all reminding me of the rain-blackened Themis on the Senate in Petersburg.

"Whose poem is that?"

"Mine."

Then he revealed to me that somnambulistic landscape in which he lived. The chief feature of this landscape was the abyss that had opened up where Russia had been. The Black Sea extended all the way to the Neva:

its waves, thick as pitch, licked at the slabs of the Isaac Cathedral and broke with mournful foam against the steps of the Senate. In this wild expanse, somewhere between Kursk and Sevastopol, swam the royal mantle of the Law, as if it were a lifebuoy, and it was not volunteers but some sort of fishermen in canoes who salvaged this queer appurtenance of the governmental toilet, about which the colonel himself could scarcely have known or guessed before the revolution.

The colonel: a nursemaid decked in the royal mantle of the Law![7]

IV. *Mazesa da Vinci*

When a phaeton with empty seats like plush medallions or a one-horse break with a wedding-pink canopy made its way into the scorching backwater of the upper town, the clopping hooves could be heard four blocks away. The horse, sweeping sparks with its legs, belabored the hot stones with such force that it seemed as if a staircase must be formed of them.

It was so dry there that a lizard would have died of thirst. A man in sandals and green socks, overcome by the appearance of the thundering carriage, stood looking after it for a long time. His face showed such astonishment one would have thought they were carting uphill the hitherto unused lever of Archimedes. Then he walked up to a woman who was sitting in her apartment and bartering goods right out of the window, which she had turned into a counter. After tapping a melon with his silver gypsy ring, he asked that it be cut in half for him. But when he had gone as far as the corner, he came back, exchanged the melon for two homemade cigarettes, and quickly made off.

In the upper town the houses have to a certain extent the character of barracks or bastions; they give the pleasant impression of stability and also of natural age, equal to that of a human life. Leaving aside archeology and not very remote antiquity, they were the first to turn this rough land into a city.

The house of the parents of Mazesa da Vinci, the artist, bashfully turned its domestic and lively rear toward the stone quarry. Soiled biblical featherbeds sprawled in the hot sun. Rabbits melted like sterilized down, running this way and that, spreading over the ground like spilled milk. And not too far, not too near, but right where it had to be, stood the hospitable booth with its door flung wide open. On the slanting yardarms of twine there flapped an enormous wash. The virtuous armada progressed under martial, maternal sail, but the wing belonging to Mazesa was overwhelming in the brilliance and wealth of its rigging: black and raspberry blouses, silk ankle-length nightshirts, such as are worn by newlyweds and angels, one of zephyr cloth, one à la Beethoven—I am of course speaking only of the shirts—and one resembling evening dress with long apelike arms to which had been added some colorful homemade cuffs.

Laundry dries quickly in the south: Mazesa walked straight into the yard, and ordered all that to be taken down and ironed at once.

He chose his name himself, and to those who inquired about it he would reply only reluctantly with the explanation that he liked the name da Vinci. In the first half of his sobriquet—Mazesa—he retained a blood link with his family: his father, a small, very decent man, having no fear of seasickness, transported drapery goods to Kerch in a powered sailboat, and he was called simply Mr. Mazes. And thus Mazesa, with the addition of the feminine ending, turned the family name into his first name.

Who does not know of the shipboard chaos of the renowned Leonardo's studio? Objects swirled in a whirlwind in the three dimensions of his ingenious workshop; pigeons got in through the dormer window and soiled with their droppings precious brocade, and in his prophetic blindness the master stumbled against the humble articles of everyday life of the Renaissance. Mazesa inherited from his involuntary godfather this fruitful uproar of the three dimensions, and his bedroom resembled a Renaissance vessel under sail.

From the ceiling there hung a large cradle basket in which Mazesa liked to rest during the day. Light flocks of down luxuriated in the dense, noble blackness. A ladder, brought into the room by the stubborn whim of Mazesa, was placed against the entresol, where there stood out among an assorted inventory the framework of some heavy bronze lamps that had hung in the days of Mazesa's grandfather in a Karaite prayer house. From the crater of a porcelain inkstand with sad synagogical lions there protruded several bearded, splintered pens, which had long been unacquainted with ink. On the shelf, under a velvet drape, was his library: a Spanish Bible, Makarov's dictionary, Leskov's *Cathedral Folk*, the entomology of Fabre and Baedeker's guide to Paris. On the night table, next to the envelope of an old letter from Argentina, there was a microscope, which gave the false impression that Mazesa would peer into it on waking up in the morning.

In the little city seized by Wrangel's condottieri, Mazesa was completely unnoticed and happy. He took walks, ate fruit, swam in the free pool, and dreamed of buying the white rubber-soled shoes which had been received at the Tsentrosoyuz. His relationship with people and the entire world was built on vagueness and sweet reticence.

He would go down the hill, select in the city some victim, cling to him for two, three, sometimes six hours and, sooner or later, bring him through the scorching zigzag streets back home. In doing this he was, like a tarantula, performing some dark instinctive act peculiar to him alone. He said the same thing to everyone: "Let's go to my place—we have a stone house!" But in the stone house it was the same as in the others: featherbeds, carnelian stones, photographs, and woven napkins.

Mazesa drew only self-portraits, and specialized in studies of the Adam's apple.

When the things had been ironed, Mazesa began to get ready for his evening's outing. He didn't wash but passionately immersed himself in the silver girlish mirror. His eyes darkened. His round feminine shoulders trembled.

The white tennis pants, Beethoven shirt, and sport belt did not satisfy him. He took out of the wardrobe his morning coat and in full evening ensemble—unimpeachable from sandals to embroidered skullcap—with black cheviot fins on his white thighs, he went out into the street, already washed in the goat milk of the Theodosia moon.

The Egyptian Stamp

I

I do not like rolled-up manuscripts. Some of them are heavy and smeared with time, like the trumpet of the archangel.

The Polish serving girl had gone into the church of Guarenghi[1] to gossip and to pray to the Holy Virgin.

That night there had been a dream of a Chinaman, bedecked in ladies' handbags, like a necklace of partridges, and of an American cuckoo duel in which the opponents fired their pistols at cabinets of chinaware, at inkpots, and at family portraits.

I propose to you, my family, a coat of arms: a glass of boiled water. In the rubbery aftertaste of Petersburg's boiled water I drink my unsuccessful domestic immortality. The centrifugal force of time has scattered our Viennese chairs and Dutch plates with little blue flowers. Nothing is left. Thirty years have passed like a slow fire. For thirty years a cold white flame has licked at the backs of mirrors, where the bailiff's tags are attached.

But how can I tear myself away from you, dear Egypt of objects? The clear eternity of dining room, bedroom, study. With what excuse cover my guilt? You wish Walhalla? The warehouses of Kokorev! Go there for salvation! Already the porters, dancing in horror, are lifting the grand piano (a Mignon) like a lacquered black meteor fallen from the sky. Bast mats are spread like the chasubles of priests. The cheval-glass floats sideways down the staircase, maneuvering its palm-tree length about the landings.

That evening Parnok had hung his morning coat on the back of a Viennese chair so that during the night it might rest its shoulders and arm holes and have out its sleep in the solid slumber of a cheviot. Who knows? Perhaps on its Viennese chair the morning coat turns somersaults, becomes young again—in short, frolics about? This invertebrate companion of young men pines for the triptych of mirrors at the fashionable tailor's. At the fitting it had been a simple sack—something like a knight's armor or a dubious camisole—which the artistic tailor had covered with designs in his Pythagorean chalk and inspired with life and fluent ease:

—Go, my beauty, and live! Strut at concerts, give talks, love, and make your mistakes!

—Oh, Mervis, Mervis, what have you done? Why have you deprived Parnok of his earthly raiment, why parted him from his beloved sister?

—Is he asleep?

—He's asleep! The scamp—it's a pity to waste electric light on him!

The last coffee beans disappeared down the crater of the coffee grinder, shaped like a barrel organ.

The abduction was accomplished.

Mervis carried it off like a Sabine woman.

We count by years, but in reality, in any apartment on Kamenoostrovsky, time is cleft into dynasties and centuries.

The management of a house is always rather grand. One cannot embrace the termini of a life: from the moment when one has comprehended the gothic German alphabet all the way to the golden fat of the university's *piroshki*.

The proud and touchy odor of gasoline and the greasy smell of the dear old kerosene protect the apartment, vulnerable as it is to attack from the kitchen, where porters break through with their catapults of firewood. Dusty rags and brushes warm up its white blood.

In the beginning there had been a workbench here—and Ilin's map of the hemispheres.

From this Parnok drew solace. He was consoled by the linen paper, which could not be torn. Poking with his penholder at oceans and continents, he plotted the itineraries of grandiose voyages, comparing the airy outlines of Aryan Europe with the blunt boot of Africa, with inexpressive Australia. In South America, beginning with Patagonia, he also found a certain keenness.

His respect for Ilin's map had remained in Parnok's blood since those fabulous years when he imagined that the aquamarine and ochre hemispheres, like two enormous balls held in the net of latitudes, had been empowered for their visual mission by the white-hot chancellery in the very bowels of the earth and that, like nutritional pills, they contained within themselves condensed space and distance.

Is it not with the same feeling that a singer of the Italian school, preparing to take off on her tour of a still young America, covers the geographical chart with her voice, measures the ocean with its metallic timbre, and checks the inexperienced pulse of the steamship engines with roulades and tremolos. . . .

Upside down on the retina of her eye are those same two Americas, like two green game bags containing Washington and the Amazon. By her maiden voyage on the salt sea she inaugurates the map as she reads her fortune in dollars and Russian hundred-rouble notes with their wintry crunch.

The fifties deceived her. No *bel canto* could have brightened them up. Everywhere the same low sky like a draped ceiling, the same smoky reading rooms, the same lances of the *Times* and the *Gazette*s plunged into the heart's core of the century. And, finally, Russia. . . .

Her little ears will begin to tickle: *kreshchatik, shchastie*, and *shcha-vel'*.[2] And her mouth will be stretched to her ears by the unheard of, the impossible sound ы.

And then the Cavalier Guards will flock to the church of Guarenghi for the singing of the requiem. The golden vultures will rend to pieces the Roman Catholic songstress.

How high they placed her! Could that really be death? Death would not dare to open its mouth in the presence of the diplomatic corps.

—We shall overwhelm her with plumes, with gendarmes, with Mozart!

At this moment the delirious images of the novels of Balzac and Stendhal flitted through his mind: young men in the act of conquering Paris and flicking at their shoes with handkerchiefs as they stand at the entrances of private residences—and off he went to recapture his morning coat.

The tailor Mervis lived on Monetnaya, right next to the lycée, but it was difficult to say whether he worked for the students; that was rather taken for granted, as it is taken for granted that a fisherman on the Rhine catches trout and not some sort of minnow. Everything indicated that the mind of Mervis was occupied by something more important than his job as tailor. It was not for nothing that his relatives came running to him from distant places while his client backed away in stupefaction and repentance.

—Who will give my children their roll and butter? said Mervis, gesturing with his hand as though he were scooping up some butter, and in the birdy air of the tailor's apartment Parnok had a vision not only of butter molded in the shape of a star and crimped with dewy petals but even of a bunch of radishes. Then Mervis cleverly turned the conversation first to the lawyer Grusenberg, who had ordered a senator's uniform from him in January, and then for some reason to his son Aron, a student at the Conservatory, became confused, began to fluster, and plunged behind a partition.

—Well, thought Parnok, perhaps it had to turn out this way. Perhaps the morning coat is no longer here, perhaps he actually did sell it, as he says, to pay for the cheviot.

Furthermore, if one thinks about it, Mervis has no real feeling for the cut of a morning coat. With him it always turns out to be a frock coat— something obviously more familiar to him.

Lucien de Rubempré[3] wore rough linen underwear and an awkward suit sewn by the village tailor; he ate chestnuts in the street and was terrified of concierges. Once, on a fortunate day for himself, he was shaving when the future came to life in his lather.

Parnok stood alone, forgotten by the tailor Mervis and his family. His gaze fell on the partition, behind which hummed a woman's contralto like viscous Jewish honey. This partition, pasted over with pictures, resembled a rather bizarre iconostasis.

There, dressed in a fur coat and with a distorted face, was Pushkin, whom some gentry resembling torchbearers were carrying out of a carriage, narrow as a sentry box, and, disregarding the astonished coachman in his archbishop's cap, were about to fling into the doorway. Alongside this the old-fashioned pilot of the nineteenth century, Santos-Dumont,[4] in his double-breasted jacket behung with pendants, having been thrown by the play of elements from the basket of his balloon, was depicted hanging by a rope and peering at a soaring condor. There was next a representation of some Dutchmen on stilts, who were running all about their little country like cranes.

II

The places where the inhabitants of Petersburg arrange their rendezvous are not so very different one from the other. They are hallowed by the remoteness of their origins, by the sea green of the sky, and by the Neva. One could mark them on a map of the city by little crosses amid the heavy-fleeced parks and cardboard streets. Perhaps they do change in the course of history; but just before the end, when the temperature of the age shot up to 37.3 and life raced out on a false alarm like a fire brigade thundering through the night along the luminous Nevsky Prospekt, they could easily be counted:

There was, to begin with, the Empire Pavilion in the Engineer Garden, where an outsider would have been ashamed to look in for fear of being involved in affairs that had nothing to do with him or of being compelled, for no reason on earth, to sing some Italian aria. Secondly, there were the Theban sphinxes across from the University. A third was the unsightly arch at the place where Galernaya Street comes out (not even good as a shelter from the rain). And, finally, there was a certain side alley in the Summer Garden, the position of which escapes me, though every knowledgeable person could immediately point it out with no difficulty. That is all. Only madmen would insist on meeting near the Bronze Horseman or the Alexander Column.

There lived in Petersburg a little man with patent leather shoes, who was despised by doormen and women. His name was Parnok. In early spring he would run out onto the street and patter along the still wet sidewalks with his little sheep hooves.

His desire was to get a position as a dragoman in the Ministry of Foreign Affairs, persuade Greece to undertake some risky adventure, and write a memorandum.

In February he fixed the following incident in his mind:

Blocks of good bottom ice were being transported through the city to the creamery. The ice was geometrically whole and salubrious, untouched by death and spring. But on the last sled there floated past a bright green pine branch frozen into the sky-blue glass like a Greek girl in an open grave. The black sugar of the snow lay spread out underfoot, but the trees stood in warm little moons of thawed earth.

A wild parabola joined Parnok with the pompous enfilades of history and music.

—They will throw you out one of these days, Parnok, throw you out with frightful scandal and shame . . . they'll take you by the arm and pf-f-t! . . . out of the Symphony Hall, out of the Society of Friends and Amateurs of the Last Word, out of the Circle for Grasshopper Music, out of the salon of Mme. Bookbinder . . . who knows where else? . . . but out you will go, disgraced, vilified. . . .

He had certain false memories: for example, he was convinced that when he was a child he had once stolen into a sumptuous conference hall and turned on the lights. All the clusters of bulbs and bunches of candles with crystal icicles had suddenly flashed out like a vacant apiary. The electricity had gushed out in such a terrifying current that it hurt his eyes, and he burst into tears.

Dear, blind, egotistical light.

He loved woodpiles and cordwood. In winter a dry log ought to be resonant, light, and hollow. And the birch should have a lemon-yellow core and weigh no more than a frozen fish. He felt a log as if it were alive in his hand.

From childhood he had been devoted to whatever was useless, metamorphosing the streetcar rattle of life into events of consequence, and when he began to fall in love he tried to tell women about this, but they did not understand him, for which he revenged himself by speaking to them in a wild, bombastic birdy language and exclusively about the loftiest matters.

Shapiro was called "Nikolay Davydych." Whence this "Nikolay" had come was not known, but its being linked to the name Davyd struck us as charming. It seemed to me that Davydovich—i.e., Shapiro himself—had drawn his head back into his shoulders and was bowing to some Nikolay from whom he wanted to borrow money.

Shapiro depended on my father. He would sit for hours in the absurd study with its copying machine and the armchair *style russe*. Of Shapiro it was said that he was honest and "a little man." I was for some reason convinced that "little people" never spent more than three rubles and always lived in the Sands.[5] The big-headed Nikolay Davydovich was a rough and kindly guest, eternally rubbing his hands together and smiling guiltily like an errand boy admitted into the house. He smelled of tailor and iron.

I was confident that Shapiro was honest and, delighted by this knowledge, secretly hoped that no one else would dare to be so. Below Shapiro on the social ladder there were only the commercial messengers—those mysterious runners whom one sent to the bank and to Kaplan. Threads passed from Shapiro through the commercial messengers to the bank and to Kaplan.

I loved Shapiro for needing my father. The Sands, where he lived, was a Sahara surrounding the dressmaking studio of his wife. My head swam at the thought that there were people who depended on Shapiro. I feared that a tornado might develop in the Sands and sweep away his seamstress wife with her single employee and the children with their infected throats—all like a little feather, like three rubles.

At night, as I lay falling asleep on my sagging mattress by the blue gleam of the night light, I pondered what to do with Shapiro: should I present him a camel and a carton of dates so that he might not perish in the Sands, or take him, together with that martyr, Mme. Shapiro, to the Kazan cathedral, where the rent air was black and sweet?

There is an obscure heraldry of moral ideas going all the way back to childhood: the ripping sound of a torn cloth can signify honesty, and the cold of madapollam cloth—holiness.

But the barber, holding above Parnok's head a pyramidal flask of Piksafon, poured the cold, brown liquid right onto his crown, which had gone bald at Scriabin's concerts—sloshed his head with that freezing sacramental oil—and Parnok, feeling the icy slap on the top of his skull, came to life. A frosty little shiver, as at a concert, ran along his dry skin and—Mother, have pity on your son!—penetrated beneath his collar.

—Not too hot? asked the barber as he followed the above treatment by dousing his head with a watering can full of boiling water, but Parnok only squinted his eyes and plunged his head deeper into the marble chopping block of the lavatory.

And his rabbit blood was instantly warmed under the shaggy towel.

Parnok was the victim of his preconceptions as to how a love affair must proceed.

On laid paper, my dear sirs, on English laid paper with watermarks and deckle edge he informed the unsuspecting lady that the distance between the Millionnaya, the Admiralty, and the Summer Garden had been polished like the carat of a diamond and brought to full combat readiness.

Such paper, dear reader, could have served for the correspondence of the Hermitage caryatids—for their notes of sympathy or esteem.

There are indeed people in the world who have never been ill with anything more dangerous than influenza and are somehow hooked on to the present age at the side like artificial corsages at a dance. Such people never feel themselves to be grown up and, at thirty, are still finding someone to be offended by, someone whose apologies they require. They were never particularly spoiled by anyone, and yet they are as corrupt as if they had received the academic ration of sardines and chocolate all their lives. They are muddle-headed people who know nothing more than a few chess moves but are still eager for a game just to see how it will turn out. They ought to spend their whole lives somewhere in a villa among agreeable acquaintances, listening to the chink of cups on the balcony, around the samovar that someone has fired with pine cones, and chatting with crab vendors and letter carriers. I should like to collect them all and settle them in Sestroretsk (since there is no longer anywhere else).

Parnok was a man of Kamenoostrovsky Prospekt—one of the lightest and most irresponsible streets of Petersburg. In 1917, after the February days, this street became still lighter with its steam laundries, its Georgian shops, where even cocoa was still to be bought, and its maniacal automobiles, the property of the Provisional Government.

Venture neither to the right nor to the left: there is bedlam, there is streetcar-less backwater. But on Kamenoostrovsky the streetcars develop an unheard-of speed. Kamenoostrovsky: a feather-brained young man with starch in his only two stone shirts and a sea breeze in his streetcar-filled head. It is a young dandy out of work, carrying its houses under its arm like an idle fop returning with his airy bundle from the laundress.

III

Nikolay Aleksandrovich, Father Bruni![6] Parnok hailed the clean-shaven priest from Kostroma, obviously not yet accustomed to his habit, who was carrying in his hand a savory package of ground, roasted coffee.

—Father Nikolay Aleksandrovich, let's walk together!

He pulled the priest by his wide lustrine sleeve and led him along like a small boat. It was difficult to speak with Father Bruni. Parnok regarded him as, to a certain extent, a lady.

It was the Kerensky summer,[7] and the lemonade government was in session.

Everything had been prepared for the grand cotillion. At one point it appeared as if the citizens would remain this way forever, like tomcats in turbans.

But the Assyrian bootblacks, like ravens before an eclipse, were already becoming alarmed, and the dentists began to run out of false teeth.

I love dentists for their love of art, for their wide horizons, their tolerance of ideas. Sinner that I am, I love the buzz of the dentist's drill, that poor earthbound sister of the airplane, which also drills holes with its little bit into the azure.

Girls were embarrassed in the presence of Father Bruni; young Father Bruni was embarrassed by trifles of cambric cloth; but Parnok, covering himself with the authority of the Church, separate as it was from the government, squabbled with the proprietress.

It was a frightful time: tailors took back morning coats and laundresses mocked young men who had lost their ticket.

The toasted mocha in Father Bruni's sack tickled the nostrils of the furious matron.

They went deeper into the hot cloud of the laundry, where six twittering girls were folding, mangling, and ironing. These crafty seraphim would take a mouthful of water and spray it on the frippery of zephyr and batiste. They played with monstrously heavy irons but did not cease their chatter for a moment. The vaudeville trumpery, spread like foam on long tables, waited its turn. The irons in the red maidenly fingers hissed as they completed their runs. The battleships promenaded along the whipped cream as the girls sprinkled.

Parnok recognized his shirt: it lay on a shelf, glistening with its piqué front, ironed, stuffed with pins, and thinly striped with the color of ripe cherry.

—Girls, whose is that?

—Captain Krzyżanowski's, answered the girls in a lying, unconscionable chorus.

—Father—the proprietress turned to the priest, who stood like some authority in the satiate fog of the laundry, while the steam condensed on his cassock as on a hatrack—Father, if you know this young man, give him some good advice! Even in Warsaw I never saw such a man. Always bringing me work to be done "urgently." He can take his "urgently" and. . . . He comes walking in here at night from the back way like I was a priest or a midwife. . . . I am not fool enough to give him the linen of Captain Krzyżanowski. He's not a policeman, he's a real lieutenant. That gentleman hid for only three days and then the soldiers themselves elected him to the regimental committee and now they carry him about on their shoulders.

No reply could be made to this and Father Bruni turned a pleading glance on Parnok.

And I would have given the girls not irons but Stradivarius violins, light as starling houses, and I would have given each a long scroll of musical notes. All of this cries out to be painted on a ceiling. The cassock in the clouds of steam would pass as the soutane of an abbot directing an orchestra. The six round mouths would open not like holes in bagels from the Petersburg Side[8] but like the astonished little circles in the *Concert at the Pitti Palace*.

IV

The dentist hung up the snout of the drill and went over to the window.

—Oh-ho. Have a look there!

A crowd was moving along Gorokhovaya Street with a rustle that sounded like a prayer. In the midst of it there had been preserved a free, square-shaped opening. But this air hole, through which shone the wooden paving blocks like chessboard squares, had its own order, its own system: there were to be seen five or six men who appeared to be the masters of ceremony of this whole procession. Their bearing was that of aides-de-camp. Between them were someone's padded shoulders and dandruff-strewn collar. The queen bee of this bizarre hive was the one whom the aides-de-camp were solicitously shoving along, cautiously guiding, and guarding like a pearl.

Could one say that this figure was faceless? No, there was a face, although faces in a crowd have no significance; only napes of necks and ears have an independent life.

Thus advanced the shoulders, like a coat hanger stuffed with wadding, the secondhand jackets, richly bestrewn with dandruff, the irritable napes and dog ears.

—All of those people, Parnok managed to think, are brush salesmen.

Somewhere between the Hay Market and Flour Lane, in the murk of chandlers and tanners, in the wild nursery of dandruff, bedbugs, and protruding ears, was the place that had engendered this strange commotion, spreading nausea and infection.

—They stink of bloated bowels, thought Parnok and was for some reason reminded of the terrible word "entrails." And he felt slightly sick as though from having remembered that an old woman standing near him in a shop recently had asked for "lungs" but in actual fact because of the terrible odor which welded that mob together.

Here mutual guarantee was the law: everyone, absolutely everyone, was ready to answer for the preservation and safe delivery of the dandruffy coat hanger to the bank of the Fontanka and the boat with the fish-well. Someone had only to try, with the most modest sort of exclamation, to come to the aid of the owner of the ill-fated collar, which was more highly treasured than sable or marten, and he himself would land in the soup, would be suspect, declared an outlaw and dragged into the empty square. This was the work of that master cooper, Terror.

The citizens (or the napes of their necks), as orderly and ceremonious as Shiahs on the day of Shakhse-Vakse,[9] advanced inexorably toward the Fontanka.

And Parnok spun like a top down the gap-toothed untended stair, leaving the dumbfounded dentist before the sleeping cobra of his drill and displacing any thought by the reiterated words:

"Buttons are made of animal blood."

Time—shy chrysalis, cabbage butterfly sprinkled with flour, young Jewess pressed to the shop window of a watchmaker—you had better not look!

It is not Anatole France whom we are burying in the ostrich-plumed catafalque, high as a poplar, like the pyramid that drives through the night to repair the streetcar poles: we are taking a little man to the Fontanka, to the fish-well boat, to drown him because of an American watch, a conductor's watch of white silver, a lottery watch.

You have had your stroll, my dear fellow, along Shcherbakov Lane, you have spat at the bad Tartar butchershops, hung for a bit on the handrails of a streetcar, taken a trip to see your friend Seryozhka in Gatchina, frequented the public baths and the Ciniselli circus; you have done a bit of living, little man—enough!

First Parnok ran into the watchmaker's, who was sitting like a hunchbacked Spinoza and peering at some springs, like insects under his Jewish magnifying glass.

—Do you have a telephone? I have to notify the police!

But how could a poor Jewish watchmaker on Gorokhovaya Street have a telephone? Daughters he had, melancholy as marzipan dolls, hemorrhoids he had, and tea with lemon, and debts—but no telephone.

Having hastily prepared a cocktail of Rembrandt, of goatish Spanish painting and the chirping of cicadas, and without even having touched this drink with his lips, Parnok dashed off.

Weaving his way sideways along the sidewalk in order to get ahead of the stately procession of lynchers, he ran into one of the mirror shops, which, as everyone knows, are all concentrated on Gorokhovaya. The mirrors threw back and forth the reflections of houses that looked like buffets; the frozen pieces of street, teeming with the beetling mob, appeared in the mirrors still more terrifying and shaggy.

To defend his business, untouched by any shame since 1881, the suspicious Czech proprietor slammed the door in his face.

At the corner of Voznesensky there appeared Captain Krzyżanowski himself with his pomaded moustache. He was wearing a military topcoat, but with a saber, and was nonchalantly whispering to his lady the sweet nothings of the Horse Guard.

Parnok raced up to him as though he were his best friend and implored him to draw his weapon.

—I appreciate the situation, the bowlegged captain coldly replied, but pardon me, I am with a lady. And skillfully seizing his companion, he jingled his spurs and disappeared into a cafe.

Parnok ran, tripping along the paving blocks with the little sheep hooves of his patent leather shoes. More than anything in the world he feared to attract upon himself the displeasure of the mob.

There are people who for some reason or other displease mobs. The mob picks them out at once, taunts them, and pulls them by the nose. Children have no special liking for them and women find them unattractive.

Parnok was among this number.

His schoolmates called him "sheep," "patent leather hoof," "Egyptian stamp," and other insulting names. For no earthly reason, the brats had circulated the rumor that he was a "spot remover," that is, that he knew some special preparation that would remove oil spots, ink spots, etc., and for fun they would filch their mother's shapeless old clothes, bring them to class, and with an innocent expression ask Parnok to "remove this little spot."

And here is the Fontanka—the Undine of ragpickers and hungry students with long, greasy hair; the Lorelei of boiled crawfish, who makes music on a comb with missing teeth; the patroness of the shabby Maly Theater with its seedy, bald Melpomene, like a witch perfumed with patchouli.

Well! The Egyptian Bridge never so much as smelled Egypt, and not a single honest man ever laid eyes on Mr. Kalinkin.[10]

The innumerable swarm of human locusts (God knows where they were coming from) blackened the banks of the Fontanka and clung round the fish-well boat, the barges loaded with cordwood, the wharves, the granite steps, and even the boats of the Ladoga potters. Thousands of eyes gazed into the water with its oily rainbows, flashing with all the hues of kerosene, mother-of-pearl filth, and peacock tails.

Petersburg had declared itself Nero and was as loathsome as if it were eating a soup of crushed flies.

Nevertheless, he telephoned from a pharmacy, telephoned the police, telephoned the government, the state, which had vanished, sleeping like a carp.

He might with equal success have telephoned Proserpine or Persephone, who had not yet had a telephone installed.

Telephones in pharmacies are made of the very finest scarlatina wood. The scarlatina tree grows in enema groves and smells of ink.

Do not telephone from Petersburg pharmacies: the instrument sloughs its skin and the voice fades. Remember that no telephone has yet been installed for Proserpine or Persephone.

My pen sketches a beautiful mustached Greek woman and someone's fox-like chin.

It is thus that arabesques spring up in the margins of first drafts and live independent, gorgeous, and perfidious lives.

Little men shaped like violins drink the milk of the paper.

Here is Babel: the fox chin and pawlike glasses.

Parnok is an Egyptian stamp.

Artur Yakovlevich Hofman—an official in the Greek section of the Ministry of Foreign Affairs.

The French horns of the Mariinsky Theater.

Another mustached Greek woman.

And a blank space for the others.

The swallows of the Hermitage chirped about the sun of Barbizon, about plein-air painting, about coloring like spinach with croutons—in short, about everything that is lacking in the gloomily Flemish Hermitage.

But I shall not receive an invitation to the luncheon of Barbizon even though in my childhood I did tear down the notched, hexagonal lanterns of the coronation and directed toward the sandy pine groves and heather now the irritatingly red trachoma, now the blue noonday cud of some alien planet, now the violet night of a cardinal.

Mother seasoned the salad with egg yolks and sugar.

The torn, crumpled ears of the salad and the marrow died together from vinegar and sugar.

The air, vinegar, and sun were kneaded together with green rags into one complete day of Barbizon, burning with salt, trellises, glass beads, gray leaves, larks, and dragonflies and loud with the sound of crockery.

The Sunday of Barbizon, fanning itself with newspapers and napkins, progressed toward its zenith, lunch, while it scattered the lawn with *feuilletons* and notes about actresses slender as pins.

Guests in wide trousers and leonine velvet vests converged upon the parasols of Barbizon. And women brushed the fruit flies from their round shoulders.

The open wagonettes of the railroad were loath to submit to the steam and, having flapped their curtains, played lotto with the field of camomile.

The top-hatted locomotive with its chicken pistons was outraged at the weight of the chapeaux-claques and muslin.

The barrel sprinkled the street with twine of frail and fragile strings.

The air itself already seemed to be a huge railroad station for the fat, impatient roses.

And brilliant black ants, like the carnivorous actors of the Chinese theater in an old play with an executioner, strutted their turpentine braids and dragged after them the martial sections of a body that had not yet been hacked to pieces as they staggered with their strong, agate rears, like military horses galloping up a hill in farthingales of dust.

Parnok shook himself.

A slice of lemon is a ticket to the fat roses of Sicily, and floor-polishers dance with Egyptian gestures.

The elevator is out of order.

The Menshevik partisans, organizing the night duty at the carriage gates, go from house to house.

Life is both terrifying and beautiful!

He is a lemon seed thrown into a crevice in the granite of Petersburg and will be drunk with black Turkish coffee by the winged night that is approaching.

V

In May Petersburg somehow reminds one of an information booth[11] that does not give out information—especially in the Palace Square area. It is positively terrifying how everything has been prepared for the opening of the historic session: white sheets of paper, sharpened pencils, and a carafe of boiled water.

I repeat once more: the grandeur of this place is that no information is ever given to anyone.

At that moment some deaf-mutes were passing through the square: with their hands they were twisting a rapid thread. They were conversing. The senior among them controlled the shuttle. They helped him. From time to time a boy would run up from one side with his fingers spread so wide that he seemed to be asking for the thread, laced diagonally upon them, to be removed lest it damage the weaving. For all of them together (there were four) it was obviously intended that there be five skeins. There was one skein extra. They were speaking the language of swallows and panhandlers and, constantly basting up the air with huge stitches, were making a shirt of it.

In a rage the chief tangled all the yarn.

The deaf-mutes disappeared into the General Staff Arch; they went on twisting their yarn, but were already much more tranquil, as if they were releasing messenger pigeons in various directions.

Musical notation caresses the eye no less than music itself soothes the ear. The blacks of the piano scale climb up and down like lamplighters. Each measure is a little boat loaded with raisins and black grapes.

A page of music is, firstly, the deployment in battle of sailing flotillas and, secondly, the plan according to which night, arranged in plum pits, sinks.

The colossal arpeggiated descents in Chopin's mazurkas, the wide staircases festooned with bells in the Liszt études, Mozart's hanging gardens with parterres, trembling on five wires—these have nothing in common with the undersized shrubbery of the Beethoven sonatas.

The mirage cities of musical notation stand like starling houses in boiling pitch.

Schubert's vineyard of notes is always pecked right down to the seeds and lashed by storms.

When hundreds of lamplighters rush about the streets with their little ladders hanging flats on rusty hooks,[12] strengthening the weathervane of sharps, taking down entire placards of stringy measures—that, of course, is Beethoven; but when the cavalry of eighths and sixteenths in their paper plumes with horse insignia and little standards throw themselves into the attack—that, too, is Beethoven.

A page of music is a revolution in an ancient German city.

Macrocephalic children. Starlings. They are unhitching the carriage of the prince. Chess players are running out of the coffee houses waving queens and pawns.

There are turtles sticking out their tender heads and competing in a race: that is Handel.

But how warlike are the pages of Bach—those astonishing sheaves of dried mushrooms.

On Sadovaya near the Church of the Intercession stands a fire tower. On freezing January days it throws out alarm signals like grapes—to assemble the brigades. It was not far from there that I studied music. They taught me how to place my hands according to the system of Leszetycki.[13]

Let the languid Schumann hang up notes as if they were linen put out to dry, while downstairs Italians stroll about with their noses in the air; let the most difficult passages of Liszt, waving their crutches about, drag the fire ladder there and back.

The grand piano is an intelligent and good-natured house animal with fibrous, wooden flesh, golden veins, and eternally inflamed bone. We protected it from catching a cold and nourished it with sonatinas, light as asparagus.

Lord! Do not make me like Parnok! Give me the strength to distinguish myself from him.

For I also have stood in that terrifying, patient line which creeps toward the yellow window of the box office—first out in the cold, then under the low, bathhouse ceiling of the vestibule of the Aleksandrinsky Theater. And I am terrified by the theater as by a hut with no chimney, as by a village bathhouse where a bestial murder was committed for the sake of a half-length coat and a pair of felt boots. And I, too, am sustained by Petersburg alone—the Petersburg of concerts, yellow, ominous, sullen, and wintry.

My pen has become insubordinate: it has splintered and squirted its black blood out in all directions, as if it were attached to the desk in the telegraph office, a public pen, ruined by scoundrels in fur coats, having exchanged its swallowy flourish, its original stroke, for such phrases as "Come for God's sake," "Miss you," "kisses," penned by unshaven lechers whispering their little message into their fur collars, warm with their breath.

The kerosene lamp existed before the primus. Mica window and collapsible lighthouse. Like the tower of Pisa the kerosene lamp nodded to Parnok, baring its patriarchal wick and relating in a good-natured way the story of the youths in the fiery furnace.

I am not afraid of incoherence and gaps.

I shear the paper with long scissors.

I paste on ribbons as a fringe.

A manuscript is always a storm, worn to rags, torn by beaks.

It is the first draft of a sonata.

Scribbling is better than writing.

I do not fear seams or the yellowness of the glue.

I am a tailor, I am an idler.

I draw Marat[14] in his stocking.

I draw martins.

In our family the thing that was most feared was "soot"—that is, lamp-black from the kerosene lamps. The cry "soot, soot" sounded like "fire, we're on fire," and everyone would run into the room where the lamp was playing tricks. Waving their arms in the air, they would stop and sniff the air, which was filled with a swarm of live, whiskered, fluttering tea leaves.

The guilty lamp was executed by lowering the wick.

Then the little dormer windows would be immediately thrown open and through them would shoot a frost like champagne, hastily chilling the whole room with the mustached butterflies of "soot," settling on the piqué bedspreads and pillowcases like an ether of grippe, a sublimate of pneumonia.

—Don't go in there—the dormer window—whispered mother and grandmother.

But even into the keyhole it forced its way—the forbidden chill, the miraculous guest from diphtherial space.

The Judith of Giorgione slipped away from the eunuchs of the Hermitage.

The trotting horse throws out its pasterns.

Little silver glasses fill up the Millionnaya.

Damned dream! Damned squares of this shameless city!

He made a weak, pleading gesture with his hand, dropped a sheet of perfumed, powdered paper, and sat down on a road marker.

He recalled his inglorious victories, his rendezvous (for which he waited ignominiously in the street), the telephones in beer halls, terrifying as the pincers of a crawfish. . . . The numbers of useless, burned-out telephones. . . .

The luxurious rattle of a droshky evaporated in a silence that was as suspect as the prayer of a cuirassier.

What is to be done? To whom can one complain? To which seraphim should one deliver the shy, concert-going soul belonging to the raspberry paradise of contrabasses and drones?

Scandal is the name of the demon discovered by Russian prose or by Russian life itself sometime in the Forties. It is not catastrophe, though it apes it: a foul transformation by which a dog's head sprouts from a man's shoulders. Scandal carries a soiled, expired passport issued by literature, of which it is the spawn, the beloved offspring. A little grain has disappeared: a homeopathic liqueur bonbon, a tiny dose of a cold, white substance. . . .

In those distant days when men had recourse to the cuckoo duel—that duel in which the opponents stood in a dark room and fired their pistols into cabinets of chinaware, into ink pots, and family portraits—that little pellet was called "honor."

Once, some bearded literati in trousers as wide as pneumatic bells climbed up on a photographer's starling house and had their picture taken in a splendid daguerreotype. Five of them were sitting, four standing behind the backs of the walnut chairs. In front of them in the picture was a little boy in a Circassian coat and a little girl with her hair in ringlets, and darting about between the legs of the company was a kitten. He was removed. All their faces expressed one alarmingly grave question: what is the current price of a pound of elephant meat?

That evening in a villa in Pavlovsk these writing gentlemen had raked a poor youngster, Ippolit, over the coals, thus spoiling his chance to finish reading his checkered notebook. Another one trying to be Rousseau!

They did not see and did not understand the charming city with its clean, shiplike lines.

And the imp, scandal, installed itself in an apartment on Razezzhaya Street, having attached a bronze plaque bearing the name of an Attorney-at-Law—that apartment remains unchanged to this day, like a museum, like the Pushkin House—it snored on the ottomans, stamped about in the entrance hall (people living under the star of scandal never know how to leave on time), made a nuisance of itself with its begging for favors, and said long, tedious good-byes as it fussed about in someone else's galoshes.

Gentlemen, litterateurs! As ballet slippers belong to ballerinas, so the galoshes—to you. Try them on, exchange them—this is your dance. It is performed in dark antechambers, but on one strict condition: disrespect for the master of the house. Twenty years of such a dance make an epoch, forty—history. That is your right.

Currant smiles of the ballerinas,

    muttering of the slippers rubbed with talc, the military complexity and insolent multitude of the string orchestra, hidden in a luminous ditch where the musicians became confused, like dryads, by the branches, roots, and fiddlesticks

    the vegetable obedience of the corps de ballet,

    the splendid disdain for motherhood:

—They've just played sixty-six with this king and queen who don't dance.

—The youthful-looking grandmother of Giselle pours milk around, probably almond milk.

—Every ballet is to a certain extent a serf ballet. No, no, you can't argue with me on this point!

The January calendar with its ballet goats, its model dairy of myriad worlds, its crackle of a deck of cards being unwrapped. . . .

Approaching from the rear the indecently waterproof building of the Mariinsky Theater:

—Detectives-scalpers, scalpers-detectives,

Why are you roving around, my dears, in the cold?

Some find a ticket to get in

Others are tricked out of their skin.

—No, no matter what you say, at the basis of the classical ballet there lies a fearful threat—a chunk of the "governmental ice."

—What do you think, where was Anna Karenina sitting?

—Consider: in the ancient world they had amphitheaters, but we, in modern Europe, have tiers. Both in the frescoes of the Last Judgment and at the Opera. One and the same worldview.

The streets, smoky with bonfires, whirled like a carousel.

—Driver, to "Giselle"—that is, to the Mariinsky!

The Petersburg cabby is a myth, a Capricorn. He should be put in the zodiac. There he would not be lost with his old woman's purse, his sleigh runners, narrow as truth, and his oaty voice.

VI

The droshky had a classic chic, rather Muscovite than Petersburg; with its high-riding body, its brilliantly polished fenders, and its tires inflated to the limit of possibility, it could not have looked more like a Greek chariot.

Captain Krzyżanowski whispered into the criminal, pink little ear:

—Don't worry about him. My word of honor, he is having a tooth filled. I will tell you what's more: this morning on the Fontanka he—I don't know which—either stole a watch or had one stolen from him. The scoundrel! A filthy story!

The white night, having stridden through Kolpina and Srednyaya Rogatka, arrived at Tsarskoe Selo. The palaces stood about, white with fright, like silken cowls. At times their whiteness resembled a shawl of Orenburg down, washed with soap and alkali. In the deep green foliage bicycles buzzed—the metal hornets of the park.

Any further whiteness was unthinkable; one minute more, it seemed, and the entire hallucination would break into pieces like fresh bonnyclabber.

A terrifying stone lady "in the high boots of Peter the Great" walks about the streets and speaks.

—Garbage in the squares . . . Simoom . . . Arabs . . . "Semyon simpered to the proseminar."[15]

Petersburg, you are responsible for your poor son!

For all this melee, for this pitiful love of music, for every gram of those liqueur bonbons, carried in a paper sack by the girl student sitting in the gallery of the Nobility Hall, you, Petersburg, will answer!

Memory is a sick Jewish girl who steals away in the night from her parents' house to the Nicholas Station thinking that perhaps someone will turn up to carry her off.

The "little old insurance man," Geshka Rabinovich, as soon as he was born, had asked for some policy forms and Ralle soap. He lived on the Nevsky in a tiny, girlish apartment. Everyone was touched by his illicit liaison with a certain Lizochka.—Genrikh Yakovlevich is asleep, Lizochka would say, putting her finger to her lips and blushing all over. She hoped, of course (insane hope), that Genrikh Yakovlevich would still grow a bit and would live long years with her, and that their rosy, childless marriage, consecrated by the archbishops of Filippov's coffeehouse, was only the beginning. . . .

But Genrikh Yakovlevich, with the bounciness of a toy dog, ran up and down stairs insuring what remained of people's lives.

In Jewish apartments there reigns a melancholy, bewhiskered silence.

It is composed of the conversations between the pendulum and the bread crumbs on the checkered tablecloth and the silver glass holders.

Aunt Vera would come to dinner and bring along her father, old Pergament. Behind Aunt Vera's shoulders there stood the myth of the ruin of Pergament. He had an apartment of forty rooms on the Kreshchatik in Kiev. "A house is a full cup."[16] On the street beneath the forty rooms beat the hooves of Pergament's horses. Pergament himself "clipped coupons."

Aunt Vera was a Lutheran and sang with the parishioners in the red church on the Moyka. She exuded the chill of a companion, reader, and hospital nurse—that strange breed of people inimically bound to someone else's life. Her thin Lutheran lips disapproved of the manner in which our household was run and her spinsterish curls hung above the chicken soup with a faint air of disgust.

On appearing at the house, Aunt Vera would mechanically begin to sympathize and offer her Red Cross services as though she were unrolling a spool of gauze and throwing out a streamer of invisible bandage.

The cabriolets drove along the hard pavement of the highway and the men's Sunday coats bristled like roofing iron. The cabriolets drove from *yarvi* to *yarvi*[17] so that the kilometers spilled out like peas and smelled of spirits and cottage cheese. The cabriolets drove, twenty-one and four more, carrying old women in black kerchiefs and in cloth skirts that were stiff as tin. They had to sing songs in the rooster-topped church, drink coffee spiked with pure alcohol, and return by the same road.

The young raven puffed himself up: Welcome to our funeral.

—That's not the way to invite people, twittered the little sparrow in the park of Mon Repos.[18]

Then the lean ravens with feathers that were hard and blue from age interposed: Karl and Amalia Blomquist announce to their family and friends the death of their beloved daughter Elza.

—That is something else again, twittered the little sparrow in the park of Mon Repos.

Boys on the street were fitted out like knights at a tourney: gaiters, wide padded trousers, and ear flaps. The ear flaps caused a buzzing in the head and deafness. In order to answer someone it was necessary to undo the laces that cut into one's chin.

He whirled about in his heavy winter armor like a deaf little knight, not hearing his own voice.

The first isolation from people and from himself and—who knows?—the sweet adumbration of sclerosis in his blood (for the time being still rubbed by the shaggy towel of the seventh year of life)—all this was brought to life in his ear flaps; and the six-year-old padded Beethoven in gaiters, armed with his deafness, was pushed out onto the stairs.

He wanted to turn around and shout, "The scullery maid is deaf as a spade."

They walked pompously along Ofitserskaya, stopping in the store to pick out a duchess pear.

Once they dropped in to Aboling's lamp store on Voznesensky, where the showy lamps thronged like idiot giraffes in red hats with festoons and flounces. Here for the first time they were overcome by the impression of grandeur and "the forest of things."

They never dropped in to Eylers's flower shop.[19]

Somewhere the woman doctor Strashuner was practicing.

VII

When a tailor delivers his finished work, you would never say that he had new clothes on his arm. He somehow resembles a member of a burial society hastening with the appurtenances of the ritual to a house marked by Azrail. Thus the tailor Mervis. Parnok's morning coat did not warm itself on his hanger long—about two hours; that was all the time it had to breathe its native caraway air. The wife of Mervis congratulated him on his success.

—That is nothing, answered the master, flattered. My grandfather used to say that a real tailor is one who, in broad daylight, on Nevsky Prospekt, can take a frock coat off a customer who won't pay.

Then he took the morning coat down from the hanger, blew on it as if it were a cup of hot tea, wrapped it up in a clean linen sheet, and carried it in its white shroud and black calico to Captain Krzyżanowski.

I must confess that I love Mervis—I love his blind face, furrowed by wrinkles that see. Theoreticians of the classical ballet devote great attention to a ballerina's smile; they regard it as an accessory to her movement, an interpretation of her leap, her flight. But sometimes a lowered lid sees more than an eye, and the tiers of wrinkles on a human face peer like a gathering of blind men.

The tailor, then, elegant as porcelain, sweeps along like a convict torn from his plank bed, beaten up by his comrades, like an overheated bath attendant, like a thief in a bazaar, ready to shout his last irresistibly convincing word.

In my perception of Mervis certain images gleam through: a Greek satyr, the unhappy singer Kifared,[20] at times the mask of an actor in a play by Euripides, at times the naked breast and sweaty body of a flogged convict, of an inmate in a Russian flophouse, of an epileptic.

I hasten to tell the real truth, I am in a hurry. The word, like aspirin powder, leaves a brassy taste in the mouth.

Cod-liver oil is a mixture of conflagrations and yellow winter mornings, and whale oil has the taste of torn-out eyes that have burst, the taste of revulsion brought to the point of ecstasy.

A bird's eye, suffused with blood, also has its own way of seeing the world.

Books melt like chunks of ice brought into a room. Everything grows smaller. Everything seems to me a book. Where is the difference between a book and a thing? I do not know life: they switched it on me as long ago as the time when I recognized the crunch of arsenic between the teeth of the amorous French brunette, the younger sister of our proud Anna.

Everything grows smaller. Everything melts. Even Goethe melts. Brief is the time allotted us. As it slips away, the hilt of that bloodless, brittle sword, broken off the drainpipe one freezing day, chills the palm.

But thought—like the hangman steel of the "Nurmis"[21] skates, which once skimmed along the blue, pimply ice—has not been blunted.

Thus skates screwed onto shapeless children's shoes, to American laced hooves, grow together with them—lancets of freshness and youth—and the shoes thus equipped, having borne their joyous weight, are transformed into the magnificent remains of a dragon, for which there is neither name nor price.

It is more and more difficult to turn the pages of the frozen book, bound in axes by the light of gas lanterns.

You, wood yards—black libraries of the city—we shall yet read, we shall still have a look.

Somewhere on Podyacheskaya was situated that renowned library whence packs of little brown volumes by Russian and foreign authors (their contagious pages so read that they seemed made of silk) were taken away to the villa. Homely young ladies chose the books from the shelves. For one Bourget, for another Georges Ohnet, for a third something else from the literary lumber room.

Across the street was a fire brigade with hermetically sealed gates and a bell in a mushroom hat.

Some pages were transparent as onion skin.

They were inhabited by measles, scarlatina, and chicken pox.

In the spines of those villa books, often forgotten on the beach, the golden dandruff of the sand had become embedded; no matter how one shook it, it appeared again.

Sometimes out would fall a piece of fern—a little Gothic fir tree, flattened and spoiled—and occasionally the mummy of some nameless northern flower.

Conflagrations and books: that is good.

We shall still see, we shall read a bit.

"Several minutes before the beginning of the agony, a fire brigade thundered along the Nevsky. Everyone dashed to the square, sweaty windows, and Angiolina Bosio—from Piemonte, the daughter of a poor strolling player, *basso comico*—was left for a moment to herself.

The martial trills and cadenzas of the firemen's crowing horns, like the unheard-of gusto of an unconditionally victorious misfortune, forced their way into the stuffy bedroom of the Demidov house. The fire horses with their barrels, carts, and ladders thundered off and the flame of the torches licked the mirrors. But in the guttering consciousness of the dying singer this bedlam of feverish, official clamor, this lunatic gallop in sheepskin coats and helmets, this armful of noises, arrested and driven off under guard, was changed into the appeal of an orchestral overture. In her small homely ears she plainly heard the final measures of the overture to *I due Foscari*, the opera of her London debut. . . .

She raised herself a bit and sang what was required, but not in that sweet voice, metallic and pliant, which had made her fame and which the newspapers had praised, but with the chesty, unpracticed timbre of a fifteen-year-old girl, with an incorrect, wasteful production of the sound, for which Professor Cattaneo had been so cross with her.

Farewell Traviata, Rosina, Zerlina. . . ."[22]

VIII

That evening Parnok did not return home to have dinner and drink tea with the little cakes which he loved like a canary. He listened to the sputter of the blowtorches as they approached the streetcar tracks with their blindingly white, shaggy roses. He received back all the streets and squares of Petersburg in the form of rough galley proofs, he composed the prospects, stitched the gardens.

He approached the raised drawbridges, which reminded him that all must come to an abrupt end, that desolation and the abyss are splendid wares, that there would be, would surely be, a leavetaking, that treacherous levers controlled masses and years.

He waited while on one side and the other the camps of the drivers and pedestrians accumulated like two hostile tribes or generations, quarreling over the wooden stone-bound book, the interior of which had been ripped out.

He thought of Petersburg as his infantile disease—one had only to regain consciousness, to come to, and the hallucination would vanish: he would recover, become like all other people, even—perhaps—get married. . . . Then no one would dare call him "young man." And he would be through with kissing ladies' hands. They'd had their share! Setting up their own Trianon, damn them! Let some slut, some old bag, some shabby feline stick her paw out to his lips and, by the force of long habit, he would give it a smack! Enough! It was time to put an end to his lapdog youth. Besides, had not Artur Yakovlevich Hofmann promised to find him a place as dragoman, even if only in Greece? And there he would see. He would have himself a new morning coat made, he would have it out with Captain Krzyżanowski, he would show him.

There was only one thing wrong—he had no pedigree. And nowhere to get one. He simply didn't have one and that was all there was to it! Of relatives he had only one, an aunt, Aunt Johanna. A dwarf. A veritable Empress Anna Leopoldovna. Spoke Russian like God knows what. As if Biron were her blood brother. Little short arms. She couldn't button anything by herself. And she had a maid, Annushka[23]—Psyche.

Yes, with such relatives one could not go far. But—wait a moment— how is that not a pedigree? How not? It is. What about Captain Golyadkin?

And the collegiate assessors, to whom "the Lord God might have given more brains and money"?[24] All those people who were shown down the stairs, publicly disgraced, insulted in the forties and fifties of the last century, all those mutterers, windbags in capes, with gloves that had been laundered to shreds, all those who do not "live" but "reside" on Sadovaya and Podyacheskaya in houses made of stale sections of petrified chocolate and grumble to themselves: "How is that possible? Not a penny to my name, and me with a university education?"

One has only to remove the film from the Petersburg air and then its hidden stratum will be revealed. Under the swansdown, the eiderdown, the far end of Gagarin, under the Tuchkov puffs of clouds, under the French *bouchées* of the dying quays, under the little plate-glass windows in the apartments of noblemen and yes-men, there will be revealed something completely unexpected.[25]

But the pen that removes this film is like a doctor's teaspoon—contaminated with a touch of diphtheria. It is better not to touch it.

The mosquito whined:

—Look what has happened to me: I am the last Egyptian—a sobber, sober tutor, simple soldier—I am a little bowlegged prince—a beggarly, blood-sucking Ramses—in the north I have become nothing—so little is left of me—I beg your pardon!

—I am the prince of ill fortune—a collegiate assessor of the city of Thebes. . . . Everything is the same—not a whit changed—Oh! I am frightened here—Excuse me. . . . I am a trifle—I am nothing. I will ask the choleric granite for a kopeck's worth of Egyptian pap, for a kopeck's worth of girl's neck.

—I—don't worry—I'll pay—Excuse me.

To calm himself, he consulted a certain small, unwritten dictionary—or rather, a register of little homey words that had gone out of use. He had long ago composed it in his mind for use in case of misfortune and shock:

"Horseshoe." That was the name for a poppy-seed roll.

"Fromuga"—his mother's name for the large, hinged dormer window, which slammed shut like the lid of a grand piano.

"Don't botch it." This was said about life.

"Do not command." One of the commandments.

These words will suffice to impart the flavor. He accustomed himself to the aroma of this little pinch of them. The past became overwhelmingly real and tickled his nostrils like a shipment of fresh Kyakhta teas.

Carriages drove across the snowy field. Above the field hung a low, police-linen sky which doled out in a miserly way the yellow and, for some reason, shameful light.

I was attached to someone else's family and carriage. A young Jew was counting some new hundred-ruble notes that crackled with a wintry sound.

—Where are we going? I asked an old woman in a gypsy shawl.

—To the city of Malinov, she replied, but with such aching melancholy that my heart contracted with an evil foreboding.

The old woman, rummaging about in her striped bundle, took out some table silver, a cloth, and velvet slippers.

The threadbare wedding carriages crawled on and on, reeling like contrabasses.

In the carriage rode Abrasha Kopelyansky, with his angina pectoris, Aunt Johanna, rabbis, and photographers. An old music teacher held on his knees a mute keyboard. Wrapped tight in the skirts of the old man's beaver coat was a fidgety rooster destined for ritual Jewish slaughter.

—Look, exclaimed someone, sticking his head out of the window. There is Malinov already.

But there was no city there. Instead, growing right in the snow were some large, warty raspberries.

—But that's a raspberry patch,[26] I gasped, beside myself with joy, and began to run with the others, filling my shoes with snow. My shoe came untied and because of that I was seized with a feeling of great guilt and disorder.

And they led me into a hateful Warsaw room and made me drink water and eat onion.

I kept bending over to tie my shoe with a double knot and put everything in its proper order—but in vain. It was impossible to recoup anything or repair anything: everything went backwards, as always happens in a dream. I scattered the featherbeds of others and ran out into the Taurid Gardens, clasping the favorite plaything of my childhood, an empty candlestick richly covered with stearin, and removed its white bark, tender as a bridal veil.

It is terrifying to think that our life is a tale without a plot or hero, made up out of desolation and glass, out of the feverish babble of constant digressions, out of the delirium of the Petersburg influenza.

Rosy-fingered Dawn has broken her colored pencils. Now they lie scattered about like nestlings with empty, gaping beaks. Meanwhile, I seem to see in absolutely everything the advance deposit of my dear prosaic delirium.

Are you familiar with this condition? When it's just as if every object were running a fever, when they are all joyously excited and ill: barriers in the street, posters shedding their skin, grand pianos thronging at the depot like an intelligent, leaderless herd, born for frenzies of the sonata and for boiled water. . . .

Then, I confess, I am unable to endure the quarantine and, smashing thermometers, through the contagious labyrinth I boldly stride, behung with subordinate clauses like happy bargain buys . . . and into the waiting sack fly the crisp pastry birds, naive as the plastic art of the first centuries of Christianity, and the *kalatch*, the common *kalatch*, no longer conceals from me that it was conceived by the baker as a Russian lyre of voiceless dough.

The Nevsky in '17: a squadron of Cossacks with their blue caps cocked on their heads, their faces turned in the direction of the sun's path like identical, oblique fifty-kopeck pieces.

Even with one's eyes shut tight, one can tell that those are cavalrymen singing.

The song rocks in the saddles like tremendous free sacks filled with the gold foil of hops.

It is the free victual served with the little trot, jingle, and sweat.

It floats along on blind, shaggy Bashkirs at the level of the plate-glass windows of the first floor as if the very squadron itself were floating on a diaphragm, trusting it more than saddle girths and legs.

Destroy your manuscript, but save whatever you have inscribed in the margin out of boredom, out of helplessness, and, as it were, in a dream. These secondary and involuntary creations of your fantasy will not be lost in the world but will take their places behind shadowy music stands, like third violins at the Mariinsky Theater, and out of gratitude to their author strike up the overture to *Leonora* or the *Egmont* of Beethoven.

What a pleasure for the narrator to switch from the third person to the first! It is just as if, after having had to drink from tiny inconvenient thimble-sized glasses, one were suddenly to say the hell with them, to get hold of oneself, and drink cold, unboiled water straight out of the faucet.

Terror takes me by the hand and leads me. A white cotton glove. A woman's glove without fingers. I love terror, I respect it. I almost said "With it, I'm not terrified!" Mathematicians should have built a tent for terror, for it is the coordinate of time and space: they participate in it like the rolled-up felt in the nomad tent of the Kirgiz. Terror unharnesses the horses when one has to drive and sends us dreams with unnecessarily low ceilings.

At the beck and call of my consciousness are two or three little words: "and there," "already," "suddenly"; they rush about from car to car on the dimly lighted Sevastopol train, halting on the platforms where two thundering frying pans hurl themselves at one another and crawl apart.

The railroad has changed the whole course, the whole structure, the whole rhythm of our prose. It has delivered it over to the senseless muttering of the French *moujik* out of *Anna Karenina*. Railroad prose, like the woman's purse of that ominous *moujik*, is full of the coupler's tools, delirious particles, grappling-iron prepositions, and belongs rather among things submitted in legal evidence: it is divorced from any concern with beauty and that which is beautifully rounded.

Yes, it is there where the beefy levers of locomotives are covered in hot oil that this dear little prose breathes, stretched out at its full length; it is there that it measures, shameless thing that it is, and winds on its own fraudulent yardstick the six hundred and nine versts of the Nikolaevsky road, with its sweating carafes of vodka.

At 9:30 P.M. the former Captain Krzyżanowski was planning to board the Moscow express. He had packed in his suitcase Parnok's morning coat and best shirts. The morning coat, having tucked in its fins, fit into the suitcase especially well, almost without a wrinkle, like a frolicsome dolphin of cheviot, to which it was related by its cut and by its youthful soul.

At Lyuban and Bologoe Captain Krzyżanowski came out to drink some vodka and kept repeating "soiré, moiré, poiré" or God knows what other officer's nonsense. He even tried to have a shave in the car, but in that he did not succeed.

At Klin he tried a cup of railroad coffee, the recipe for which has not changed since the days of Anna Karenina: chicory, with a slight admixture of cemetery earth or some other such nastiness.

In Moscow he stopped at the Hotel Select—an excellent hotel on Malaya Lubyanka—where he was given a room that had formerly been used as a store; in place of a regular window it had a fashionable shop window, heated by the sun to an improbable degree.

A Note on *Fourth Prose* and *Journey to Armenia*

The story behind both *Fourth Prose* (*Četvërtaja Proza*) and *Journey to Armenia* (*Putešestvie v Armeniju*) is that of a sordid defamatory campaign against Mandelstam. In outline, the facts are as follows. At the end of the 1920s, Mandelstam, who had been publishing his poetry and criticism for some two decades, was at the height of his fame. On the grounds of his poetry he was for the moment nearly invulnerable. But he belonged to that camp of free intellectuals and artists whose sympathies, always on the side of the Revolution, had never been with the Bolsheviks' brutal perversion of the dream; and he was thus, with many others, the constant object of attack, usually private, behind the scenes in writers' organizations and editorial offices, but also, as in the present case, public. Since about the middle of the twenties, Mandelstam had been driven to support himself and buy time for his real concerns by a backbreaking load of literary hackwork—as publisher's reader, reviewer, interviewer, consultant, translator.

Probably no writer of our time, except possibly Ezra Pound, has had a higher conception of the writer's calling, his obligations to his art and to his reader. One can only imagine his exertions, as he ploughed through the general literary muck from which he wrested a living, to keep what he could of his artistic standards or to salvage what he could of the work in hand. In one letter of 29 June 1928 we find the poet, whose wife was ill and had just undergone an operation, helplessly begging a certain Venediktov to send the money promised him for his work on a volume of Mayne Reid![1] The money was being withheld, another document tells us, pending someone's approval of Mandelstam's Mayne Reid.

But even in this arena he was not really vulnerable, and so the occasion for an attack on him had to be manufactured. It was done as follows. The publishing house ZIF (initials for *Zemlja i Fabrika* [Land and Factory]) had commissioned him in 1927 to revise and edit two existing Russian versions of Charles de Coster's *La légende de Thyl Ulenspiegel*. These were a translation by V. Karyakin, made in 1916, and another by the prominent literary critic A. G. Gornfeld, which had come out in 1920. An editor at the State Publishing House, A. Gorlin, warned Mandelstam to have nothing to do with the project, asserting that Gornfeld regarded de Coster as his personal property, a warning which, even in the phrase about personal property, proved grimly prophetic.

When his revision appeared in 1928, the unsuspecting Mandelstam was horrified to find his own name on the title page as sole "translator." Had certain other things not happened recently, this might have seemed nothing more than the habitual sloppiness of the publishers. But there was the abrupt dismissal from ZIF (and from the Party) of his old friend and former Acmeist colleague Vladimir Narbut, who was in fact also the editor who had suggested the de Coster project. Then there was the increasing difficulty about getting writing assignments and about being paid for them. It seemed, and it was, part of a pattern. The ground for the attack had been prepared.

Mandelstam demanded at once that the publishers rectify their error by pasting in a slip with the correct information on the title page, but this was refused. It was Mandelstam also who immediately telegraphed Gornfeld, explaining the circumstances and offering to turn over to him his own fee, thus taking upon himself a moral responsibility that, in all reason, belonged to the publisher alone. But reason had nothing to do with it.

Gornfeld's role is not clear to me. Mandelstam's senior by some twenty-four years, he was not a creature of the new order; his career in literary journalism had been, if unspectacular, at least honorable; as a translator he evidently strove for a certain wooden literalness, which is at worst a lapse of taste. But, leaving aside the question whether he willingly offered himself as a utensil, he did play a rather supine role by printing, in a newspaper where the publisher's belated and more or less *pro forma* correction of the title page had appeared, an attack on Mandelstam, depicting him (though not in so many words) as a petty thief of literary property.

The poet, struggling to live from day to day, was enraged by the figurative charge (foreseen by Gorlin) that he had stolen Gornfeld's fur coat and tried to fence it at a rummage shop. If Mandelstam despised "Authors" and "Literature" as he had come to know them in their official aspect, he nevertheless cherished a lofty ideal of the writer and of the fellowship of writers: one cannot read his work without a sense of the covenant that he felt to exist between himself and Ovid, Dante, Villon, Goethe, Pushkin,

Herzen. Gornfeld's remark about the stolen coat (the charge of plagiarism having been made only in this equivocal form) seemed to Mandelstam so perfidious and contemptible a thing to have been said by one writer of another that he blazoned it as the epigraph in a letter to the editor where he answered the charges.

A few months later the persecution of Mandelstam took an alarming turn—even though it was only 1929, that "relatively vegetarian" period in Akhmatova's bitter phrase—with the entry into the affair of David Zaslavsky. In the interval, Mandelstam had written a newspaper article deploring the slapdash treatment of translation and translators in the Soviet press, and Zaslavsky seized upon it as a device for reopening the charges in the *Ulenspiegel* case. Zaslavsky is one of the most odious figures in the history of Stalinist journalism. A reliable scourge, he took a prominent part in campaigns against his own former associates, the Mensheviks, and his fellow Jews (in the notorious persecution of the "cosmopolites" after the war). One of his last services to the regime—he died in 1965—was the public savaging of Pasternak during the *Zhivago* affair. Mandelstam, feeling perhaps that Zaslavsky was beneath notice in a dispute between men of letters, does not even mention him. But his participation may help explain why the Mandelstams took to calling the whole affair their own "Dreyfus case."

Such, in general contour, was the bloated and at times—had it not been so sinister in intent—almost comic personal and political campaign against one Russian poet. The *odium sovieticum* spread like a stain through the two capitals. Certain Leningrad writers planned a letter in Mandelstam's defense, then lost their nerve, to his enduring disgust. Moscow writers—among them Vsevolod Ivanov, Pilnyak, Fadeev, Pasternak, Kataev, Fedin, Olesha, Zoshchenko, and Leonov—did publish a warm letter in his defense. The matter now became a *cause célèbre*. Various legal and quasi-legal proceedings were initiated and dragged on through the next year and a half. Mandelstam was subjected to endless gruelling and exhausting interrogations, which grew increasingly sinister in tone as they covered his entire lifetime and seemed for some reason to concentrate on the period of the Civil War. An arbitration court of FOSP, the federation of Soviet writers' organizations, eventually produced an ambiguous decision: Mandelstam had been treated unfairly, but, on the other hand, he bore the moral responsibility for the publisher's having made no suitable arrangement with the earlier translators.

The matter might not have ended there, however, had not a powerful protector of Mandelstam, the ill-fated Nikolay Ivanovich Bukharin,[2] intervened. He saw to it that the persecution was stopped, and then he arranged that the poet and his wife be sent on a trip to Armenia.

II

Armenia was a godsend. But it was *Fourth Prose* that effected in artistic terms an even more startling cure. It was a desperate act of self-therapy. By this outburst Mandelstam seems to have defined himself, and also the "new reality" that now obtained in his country, in a kind of transport of fury. It was an explosion, a scream, a howl of his injured humanity—and, whatever else it may have accomplished, it cleared his lungs. His breathing freed, an awful five-year period of poetic silence, the "deaf-mute" time as he called it, came suddenly to an end. The *Fourth Prose* is what preceded and largely made possible the poems dated "1930" and onward in his collected works.

Like *The Noise of Time* and *The Egyptian Stamp*, *Fourth Prose* is a blend of fiction and autobiography. (It differs from them in that it was never published while he was alive and it has never been published in the USSR.) It scarcely has a title. Nadezhda says that *Fourth Prose* was simply one of those household nicknames by which so many writings were pigeonholed. If one takes *Noise* as the first, *Stamp* as the second, and the critical essays lumped together as the third, then *Fourth* is fourth. *Journey to Armenia*, by this logic, might bear the subtitle "Fifth Prose."

The numeral appealed to Mandelstam on other grounds as well. It carried overtones of "fourth estate," a term that he vastly preferred to the despised "Literature" as the focus of his allegiance. The original first chapter, Nadezhda writes, contained certain political observations that were deemed too dangerous for retention even in a work never intended for publication.

Though Mandelstam no doubt expected that *Fourth Prose* would eventually be published somewhere (such was his faith in the future), he certainly knew that it would never see the light of day in his lifetime. Why then did he write it?

The answer may lie in the mystery of journal-keeping and in that of letters written (and kept) though never sent. And perhaps to some extent also in the phenomenon known as *esprit de l'escalier* (or *Treppenwitz*)— the rejoinder that one thinks about one or two beats after the psychological moment has passed. In his fascinating study of diarists of all kinds (*A Book of One's Own*) Thomas Mallon has convincingly argued that no inveterate recorder of his own life—not even the one who resorts to codes, concealment, or testamentary instructions that the work be destroyed—ever writes for himself alone.

To write at all is a kind of infinitely clandestine sort of publication, or at least publication *in posse*, something in between silence and being read. Just to unburden one's heart with words is a relief, and if the words are not borne away on the wind but traced on paper, so much greater the relief. And how much greater still the relief if the words are well selected and fall into a pattern that suggests a permanence beyond their temporary means of preservation.

The theme of *Fourth Prose* is wider than Mandelstam's personal outrage at the injustice done him by publishers, professional writers' organizations, and the courts. It is an appeal against violence of all kinds, especially the violence of the mob against the helpless individual (cf. *The Egyptian Stamp*, with its central episode of the lynch mob). But it was the violence committed by that ultimate mob, the State, against the individual sentenced to capital punishment that most horrified Mandelstam. In parts two and three he traces the growth of such violence from the childhood scene of little Vasenka being egged on to beat up some servant boy to its adult and socially approved form in the "sacred law of lynching." Mandelstam was far from the scene in 1921 when he learned that his old colleague and friend Nikolay Gumilev had been shot by a firing squad for complicity in a counterrevolutionary plot. There was nothing he could have done, but an episode some years later suggests that he might have tried.

In the spring of 1928, while he was at work revising the novel of de Coster, Mandelstam got word that five elderly bank clerks had been arrested on some charge or other and had been sentenced to death. Putting to the test his prestige, which was then at its height, he did the "wirepulling" mentioned in the second paragraph of *Fourth Prose* and managed to have their sentence commuted. Nadezhda recalls as the decisive move his having sent Bukharin a copy of his recently published collection of poetry with the inscription: "Every line in this book argues against what you are planning to do."

III

The journey to Armenia that Bukharin arranged for Mandelstam is known in Russian as a *komandirovka*—a trip taken on official business, a mission. It was not a vacation or a junket, since the end in view was a piece of writing that would be of practical use in the furtherance of government policy. Mandelstam's task was to bring back an optimistic report on the pleasure that the ancient land of Armenia was experiencing as it settled into its new, Soviet, identity. Whether the intelligent Bukharin ever really expected to see such a document from the hand of his friend cannot be known. What is known is that when *Journey to Armenia* finally achieved publication in the fifth number of the journal *Zvezda (Star)* for 1933, after much dickering with the censor, the editor responsible, Caesar Volpe, was sacked for not excising the offending passages (principally the folkloric ending, which must be one of the most unmistakably derogatory references to Stalin published in the Soviet Union in the 1930s), and that no syllable of Mandelstam's thereafter appeared in the Soviet Union during his lifetime. Mission not exactly accomplished.

Since every reader will immediately notice that *Journey* is anything other than conventional travel writing, it is perhaps worth calling attention to the fact that there *are* passages of description and narration. It is because they are so overshadowed by the astonishing meditations on painting and natural science, etc., that they require pointing out. The very first sentence, for instance, though it suffers from an almost Gogolian viscosity, seems determined, in the best tradition of Baedeker, to overwhelm the reader with numbers: *two very worthy architectural monuments, the seventh century, a month, four thousand feet above sea level, two or three dozen tombs*. And the opening passage continues with this numerical precision, which the reader will easily find for himself. It is perhaps worth mentioning also that many of the most plainly described episodes are not set in Armenia at all, but in Moscow.

At its two extremes the book has a rather conventional shape: at the beginning we have just arrived in the exotic place promised by the title, and at the end, the final sentence with its points of suspension fades into silence and betokens in the classical manner of travel-writing that one journey has come to an end but will be succeeded on the morrow by another, as yet unknown. . . . The interior of the book, however, wanders back and forth without warning between Moscow and Armenia, though a minimal alertness will suffice to keep one oriented. At the section entitled "Ashot Ovanesian," for instance (signaled, if not by the Bersenev Embankment, then by mention of the River Moscow), we return to Moscow and do not resume the picture of the island of Sevan for some dozen pages.

This contrast between Moscow and one of the more recent of her acquisitions is never too much insisted upon, but it is essential to the great overriding theme of the *Journey*, which it is now time to specify. At the highest level of abstraction, it might simply be called that of Life against Death. Put simply, everything associated with Armenia represents Life, while everything associated with Moscow represents the rigidity and staleness of Death—not only the actual death of capital punishment as decried in *Fourth Prose*, but the death of the imagination, of honor, of all the humane values, which Mandelstam had discerned in his tormentors. Note that it is not Russia, but Moscow, the governmental, bureaucratic, official heart of Russia that denotes the evil. Not for nothing did the writer who vituperated *Journey to Armenia* in *Pravda* (30 August 1933) entitle his article "Shades of Old Petersburg" (*Teni starogo Peterburga*), for, without stating it in so many words, he rightly detected the ancient animosity against Moscow that always emanated from the other capital.

Here is a sample of those elements large and small that might be contrasted under the rubrics of this principal theme; some are large and pervasive, such as "vegetable life" opposed to "development" (a term by which Mandelstam referred to the sterility of Marxist dogma), and some are single, telling images, such as the burning poppies set over against the skull-like cabbages. The list might be greatly extended.

LIFE	DEATH
Lamarck (free, volitional evolution)	Darwin (determinism, lack of freedom)
Biology and the naturalists	"Literature" and "Writers"
pagan burning of poppies	pale green cabbage bombs [reminiscent of the mounds of human skulls in Vereshchagin's famous painting]
vegetable life	"boring, bearded development" [This was taken as a derogation of Marxism.]
Impressionism	naive realism
light Moslem slippers	hooflike, dusty city shoes
The vitality of Armenia	The "watermelon emptiness" of Russia.

The character portraiture in the *Journey* continues that to be found in *The Noise of Time*. Yuly Matveich, Ostrogorsky, and Sergey Ivanych, that "tutor of the Revolution," are now joined by Professor Khachaturian, Dr. Herzberg (who seems like "the pale shadow of an Ibsen problem"), and Arnoldi, the "Tamerlane of good nature." To these should be added the great naturalists—Linnaeus, Lamarck, and Pallas—whom of course Mandelstam did not encounter in the flesh but into whose biography he felt obliged to enter; for he could never conceive of any great creative genius of the past—Socrates, Ovid, Dante, Bach, or Beethoven—bereft of his human traits and history.

But the principal character, after Mandelstam himself, is the biologist (and devotee of Lamarck) Boris Sergeevich Kuzin, referred to only by his initials. Kuzin incarnated for Mandelstam a kind of ideal: a humane and literate man, and a realist to the core of his being; a man of exact knowledge, deeply learned in the lore of actual matter, living and inert; a man beyond the filth of politics and ideology; he was everything that was *not* meant by the now detestable name of *writer*. On those occasions when *Journey* seems to be a dialogue or a letter, Kuzin is the addressee.

Armenia held for Mandelstam, finally, one immense attraction about which he could not write, or at least did not write in this already sufficiently dangerous work. For our knowledge of it we depend upon the memoirs of Nadezhda Yakovlevna. A Jew by birth, Mandelstam was in his youth, as we read in *The Noise of Time*, merely puzzled and discomfited by his heritage. By the beginning of the thirties, however, he had more than made his peace with his Jewishness and declared a defiant pride in his blood "with its inheritance from sheep breeders, patriarchs, and kings" (*Fourth Prose*). But in his religious faith Mandelstam was a Christian. He was baptized in the Methodist church in Vyborg, then a part of Finland, in May 1911.

He had always been attracted to the South, first to the Crimea, the only outpost of the classical world on the soil of what came to be his country (his second book of poems was entitled *Tristia*, after the poems written by Ovid in his exile on the shores of the Black Sea), then to Georgia, and finally to Armenia. Armenia, Nadezhda says, came to replace the others, and the reason was its ancient association with all the components of what Mandelstam took to be genuine civilization—the Judaic, the Hellenic, and the Christian. In the shadow of Ararat, Old Testament reminiscences are scarcely avoidable, and one of the dynasties of Armenia, that of the Bagratidae, founded in 885 A.D., claimed descent from King David of Israel. It was, as Mandelstam wrote, "the younger sister of the land of Judea" and the "Sabbath land." But Armenia was also Christian. From the time when

King Tiridates III was baptized by St. Gregory the Illuminator (c. 300 A.D.—some seven centuries, that is, before Vladimir I sent for Greek clergy to evangelize Russia), Armenia became the bulwark of Christianity in Asia. Mandelstam's closest approach to acknowledging this attraction was the delight that he took in describing the ancient Christian churches

Fourth Prose

I

Venyamin Fyodorovich Kagan[1] approached this matter with the sage frugality of a sorcerer or of some Odessa-born Newton. All the conspiratorial activity of Venyamin Fyodorovich rested upon a basis of infinitesimals. Venyamin Fyodorovich saw the law of salvation as a matter of keeping to a turtle's pace. He allowed himself to be shaken out of his professorial cubicle, answered the telephone at all hours, made no promises in advance, would not say no to anything; but the main thing he did was try to retard the dangerous course of the disease.

The fact that a professor, and a mathematician at that, was involved in the improbable affair of saving five lives by means of those cognizable, absolutely weightless integral moves known as pulling wires, was a source of general satisfaction.

Isai Benediktovich[2] behaved himself from the very first as if the illness were infectious, something catching, like scarlet fever, so that he too, Isai Benediktovich, might, for all he knew, be shot. There was not the least sense in the way Isai Benediktovich bustled about. It was as if he were racing from one doctor to another imploring them to disinfect him at once.

If Isai Benediktovich had had his way he would have taken a taxi and raced all over Moscow at random, without a shadow of a plan, for that, as he imagined, was the ritual.

Isai Benediktovich was forever repeating and constantly recalling that he had left behind him, in Petersburg, a wife. He even set himself up with something like a secretary—a small, stern, very commonsensical companion—a relative who had already begun to fuss over him, Isai Benediktovich, as though he were a child. To make a long story short, Isai Benediktovich, by appealing to various people and at various times, was, so to speak, vaccinating himself against execution.

All the relatives of Isai Benediktovich had died in their Jewish beds of walnut wood. As the Turk travels to the black stone of the Kaaba, so these Petersburg bourgeois, descended from rabbis of patrician blood and, via the translator Isai, brought into touch with Anatole France, made pilgrimages to the most unimaginably Turgenevian and Lermontovian watering places where they prepared themselves, by taking the cure, for the transition to the hereafter.

In Petersburg Isai Benediktovich lived like a pious Frenchman, ate his *potage*, chose for acquaintances people no more offensive than the croutons in his bouillon, and, in his professional capacity, made calls on two traffickers in junk translations.

Isai Benediktovich was good only at the very beginning of the wire-pulling, during the mobilization and, as it were, the sounding of the alarm. Afterwards he faded, drooped, stuck out his tongue, and his relatives themselves pooled their money and sent him to Petersburg.

I have always been interested in the question where the bourgeois gets his fastidiousness and his so-called decency. His decency is what makes the bourgeois kin to the animal. Many Party members are at ease in the company of a bourgeois for the very same reason that grownups require the society of rosy-cheeked children.

The bourgeois is of course more innocent than the proletarian, closer to the womb world, the baby, the kitten, the angel, the cherub. In Russia there are very few of these innocent bourgeois, and that has a bad effect on the digestion of true revolutionaries. The bourgeoisie must be preserved in its innocent aspect, it must be entertained with amateur theatricals, lulled on the springs of Pullman cars, tucked into envelopes of snow-white railway sleep.

II

A little boy in goatskin boots and velveteen Russian coat, his hair brushed carefully back, is standing in the midst of mammas, grannies, and nannies, and beside him stands some cook's or coachman's whelp, some urchin from the servants' quarters. And that whole pack of lisping, hooting, spluttering archangels is urging the young master on:

"Hit 'im, Vasenka, hit 'im!"

Vasenka gets in a blow, and the old maids, the disgusting old toads, poke each other and hold on to the mangy coachman's brat:

"Hit 'im, Vasenka, hit 'im, while we hold his curly head, while we dance around him. . . ."

What is this? A genre painting in the style of Venetsianov? An étude by some peasant artist?

No, this is the way they train some shaggy shrimp from the Komsomol under the supervision of the agit-mammas, grannies, and nannies so that he can stomp 'im, Vasenka, hit 'im, Vasenka, while we hold him by his black hide, while we dance around. . . .

"Hit 'im, Vasenka, hit 'im. . . ."

III

The lame girl came into us from a street as long as a night with no street-cars. She put her crutch to one side and quickly took her seat so as to look like everyone else. Who is this husbandless girl?—The light cavalry . . .[3]

We cadge cigarettes from each other and correct our Chinese gibberish, enciphering in formulas of animal cowardice the great, powerful, and forbidden notion of class. Animal fear taps on the typewriters, animal fear proofreads the gibberish on sheets of toilet paper, scribbles denunciations, hits men when they're down, demands execution for prisoners. As urchins drown a kitten in the river Moscow in plain view of everyone, so our grown-up boys playfully put the screws on, at noon recess play back-to-the-wall: "Hey, pile on, press till you can't see him anymore. . . ." Such is the sacred law of the vigilante.

A shopkeeper on the Ordynka gave a woman short weight: kill him!

A cashier came out a nickel short: kill her!

A director foolishly signed some junk or other: kill him!

A peasant hid some rye in a barn: kill him!

The girl comes to see us, dragging along on her crutch. One of her legs is short, and the crude prosthetic boot looks like a wooden hoof.

Who are we? We are schoolchildren who do not go to school. We are Komsomol freebooters. We are bullyboys by leave of all the saints.

Filipp Filippich has developed a toothache. Filipp Filippich has not and will not come to class. Our notion of studying has as much to do with science as the hoof with the foot, but that does not embarrass us.

I have come to you, my artiodactylous friends, to stamp my wooden stump in the yellow socialist arcade-combine created by the frantic fantasy of the daredevil business executive, Giber, from elements of the chic hotel on the Tverskoy, from the night telephone or telegraph exchange, from a dream of universal bliss—realized as a permanent foyer with buffet—from an office with saluting clerks that never closes, from the postal-telegraph aridity of air that makes one's throat tickle.

Here there's an unbroken bookkeeper's night beneath the yellow flame of the second-class bulbs of the railway station. Here, as in Pushkin's fairy tale, a Yid is betrothed to a frog, that is to say, there's an endless wedding ceremony between a goat-footed fop, spawning theatrically, and a well-matched devil from the same stew, a Moscow editor-cum-coffinmaker turning out silk brocade coffins for Monday, Tuesday, Wednesday, and Thursday. He rustles his paper shroud. He opens the veins of the months of the Christian year that still preserve their pastoral Greek names: January, February, March. . . . He is the terrifying and illiterate horse doctor of happenings, deaths, and events, and is tickled pink when the black horse blood of the age spurts forth in a gushing fountain.

IV

I went to work for the newspaper *Moscow Komsomol Member* straight from the caravanserai of the TSEKUBU.⁴ There were twelve pairs of earphones there, almost all of them broken, and a reading room made over from a church, with no books, where people slept like snails on little curved divans.

The staff at TSEKUBU despised me for my straw baskets and because I was not a professor.

In the afternoon I would go look at the high water and firmly believed that the obscene waters of the river Moscow would flood the learned Kropotkin Embankment and that TSEKUBU would telephone for a boat.

In the mornings I would drink sterilized cream right on the street from the mouth of the bottle.

I would take someone else's soap from the professors' shelves and wash myself at night and was never caught once.

People from Kharkov and Voronezh would come and all of them wanted to go to Alma-Ata. They took me for one of their own and asked my advice which republic was the best deal.

At night TSEKUBU was locked up like a fortress and I would rap on the window with my stick.

Every decent man got his telephone calls at TSEKUBU and in the evening the servants would hand him a note as if giving a priest the list of those to be prayed for. The writer Grin,[5] whose clothes the servants used to brush, lived there. I lived at TSEKUBU like everyone else, and no one bothered me until I myself moved out in the middle of the summer.

When I was moving to another apartment, my fur coat lay across the carriage as it does when people leave the hospital after a long stay or have just been let out of prison.

V

Things have come to the point where I value only the proud flesh around the wound in the word trade, only the insane excrescence:

> And the whole ravine was cut
> To the bone by the falcon's scream

That is what I need.

I divide all the works of world literature into those written with and without permission. The first are trash, the second—stolen air. As for writers who write things with prior permission, I want to spit in their faces, beat them over the head with a stick and set them all at a table in the Herzen House,[6] each with a glass of police tea in front of him and the analysis of Gornfeld's urine in his hand.

I would forbid these writers to marry and have children. After all, children must carry on for us, must say to the end for us what is most important to say. But their fathers have sold out to the pockmarked devil[7] for three generations to come.

Now that's a little literary page.

VI

I have no manuscripts, no notebooks, no archives. I have no handwriting because I never write. I alone in Russia work from the voice while all around the bitch pack writes. What the hell kind of writer am I!? Get out, you fools!

On the other hand, I have a lot of pencils and they are all stolen and of different colors. You can sharpen them with a Gillette blade.

The blade of the Gillette razor with its faintly serrated beveled edge has always seemed to me one of the noblest products of the steel industry. The good Gillette blade cuts like sedge grass, bends but doesn't break in the hand—something like a calling card from a Martian or a note from a dapper devil with a hole drilled in the middle.

The blade of the Gillette razor is the product of a dead trust, the shareholders of which are packs of American and Swedish wolves.

VII

I am a Chinaman, no one understands me. Idiot-shmidiot! Let's go to Alma-Ata where the people have raisin eyes, the Persian has eyes like fried eggs, the Sart has sheep's eyes.

Idiot-shmidiot! Let's go to Azerbaijan!

I had a patron—People's Commissar Mravyan-Muravyan,[8] most pissantic People's Commissar of the land of Armenia, that younger sister of the Land of Judah. He sent me a telegram.

Dead is my patron, the People's Commissar Mravyan-Muravyan. Gone from the Erevan anthill is the black People's Commissar. He will no longer come to Moscow in the international car of the train, naive and curious as a priest from a Turkish village.

Idiot-shmidiot! Let's go to Azerbaijan!

I had a letter for People's Commissar Mravyan. I took it to the secretaries in the Armenian residence in the cleanest, most ambassadorial street in all Moscow. I was just on the point of leaving for Erevan under the auspices of the ancient People's Comissariat of Education to conduct a terrifying seminar for those roundheaded youths in their poor monastery of a university.

If I had gone to Erevan I should have run for three days and three nights to the large buffets in the railway stations to eat buttered bread with black caviare.

Idiot-shmidiot!

On the way I should have read Zoshchenko's[9] very best book and been as happy as a Tartar who'd stolen a hundred rubles.

Idiot-shmidiot! Let's go to Azerbaijan!

I should have taken courage with me in my yellow straw basket with its great heap of linen smelling of alkali soap, and my fur coat would have hung on a golden nail. And I should have got out at the railway station in Erevan with my winter coat in one hand and my senile cane—my Jewish staff—in the other.

VIII

There is a splendid line of Russian poetry which I never tire of repeating in the bitch-loud nights of Moscow. Which, like a spell, disperses evil spirits. Guess what line, friends. It writes on the snow like sleigh runners, clicks in the lock like a key, shoots into a room like frost:

. . . didn't shoot the wretches in the dungeons . . .[10]

There is the symbol of faith, there is the genuine canon of the true writer, the mortal enemy of literature.

In the Herzen House there is a milksop vegetarian, a philologist with a Chinese noodle, a Chink of that breed that tiptoes about the blood-stained Soviet land twittering *hao-hao shango-shango* when heads are being lopped off, a certain Mitka Blagoy,[11] a piece of trash from the lycée, authorized by the Bolsheviks for the benefit of learning; in a special museum he guards the length of cord with which Seryozha Esenin hanged himself.

And I say: Blagoy for the Chinese! To Shanghai with him! To the Chinks, where he belongs! To think what Mother Philology was and what she has become. Full-blooded and implacable she was, and now she's become fool-blooded and in everything placable.

IX

To the number of murderers of Russian poets, or of aspirants to join these murderers, has been added the murky name of Gornfeld. This paralytic D'Anthès,[12] this Uncle Monya from Basseyny Street, preaching morality and the State, carried out the orders of a regime totally alien to himself, which is, to him, more or less the same as a touch of indigestion.

To die from Gornfeld is as silly as to die from a bicycle or a parrot's beak. But a literary murderer can also be a parrot. I, for instance, was nearly killed by a polly named after His Majesty King Albert and Vladimir Galaktionovich Korolenko.[13] I am very glad that my murderer is alive and has in a sense survived me. I feed him sugar and take pleasure in hearing him repeat, from *Thyl Ulenspiegel*, "The ashes are knocking at my heart," a sentence which he alternates with another, no less pretty, "There is no torment in the world greater than the torment of the word. . . ." A man capable of calling his book *Torments of the Word*[14] was born with the mark of Cain, as the sign of the literary murderer, on his brow.

I met Gornfeld only once, in the dirty editorial office of some unprincipled rag where, as in the buffet of Kvisisan, a crowd of spectral figures had gathered. There was as yet no ideology then and no one to complain to when you were insulted. When I recall that deprivation—how could we have lived then?!—huge tears well up in my eyes. Someone introduced me to the biped critic, and I shook his hand.

Papa Gornfeld, why did you complain to the *Bourse News*, I mean to the *Evening Red Gazette*, in the year of Our Soviet 1929? You would have done better to weep into the pure literary Jewish waistcoat of Mr. Propper. Better to have told your woe to your banker with sciatica, kugel, and tallith. . . .

X

Nikolay Ivanovich[15] has a secretary who is, really and truly, an absolute squirrel, a little rodent. She gnaws a nut with every visitor and runs to the telephone like an inexperienced young mother to a sick baby.

A certain scoundrel told me that truth was *mria* in Greek.

So that little squirrel is genuine truth with a capital letter in Greek; and at the same time she is that other truth, that stern card-carrying virgin—Party Truth.

The secretary, frightened and compassionate, like a hospital nurse, does not merely work but lives in the antechamber of the office, in the telephone dressing-room. Poor Mria from the connecting room with her telephone and her classical newspaper!

This secretary differs from others in that she sits like a night nurse on the threshold of power, defending the wielder of that power as if he were gravely ill.

XI

No, really, let me be tried! Allow me to enter in evidence! . . . Permit me, as it were, to file myself. Do not, I implore you, deprive me of my trial. . . . The legal proceedings are not yet at an end and, I make so bold as to assure you, will never be at an end. What happened before was only the overture. Bosio[16] herself is going to sing at my trial. Bearded students in checkered plaids, mingling with caped policemen and, under the direction of their goat precentor, ecstatically chanting a syncopated version of the Eternal Memory, will carry the police coffin with the remains of my case out of the smoke-blackened hall of the district court.

Papa, Papa, Papochka,
Where, Oh where's your Mamochka?

The Writers' Union is too close—
She will come back with a dose.

Mama's blind in one eye, right?
And this case is sewn up tight.

Aleksandr Ivanovich Herzen! . . . Allow me to introduce myself. . . . It was, it seems, in your house. . . . As host, you are in some sense responsible. . . .

You were so good as to go abroad, were you? . . . Meanwhile, something disagreeable has happened here. . . . Aleksandr Ivanovich! Sir! What am I to do? There is absolutely no one to turn to!

XII

In a certain year of my life, grown men from that tribe which I despise with all the strength of my soul, and to which I neither wish to belong nor ever shall, conceived the intention of jointly committing against me an ugly and repellent ritual. The name of this ritual is literary pruning or dishonoring, and it is performed in accordance with the customs and the calendrical needs of the writers' tribe, the victim being selected by vote of the elders.

I insist that writerdom, as it has developed in Europe and above all in Russia, is incompatible with the honorable title of Jew, of which I am proud. My blood, burdened with its inheritance from sheep breeders, patriarchs, and kings, rebels against the shifty gypsyishness of the writing tribe. A creaking camp of unwashed Romanies kidnapped me as a child and for a certain number of years dawdled along its obscene routes, vainly striving to teach me its one craft, its one art: theft.

Writerdom is a race with a revolting smell to its hide and the filthiest known means of preparing its food. It is a race that wanders and sleeps in its own vomit, one that is expelled from cities and hounded in villages, but it is always and everywhere close to the authorities, who grant them a place in red-light districts, as prostitutes. For literature always and everywhere carries out one assignment: it helps superiors keep their soldiers obedient and it helps judges execute reprisals against doomed men.

A writer is a mixture of parrot and pope. He's a polly in the very loftiest meaning of that word. He speaks French if his master is French, but, sold into Persia, he will say, "Pol's a fool," or, "Polly wants a cracker," in Persian. A parrot has no age and doesn't know day from night. If he starts to bore his master he's covered with a black cloth and that, for literature, is the surrogate of night.

XIII

There were two brothers named Chenier. The despicable younger brother belongs entirely to literature; the elder, who was executed, executed literature himself.

Jailers love to read novels and, of all men, have the greatest need of literature.

In a certain year of my life grown men with beards and wearing horned fur caps brandished a flint knife over me, with which they meant to castrate me. Judging by the evidence, they were priests of their tribe: they smelled of onion, novels, and goat meat.

And it was all as terrifying as in a child's dream. *Nel mezzo del cammin di nostra vita*—midway on the path of life—I was stopped in the dense Soviet forest by bandits who called themselves my judges. They were old men with scrawny necks and little goose heads unfit to bear the burden of years.

For the first and only time in my life, literature had need of me, and it crumpled me, pawed me, squeezed me, and it was all as terrifying as in a child's dream.

XIV

I am morally responsible for the fact that the ZIF Publishing House did not make a contract with the translators Gornfeld and Karyakin. I—furrier of precious furs, and practically suffocated with literary hides—I am morally responsible for having inspired a Petersburg cad with the desire to allude in a libelous anecdote to that warm Gogolian fur coat, torn by night from the shoulders of that most ancient member of the Komsomol, Akaky Akakievich. I tear off my literary fur coat and trample it under foot. In nothing but my jacket and in a thirty-degree frost I shall run three times around the boulevard rings of Moscow. I shall escape from the yellow hospital of the Komsomol arcade straight into a fatal chill, if only not to see the forty bright Judas holes of that obscene building[17] on Tverskoy Boulevard, if only not to hear the clinking of the pieces of silver and the counting of the printer's sheets.

XV

My dear Romanies of the Tverskoy Boulevard, you and I together have written a novel of which you have not even dreamt. I am very fond of coming across my name in official papers, bailiff's subpoenas, and other stern documents. Here the name has an absolutely objective ring to it, a sound novel to the ear and, I must say, most interesting. From time to time I am myself curious to know what it is I am forever doing wrong. What sort of pineapple is this Mandelstam, anyway, who for so and so many years was supposed to have done such and such and, like the scoundrel that he is, keeps dodging it? . . . How much longer is he going to keep on dodging it? That's why the years are wasted on me; others accumulate more respect with every passing day, but for me it's the reverse—time is flowing backwards.

I'm to blame. No two ways about it. I shan't wriggle out of this guilt. I live in insolvency. I save myself by dodging. How much longer am I to go on dodging?

When that tin subpoena arrives or that reminder, Greek in its clarity, from the social organization; when they demand that I name my accomplices, cease my skulduggery, tell where I get the counterfeit money, and sign an undertaking not to travel beyond certain specific limits, I agree on the spot; but immediately, as if nothing had happened, I start dodging again—and so it goes.

In the first place: I ran away from somewhere and I must be sent back, extradited, found, and returned. In the second place, I am being mistaken for someone else. No hope of proving identity. Pockets full of trash: cryptic jottings from a year ago, telephone numbers of dead relatives, and addresses of persons unknown. In the third place, I signed with Beelzebub or with the State Publishing House a grandiose, unfulfillable contract on Whatman paper smeared with mustard and emery powder pepper in which I undertook to return twice over everything that I acquired, to belch back fourfold what I misappropriated, and to perform sixteen times running that impossible, unimaginable, that unique thing that might, in part, acquit me.

With every passing year I am more incorrigible. As though by a conductor's steel punch I am riddled with holes and stamped with my own surname. Every time someone calls me by my first name I tremble, I simply cannot get used to it, such an honor! For once in one's life to be called Ivan Moyseich by somebody! Hey, Ivan, go scratch the dogs![18] Mandelstam, go scratch the dogs! To some Frenchy, it's *cher maître*, dear teacher; but me? Mandelstam, go scratch the dogs! To each his own.

An ageing man, I scratch the master's dogs with the bitten stump of my heart, and it's not enough for them, it's not enough. The eyes of Russian writers look at me with canine tenderness and implore me: drop dead! Where does this cringing spite, this grovelling contempt for my name come from? The gypsy at least had his horse, but I am horse and gypsy in one person. . . .

Tin subpoenas under the little pillow . . . the forty-sixth contract in place of the wreath of burial ribbon on my forehead, and a hundred thousand lighted cigarettes instead of little candles. . . .

XVI

No matter how much I work, if I carry horses on my back, if I turn mill-stones, still I shall never become a worker. My work, whatever form it may take, is seen as mischief, as lawlessness, as an accident. But that's how I like it, so I agree. I subscribe to it with both hands.

It is a question of how you look at it. What I prize in the doughnut is the hole. But what about the dough of the doughnut? You can gobble up the doughnut, but the hole will still be there.

Real work is Brussels lace, the main thing in it is what holds the pattern up: air, punctures, truancy.

But in my case, brethren, work's of no benefit; it doesn't go on my record.

We have a bible of work, but we don't appreciate it. It's Zoshchenko's stories. The only man who ever showed us a worker has been trampled in the dirt. But I demand monuments to Zoshchenko in every city and town of the Soviet Union, or at least, as for Papa Krylov, in the Summer Garden.

That's a man whose work breathes truancy, in whose work Brussels lace lives!

At night on the Ilyinka when the department stores and the trusts are asleep and talking in their native Chinese, at night jokes run along the Ilyinka. Lenin and Trotsky walk about with their arms around each other as though nothing had happened. One has a little pail and a fishing rod from Constantinople in his hand. Two Jews walk about, an inseparable pair—one inquirer and one responder, and the one keeps asking, but the other keeps evading and evading, and there's no way for them to part.

A German organ-grinder walks by with his Schubertian barrel organ, such a failure, such a sponger . . . *Ich bin arm*. I am poor.

Sleep, my darling . . . M . . . S . . . P . . . O.[19]

The Viy[20] is reading the telephone directory on Red Square. Lift up my eyelids . . . Connect me with the Central Committee. . . .

Armenians from Erevan walk by with green-painted herrings. *Ich bin arm*—I am poor.

And in Armavir on the city coat of arms it is written: the dog barks, the wind carries.

Journey to Armenia

I. Sevan

On the island of Sevan,[1] which is distinguished by two very worthy architectural monuments of the seventh century and also by the mud huts of some lice-bitten hermits who recently died off, now thickly overgrown with nettles and thistles and no more frightening than the neglected cellars of summer houses, I spent a month enjoying the lake water standing at a height of four thousand feet above sea level and schooling myself to contemplate the two or three dozen tombs that lie scattered about, a kind of flower bed among the dormitories of the monastery, which repairs have made young again.

Every day at precisely five o'clock the lake, which teems with trout, would boil up as though a huge pinch of soda had been flung into it. It was in the fullest sense of the word a mesmeric seance of changing weather, as if a medium had cast a spell on the normally tranquil limewater, producing first a silly little ripple, then a sort of twittering boiling, and finally a stormy Ladogan fit of frenzy.

It was then impossible to deny oneself the pleasure of measuring off some three hundred paces along the narrow path of the beach, which lies opposite the gloomy Gunei shore.

At this point the configuration of Gokcha forms a strait some five times broader than the Neva. The magnificent freshwater wind would tear into the lungs with a whistle. The clouds moved with a velocity that kept increasing by the minute and the incunabular surf would hasten to publish by hand in half an hour's time a plump Gutenberg Bible under the gravely glowering sky.

No less than seventy percent of the island population consisted of children. They would clamber about like little wild animals over the monks' tombs, bombard some peaceful snag on the lake bottom, the icy spasms of which they took for the writhing of a sea serpent, bring out of their damp lairs the bourgeois toads and the green snakes with their gemlike feminine heads, and chase back and forth a ram that had lost its mind, couldn't for the world make out whom it was bothering with its poor body, and kept shaking its tail, grown fat in freedom.

The tall steppe grasses on the lee hump of the island of Sevan were so strong, juicy, and self-confident that one felt like coiffing them with an iron comb.

The whole island is Homerically bestrewn with yellow bones—remnants of the local people's devout picnics.

Besides that, it is literally paved with the fiery red slabs of nameless graves, some sticking up, others knocked over, and others crumbling away.

At the very beginning of my stay the news came that some stonemasons digging the foundation for a lighthouse on the long and melancholy spit of land called Tsamakaberda had come across the urn burial ground of the ancient Urartu[2] people. Earlier, in the Erevan Museum, I had already seen a skeleton crammed into a sitting position in a large clay amphora and with a little hole drilled in the skull for the evil spirit.

I was waked up early in the morning by the chirring of a motor. The sound kept jumping up and down in one place. A pair of mechanics were warming the tiny heart of an epileptic engine, pouring black oil into it. But the moment it got going, its tongue twister—something like "Not Peter not Helena, not Peter not Helena"—would expire and melt in the water.

Professor Khachaturian, whose face was stretched over with eagle skin beneath which all the muscles and ligaments stood out, numbered and with their Latin names, was already strolling along the wharf in his long black frock coat, cut in the Ottoman style. Not only an archeologist but also a teacher by calling, he had spent a great part of his career as director of a secondary school, the Armenian Gymnasium in Kars. Invited to the chair of archeology in Soviet Erevan, he brought along with him his devotion to the Indo-European theory, his blind hatred of Marr's Japhetic fabrications[3] as well as his astonishing ignorance of the Russian language and of Russia, where he had never been.

When we had somehow struck up a conversation in German, we got into a launch with Comrade Karinian, former chairman of the Armenian Central Executive Committee.

This proud, sanguineous man, whose fate it was to be idle, to smoke Russian cigarettes, and waste his time in the gloomy occupation of reading Onguardist[4] literature, evidently found it difficult to give up the habit of his official duties, and boredom had planted fat kisses on his ruddy cheeks.

The motor muttered "Not Peter not Helena" as if it were reporting to

Comrade Karinian, the little island dropped away behind us and straightened out its bearish back with the octagons of the monasteries. A swarm of midges kept pace with the launch, and we sailed along in it as in a bit of muslin across the morning lake of milk and honey.

At the excavation we did in fact discover both clay crocks and human bones, and in addition to that we found the haft of a knife stamped with the ancient trademark of the Russian N. N. factory.

As for me, I respectfully wrapped up in my handkerchief the porous calcified little crust of someone's cranium.

On every island—be it Malta, Saint Helena, or Madeira—life flows past in a sort of noble expectation. This has its own charm and inconvenience. In any case, everyone is constantly busy, everyone slightly loses his voice and is a little more considerate of others than on the mainland with its fat-fingered roads and negative freedom.

The helix of the ear becomes finer and is whorled in a different way.

It was my good fortune that a whole gallery of clever, thoroughbred old men had collected on Sevan: there was the respected expert in regional lore Ivan Yakovlevich Sagatelian, the archeologist Khachaturian whom I mentioned, and finally a buoyant chemist named Gambarian.

I preferred their peaceful company and the strong black coffee of their talk to the commonplace conversation of the young people, which revolved, as it does everywhere in the world, around examinations and physical culture.

The chemist Gambarian speaks Armenian with a Moscow accent. He has voluntarily and gaily Russified himself. His heart is young and he has a dry, stringy body. Physically, he is the pleasantest of men, and a wonderful partner at games.

He was anointed with a holy oil that had something military about it, as though he'd just come back from the regimental chapel; this proves nothing, though, and often happens with splendid Soviet people.

With women he is a chivalrous Mazeppa, caressing Maria with his lips alone; in the company of men he is the sworn enemy of biting remarks and touchiness, but if someone insults him in a quarrel he flares up like a Frankish fencer.

The mountain air had made him younger, and he would roll up his sleeves and throw himself at the little fishnet on the volleyball court, drily waving his small hands.

What is there to say about the climate on Sevan?

The golden currency of cognac in the secret cupboard of the mountain sun.

The little glass stick of the thermometer was carefully passed around from hand to hand.

Doctor Herzberg was frankly bored on this island of Armenian mothers. He struck me as the pale shadow of an Ibsen problem, or an actor of the Moscow Art Theater at his summer house.

The children would show him their slender little tongues, sticking them out for an instant like slices of bear meat. . . .

But toward the end of our stay we did have a visit from the foot-and-mouth disease, which was brought in via the milk cans from the far shore of Zeinal, where some ex-Flagellants, their zeal having long since run out, were keeping themselves to themselves in dismal Russian huts.

For the sins of the grownups, however, the sickness struck only the godless children of Sevan.

One by one, the wiry-haired, pugnacious children would droop with a ripe fever onto the arms of the women, onto pillows.

Once Gambarian ventured to compete with Kh., a youngster from the Komsomol, in swimming completely around the island of Sevan. His sixty-year-old heart couldn't hold out and Kh., who was himself exhausted, had to leave his friend and return to the starting point, where he threw himself out half alive onto the pebbles of the beach. The witnesses to the accident were the volcanic walls of the island fortress, which precluded any thought of mooring there. . . .

Then what an alarm was raised! There turned out to be no lifeboat on Sevan, though an order for one had long ago been signed.

People rushed about the island, proud of knowing that an irreparable accident had taken place. The unread newspaper rattled like tin in the hands. The island was nauseated, like a pregnant woman.

We had neither telephone nor pigeon post to communicate with the shore. The launch had left for Elenovka about two hours ago, and no matter how you strained your ear, not the least chirring could be heard on the water.

When the expedition headed by Comrade Karinian, armed with a blanket, a bottle of cognac, and so on, returned with Gambarian, whom they had picked up on a rock, stiff with cold but smiling, he was met with applause. That was the most splendid hand-clapping that I have ever heard in this life: a man was being congratulated on the fact that he was not yet a corpse.

At the fishing wharf of Noraduz, where we were taken for an excursion that went off, fortunately, without any choral singing, I was struck by the hull of a completely finished barge that had been pulled up in its raw state onto the trestle of the dockyard. It was a good Trojan Horse in size, and its fresh musical proportions resembled the box of a bandore.

Curly shavings lay around. The salt was eating into the earth, and the fish scales twinkled like little discs of quartz.

In the cooperative dining room, which was just as log-cabin and Mynheer-Peter-the-Great as everything else in Noraduz, we sat side by side to eat the thick artel soup of cabbage and mutton.

The workers noticed that we had no wine with us and, as befits true hosts, filled our glasses.

In my thoughts I drank a toast to the health of young Armenia with its houses of orange stone, to its commissars with their white teeth, to its horse sweat and the stamping of queues, and to its mighty language, which we are unworthy to speak and can only steer clear of in our feebleness. *Water* in Armenian is *dzhur*. *Village* is *g'iur*.

I shall never forget Arnoldi.

He was lame and walked on an orthopedic claw, but in such a manly way that everyone envied him his walk.

The learned leadership of the island resided on the high road in Molokan Elenovka, where in the half shadow of the scientific Executive Committee one could make out the light blue policemanly phizzes of giant trout, preserved in alcohol.

Oh, these visitors!

They were brought to Sevan by an American yacht, quick as a telegram, which cut through the water like a lancet—and Arnoldi, the terror of science, the Tamerlane of good nature, would step out onto the shore.

I got the impression that a blacksmith lived on Sevan who used to shoe him, and that that was why he frequented the island—to consult with him.

There is nothing more edifying and pleasant than to bury yourself in the society of people who belong to an entirely different race, whom you respect, with whom you sympathize, of whom you are, however alien, proud. The Armenians' fullness with life, their rude tenderness, their noble inclination for hard work, their inexplicable aversion to anything metaphysical, and their splendid intimacy with the world of real things— all of this said to me: you're awake, don't be afraid of your own time, don't be sly. . . . Wasn't this because I found myself among a people who, though renowned for their fervent activity, nevertheless lived not by the clock in the railway station nor by that in some institution, but by the sundial such as I saw among the ruins of Zvartnots in the form of an astronomical wheel or rose inscribed in stone?

II. *Ashot Ovanesian*

The Institute of Eastern Peoples is located on the Bersenev Embankment next door to the pyramidal Government House. A little further along, a ferryman used to ply his trade, levying three kopecks for a crossing and sinking his overloaded skiff right up to the oarlocks in the water.

The air on the Moscow River embankment is viscid and mealy.

A bored young Armenian came out to greet me. Among the Japhetic books with their spiny script there also existed, like a cabbage butterfly in a cactus library, a blonde young lady.

My amateurish arrival gladdened no one. A request for help in studying Old Armenian did not touch any hearts among these people, and the woman, moreover, lacked this key of knowledge herself.

Owing to my incorrect subjective orientation, I have fallen into the habit of regarding every Armenian as a philologist. Which is, however, partly right. These are people who jangle the keys of their language even when they are not using them to unlock any treasures.

My conversation with the young doctoral candidate from Tiflis flagged and ended on a note of diplomatic reserve.

I inserted the names of highly esteemed Armenian writers, I mentioned Academician Marr, who had just dashed through Moscow on his way from the Udmurt or Vogul Oblast to Leningrad, and I praised the spirit of

Japhetic philosophy, which penetrated to the structural depths of every language. . . .

I was already getting bored and glancing out the window more and more often at a bit of overgrown garden when there entered the library an old man with the manners of a despot and a lordly bearing.

His Promethean head radiated a smoky ash-blue light like the most powerful quartz lamp. The blue-black locks of his wiry hair, whipped up with a certain disdain, had something of the rooty strength of an enchanted feather.

There was no smile on the wide mouth of this sorcerer, who never forgot that talking is working. Comrade Ovanesian's head had the capacity of distancing itself from the person to whom he was talking, like the top of a mountain that only chanced to resemble a head. But the dark blue quartz grimace of his eyes was better than a smile.

Thus deafness and ingratitude, bequeathed to us by the Titans. . . .

Head in Armenian is *glukh'e*—with a puff of breath after the "kh" and a soft "l". It's the same root as in Russian [*glava*, or *golova*]. . . . And what about a Japhetic novella? Be my guest:

"To see," "to hear," and "to understand"—all these meanings coalesced at one time into a single semantic bundle. At the very deepest stages of language there were no concepts, only directions, fears and longings, only needs and apprehensions. The concept of "head" was fashioned over a dozen millennia out of that foggy bundle of meanings, and its symbol became . . . deafness [glukhota].

But, reader, you'll get everything mixed up anyway—and who am I to teach you?

III. *Zamoskvorechie*

Not long before that, as I was rooting about under the staircase in the dusty-rose-colored house on the Yakimanka, I found a ragged book by Signac defending Impressionism. The author explained the "law of optical blending," glorified the method of working with little dabs of the brush, and impressed upon one the importance of using only the pure colors of the spectrum.

He based his arguments on citations from Eugène Delacroix, whom he idolized. He would constantly refer to Delacroix's *Journey to Morocco* as if he were leafing through the codex of visual training that every thinking European was obliged to know.

Signac was trumpeting on his chivalric horn the final, ripe gathering of the Impressionists. Into the bright camps he summoned Zouaves, burnooses, and the red skirts of Algerian women.

At the very first sounds of this theory, which inspires one and strengthens the nerves, I felt the shiver of novelty; it was as if someone had called me by name. . . .

It seemed to me as though I had exchanged my hooflike dusty city shoes for light Moslem slippers.

In all my long life I have seen no more than a silkworm.

What is more, an easiness invaded my life, my always dry and disorderly life, which I imagine to myself as a kind of titillating waiting for some all-prize lottery from which I might win whatever my heart desired: a piece of strawberry soap, a spell of sitting in the archive of the Archprinter's chambers, or the long-desired journey to Armenia, of which I would not stop dreaming. . . .

It must be the greatest impertinence to speak with the reader about the present in that tone of absolute courtesy that we have for some reason yielded to the memoirists.

I think that comes from the impatience with which I live and change my skin.

The salamander doesn't even suspect the presence of the black and yellow spots on its back. The thought never entered its head that these spots are arranged in two chains or else fused together into one solid path, depending on the humidity of the sand, or on whether the papering in the terrarium is cheerful or gloomy.

But as for the thinking salamander, Man, who can guess tomorrow's weather . . . if only he could choose his own coloration.

Next door to me there lived some stern families of philistines. God had not endowed these people with affability, which does, after all, make life more pleasant. They had morosely hooked themselves together into a sort of passionate consumer association, would tear off the days due them in the ration coupon booklet and smile as though they were saying "cheese."

Inside, their rooms were stocked like handicraft shops with various symbols of kinship, longevity, and domestic fidelity. For the most part, these were white elephants, both large and small, artistic renditions of dogs, and seashells. They were no strangers to the cult of the dead, and also felt a certain respect for those who were absent. It seemed to me that these people with their fresh, cruel Slavic faces ate and slept in a photographer's prayer-room.

And I thanked the circumstances of my birth that I was merely an accidental guest of the Zamoskvorechie and I would not spend my best years there.[5] Nowhere, never, have I felt so strongly the watermelon emptiness of Russia; the brick-colored sunsets over the River Moscow, the color of the brick-tea, brought to mind the red dust from the blast furnace on Ararat.

I felt like hurrying back to the place where people's skulls are equally beautiful in the grave and at work.

All around there were such (God forbid) cheery little houses with nasty little souls and cowardly windows. It was no more than seventy years ago that serf girls who were quiet and quick to catch on, who had been taught to sew and stitch hems, used to be sold here.

Two stale lindens, deaf with age, raised their brown pitchforks in the courtyard. Frightful in their somehow governmental thickness, they heard and understood nothing. Time fed them with lightning and watered them with downpours; thunder—shmunder: it was all the same to them.

Once a meeting of the adult men who populated the house passed a resolution to fell the older linden and cut it up into firewood.

They dug a deep trench around the tree. The axe began to hack at the indifferent roots. Doing a woodcutter's job requires a certain knack. There were too many volunteers. They fretted about like incompetents trying to carry out some vile death sentence.

I called my wife: "Look, it's about to fall."

Meanwhile, however, the tree was resisting with a kind of sentient force; it seemed to have become fully conscious again. It despised its attackers and the pike's teeth of the saw.

Finally, they threw a noose made of thin laundry twine around the dry place where the trunk forked—the very place from which the tree's great age, its lethargy, and its verdant obscenity proceeded—and began to rock it gently back and forth. It shook like a tooth in a gum, but still continued cock of the walk. Another second . . . and children ran up to the toppled idol.

That year the directors of Tsentrosoyuz[6] approached Moscow University with the request that they recommend a man who could be sent to Erevan. What they had in mind was someone to oversee the production of cochineal, an insect that few people have ever heard of. A superlative carmine dye is made from the cochineal when you dry it and reduce it to powder.

The university selected B. S. K.,[7] a well-trained young zoologist. B. S. lived with his old mother on Bolshaya Yakimanka, belonged to the trade union, would snap to attention, out of pride, before anyone and everyone, and reserved his highest regard, out of the entire academic milieu, for old Sergeev, who had made and installed the tall red cabinets in the zoology library with his own hands and who could unerringly name the wood of already finished lumber—whether it was oak, ash, or pine—merely by rubbing his palm over it, eyes closed.

B. S. was anything but a bookworm. He studied science on the run, was involved in some way with the salamanders of the famous Viennese professor (and suicide) Kammerer,[8] and loved the music of Bach more than anything else on earth, especially one invention for wind instruments that would go flying upward like some Gothic firework.

B. S. was a fairly experienced traveler within the USSR. In both Bukhara and Tashkent his field shirt had been seen and his infectious military laugh had resounded.

Hooray for the living! Every form of work is honorable!

B. S. went about his preparations for Armenia with reluctance. He was forever running after poles and pails for collecting the cochineal and complaining about the slyness of officials who made trouble over his packing.

Parting is the younger sister of death. For those who respect fate's arguments, the rite of seeing someone off contains a sinister nuptial animation.

The front door kept slamming and up the mousey stairs from the Yakimanka guests of both sexes kept arriving: students from the Soviet aviation schools—carefree skaters through the air; workers from distant botanical stations; specialists in mountain lakes; people who had been in the Pamirs and in Western China; and others who were simply young people.

The filling of goblets with Muscovite wines began, and the sweet de-
murrals of the ladies and girls; tomato juice was splashed about, and so
was the incoherent general muttering: about flying, about the maneuver
called the loop, when you don't notice you've been turned upside down
and the earth, like some huge brown ceiling, comes rushing at your head,
about the high cost of living in Tashkent, about Uncle Sasha and his
grippe, about everything. . . .

Someone told the story about the man ill with Addison's disease who
lay sprawled down below on the Yakimanka and lived right there: he drank
vodka, read the newspaper, played dice with a passion, and at night took
his wooden leg off and slept on it for a pillow.

Someone else compared this Diogenes of the Yakimanka with a medi-
eval Japanese woman, and a third party shouted that Japan was a country
of spies and bicycle riders.

The subject of the conversation kept gaily slipping away like the ring
passed around the back, and the knight's move, always swerving to one
side, reigned over the table talk. . . .

I don't know how it is with others, but for me the charm of a woman
increases if she is a young traveler, has spent five days on a scientific trip
lying on a hard bench of the Tashkent train, knows her way around in
Linnaean Latin, knows which side she is on in the dispute between the
Lamarckians and the epigeneticists, and is not indifferent to the soybean,
cotton, or chicory.

And on the table there is an elegant syntax—of confused, heteroalpha-
bet, grammatically wrong wildflowers, as though all the preschool forms
of vegetative nature were coalescing into a pleophonic anthology poem.

When I was a child a stupid sort of touchiness, a false pride, kept me from
ever going out to look for berries or stooping down over mushrooms.
Gothic pinecones and hypocritical acorns in their monastic caps pleased
me more than mushrooms. I would stroke the pinecones. They would
bristle. They were trying to convince me of something. In their shelled
tenderness, in their geometrical gaping I sensed the rudiments of architecture, the demon of which has accompanied me throughout my life.

I have practically never spent any time in summer houses near Moscow.
Of course, one can't count automobile trips to Uzkoe along the Smolensk
highway, past the wide-trousered log huts where the truck-farmers' cabbage allotments looked like cannon balls with green fuses. Those pale

green cabbage bombs, heaped up in godless abundance faintly reminded me of the pyramid of skulls in Vereshchagin's tiresome picture. Things are changed now, but it may be that the break came too late.

Only last year on the island of Sevan in Armenia, as I was strolling in the waist-high grass, I was captivated by the pagan burning of the poppies. Bright to the point of surgical pain, looking like pseudo-cotillion badges, big, too big for our planet, fireproof, gawking butterflies, they grew on disgusting hairy stalks.

I envied the children. . . . They zealously hunted for poppy wings in the grass. Stoop once, stoop again . . . and there's already fire in my hands, as if a smith had lent me some coals. Once in Abkhazia I happened upon a whole field of northern strawberries.

At a height of a few hundred feet above sea level. Young forests clothed all the hilly region. The peasants hoed the sweet reddish earth, preparing little holes for the botanical seedlings.

How glad I was at this coral coinage from the northern summer. The ripe glandular berries hung in triads and pentads, singing in broods and in tune.

So, B. S., you are leaving first. Circumstances don't yet permit me to follow you. I hope they'll change.

You are going to stay at No.92 Spandarian Street, with those very nice people, the Ter-Oganians. Do you remember how it was? I would come running to see you "down Spandarian," swallowing the caustic construction dust for which young Erevan is famous. I still found pleasure and novelty in the roughnesses, crudenesses, and solemnities of the valley of Ararat, which had been repaired right down to its wrinkles; in the city, which seemed to have been upended by divinely inspired plumbers; and in the widemouthed people with eyes that had been bored straight into their skulls—the Armenians.

Past the dry pump-houses, past the conservatory, where a quartet was being rehearsed in the basement and one could hear the angry voice of the professor saying, "Lower! Lower!"—that is, make a diminuendo in the adagio—to your gateway.

Not a gate, but a long cool tunnel cut into your grandfather's house and into it, as into a spyglass, there glimmered a little door covered with greenery that was so unseasonably dull one would have thought it had been burnt with sulphuric acid.

In that vicinity the eyes need more salt. You pick out forms and colors but it's all unleavened bread. Such is Armenia.

On the little balcony you showed me a Persian pen case covered with a lacquer painting the color of blood coagulated with gold. It was offensively empty. I wanted to smell its venerable musty little panels which had served Sirdar justice and the instantaneous sentencing of men to have their eyes put out.

Then you went off again into the walnut twilight of the Ter-Oganians' apartment and returned with a test tube to show me the cochineal. Tawny red peas lay on a little wad of cotton.

You had taken that sample from the Tartar village of Sarvanlar, about twenty versts from Erevan. From there you can see Father Ararat, and in the arid borderland atmosphere you can't help feeling like a smuggler. Laughing, you told me about a splendid girl glutton who belonged to a friendly Tartar family in Sarvanlar. . . . Her sly little face was always smeared with sour milk and her fingers greasy with mutton fat. . . . At dinner you, who are not in the least subject to dyspeptic fastidiousness, would still quietly put aside a sheet of the lavash for yourself, because the little glutton would rest her feet on the bread as if it were a stool.

I would watch the accordion of your forehead as the infidel wrinkles came together and drew apart; it must be the most inspired part of your physical appearance. These wrinkles—polished, it seemed, by your lamb-skin cap—reacted to every significant phrase and strolled over your forehead staggering and swaggering and stumbling about. You were some-what Godunov, my friend, and somewhat Tartar.

I would compose similes to convey an idea of your nature and got more and more accustomed to your anti-Darwinian essence; I studied the living language of your long ungainly arms, created to provide a handshake in some moment of peril, and given to passionate protestations, on the run, against natural selection.

In Goethe's *Wilhelm Meister* there is a little man named Jarno, a scoffer and naturalist. He disappears for weeks at a time in the latifundia of his exemplary world, spends his nights in tower rooms on chilly sheets, and comes to dinner from out of the depths of his well-meaning castle.

This Jarno belonged to a peculiar order founded by a large landowner named Lothario for the purpose of educating his contemporaries in the spirit of *Faust*, Part Two. The society had an extensive network of secret agents, which reached all the way to America, and as an organization was not far from jesuitical. Secret lists of merits and demerits were kept, tentacles would stretch out, and people would get caught.

It was this Jarno who had the job of keeping Meister under surveillance.

Wilhelm was travelling about with his little boy, Felix, the son of the unfortunate Marianna. One paragraph of his novitiate forbade him to spend more than three days in any one place. The rosy-cheeked Felix—a frisky, didactic child—spent his time herbalizing, heaping questions upon his father—with the exclamation "Sag mir, Vater . . ."—breaking off bits of rock, and striking up one-day acquaintances.

Goethe's well-behaved children are in general exceedingly tiresome. Children in his depiction are little Cupids of curiosity with a quiver of pointed questions slung over their shoulders. . . .

And so Meister encounters Jarno in the mountains.

Jarno literally snatches Meister's three-day pass out of his hands. Behind them and before them lie years of separation. So much the better! All the better acoustics for the geologist's lecture in his sylvan university!

That is why the warm light shed by oral instruction, the clear didactic of the friendly talk, so greatly surpasses the reasonable and edifying action of books.

I gratefully recall one of my Erevan conversations, which are today, some twelve months later, already made to seem old by the certitude of my personal experience, and which possess that truth which helps us form some sense of our own selves in the tradition.

The talk turned around the "theory of the embryonic field," proposed by Professor Gurvich.

The embryonic leaf of the nasturtium has the form of a halberd or of an elongated, bifoliate purse that begins to resemble a little tongue. It also looks like a flint arrowhead from the Paleolithic. But the tension in the field of force that rages around the leaf first transforms it into a five-segmented figure. The lines of the cave arrowhead get stretched into the shape of an arc.

Take any point and join it by a bunch of coordinates to a straight line. Then extend these coordinates, intersecting the line at various angles, to a section of identical length, then join them together again, and you get convexity!

But later the force field sharply changes its game and drives the form to its geometrical limit, the polygon.

A plant is a sound evoked by the wand of a termenvox[9] and it coos in a sphere oversaturated with wave processes. It is the envoy of a living thunderstorm that rages permanently in the universe—akin in equal measure to stone and lightning! A plant in the world is an event, a happening, an arrow, and not a boring, bearded development.

Only a little while ago, B. S., a certain writer repented in public for having been an ornamentalist, or for having tried to be one to the extent that his sinful powers would allow it.*

I think that a place is prepared for him in the seventh ring of Dante's Hell, where the bleeding thornbush grew. And when out of curiosity some tourist breaks a twig off that suicide, he will beg in a human voice, like Pier della Vigna: "Don't touch me! you're hurting me! Or have you no pity in your heart? We were men, that are now trees. . . ."[10]

And a drop of black blood will fall. . . .

What Bach, what Mozart does variations on the theme of the nasturtium leaf? Finally, a phrase flared up: "the world-record speed of a nasturtium's bursting pod."

Who has not felt envious of chess players? You sense in the room a peculiar field of alienation from which a chill inimical to nonparticipants flows.

But these little Persian horses made of ivory are immersed in a solution of power. The same thing happens to them as happens to the nasturtium of E. S. Smirnov, the Moscow biologist, and the embryonic field of Professor Gurvich.

The threat of displacement hangs over each figure throughout the game, during the whole stormy event of the tournament. The chessboard swells up from the concentrated attention. When the rays of a combination focus upon the chess figures they grow like mushrooms in Indian summer.

The problem is solved not on paper, and not in the camera obscura of causality, but in a live Impressionist milieu in Édouard Manet's and Claude Monet's temple of air, light, and glory.

*M. E. Kozakov—author's footnote.

Is it true that our blood emits mitogenetic rays, which the Germans have captured on a phonograph disc, rays that, I was told, help to intensify the cell division of tissue?

We are all, without suspecting it, carriers of an immense embryological experiment: for the very process of remembering, crowned with the victory of memory's effort, is amazingly similar to the phenomenon of growth. In both of them there is a sprout, an embryo, some facial feature, half a character, half a sound, the ending of a name, something labial or palatal, some sweet pea on the tongue—which doesn't develop out of itself but only answers an invitation, only stretches out, justifying one's expectation.

With these belated reflections, B. S., I hope to repay you, if only in part, for having disturbed your chess game in Erevan.

IV. *Sukhum*

Early in April I arrived in Sukhum—a city of mourning, tobacco, and fragrant vegetable oils. This is the place to begin studying the alphabet of the Caucasus: every word begins with *a*. The language of the Abkhazians is powerful and pleophonous, but it abounds in the upper and lower gutteral compound sounds, which impede the pronunciation; one might say that it was torn out of a larynx overgrown with hair.

I'm afraid that the kindly bear Baloo has not yet been born to teach me, as he did the boy Mowgli of Kipling's jungle, the splendid language of "ahchoo"—although in the distant future I foresee academies for the study of Caucasian languages scattered about the entire earth. The phonetic ore of Europe and America will dry up. Its deposits have limits. Even now young people read Pushkin in Esperanto. To each his own.

But what a sinister warning!

It is easy to see a panorama of Sukhum from Mount Chernyavsky, as it is called, from Ordzhonikidze Square. It is completely linear, flat, and, to the tune of Chopin's funeral march, it sucks into itself a great crescent of the sea with a heave of its Kurortly colonial breast.

It lies down below like a case of drawing instruments where, ensconced in the velvet, there is a compass that has just described the bay, sketched the eyebrows of the hills, and closed up.

Although the public life of Abkhazia contains much that is naïvely crude and many abuses, one cannot help being captivated by the administrative and economic elegance of this little maritime republic, proud of its valuable soils, its box tree forests, its Sovkhoz olive grove at New Athos, and the high quality of its Tkvarchel coal.

Rose thorns punctured one through a kerchief and the tame bear cub with the gray Old Russian snout of some dunce-capped Ivan the Fool screamed a scream that shattered glass. Fresh automobiles were rolled up straight from the sea, their tires slicing up the eternally green mountain. . . . The gray bast of theatrical wigs was obtained from underneath the bark of the palm, and in the park the flowering agave plants, like candles weighing six poods, shot up another inch and a half every day.

Ley gave sermons on the mount against smoking and reproved the gardener in a fatherly way. He once asked me a question by which I was profoundly struck: "What was the mood of the petty bourgeoisie in Kiev in 1919?"

I think that his dream was to quote Karl Marx's *Kapital* in the hut of Paul and Virginie.

In my twenty-verst strolls, accompanied by silent Latvians, I developed a feeling for the relief of the locale.

Theme: a race to the sea of gently sloping volcanic hills, joined by a little chain—for pedestrians.

Variation: the little green key of altitude is passed from hilltop to hilltop and each new ridge locks up its depression.

We went down to the Germans in their hollow—their "Dorf"—and got thoroughly barked at by the sheepdogs.

I visited Beria,[11] the president of the Society of Friends of Caucasian Literature, and came very near giving him the regards of Tartarin and the Armourer Costecalde.

A marvellous figure from Provence!

He complained about the difficulties entailed by inventing the Abkhazian alphabet, and spoke with respect about that jolly person from Petersburg, Evreinov,[12] who got carried away in Abkhazia by the cult of the goat and was unhappy about not being able to obtain any serious scientific studies owing to the remoteness of Tiflis.

The hardheaded knocking together of billiard balls is just as pleasant to men as the clicking of ivory knitting needles is for women. The bandit cue would lay waste the pyramid, and a quartet of epically sturdy lads from Blücher's army—as alike as brothers, on duty, precise, with a bulb of laughter in their chests—found the game charming to the point of "Ach!"

And the old men, Party members, didn't lag behind them.

Looking from the balcony with army binoculars you got a clear view of the track and bleachers on a swampy parade ground the color of billiard cloth. Once a year there are great horse-races to test the endurance of anyone who wants to compete.

A cavalcade of biblical elders would follow the boy who won.

Relatives scattered around the many versts of the ellipse would deftly hand the flushed horsemen wet towels on the end of poles.

In a distant swampy meadow a lighthouse kept turning like the Tate diamond.

And I somehow saw the dance of death, the marriage dance of phosphorescent insects. First it seemed that the tips of very thin little roving cigarettes were being puffed to a glow, but their flourishes were too venturesome, free, and bold.

The Devil only knows where they were blown away!

On closer inspection: insane electrified ephemera winking, twitching, tracing, devouring the black hackwork of the present moment.

Our heavy fleshly body decays in just the same way, and our activity will turn into just such a devil's sabbath of signals if we don't leave behind us some material proof of having existed.

It is frightening to live in a world that consists only of exclamations and interjections!

Bezymensky,[13] the strongman who lifts cardboard weights, a round-headed, gentle, inkstained blacksmith—no, not blacksmith—vendor of birds—and not even birds, but the balloons of RAPP—Bezymensky was forever stooping, humming, and butting people with his blue eyes.

An inexhaustible operatic repertoire gurgled in his throat. His open-air-concert, mineral-water heartiness never left him. A sluggard with a mandolin in his soul, he lived on the string of a song, and his heart sang under the needle of a phonograph.

V. *The French*

Now I stretched out my vision and sank my eye into the wide goblet of the sea, so that every mote and tear should come to the surface.

I stretched my vision like a kid glove, stretched it onto a shoe tree, onto the blue neighborhood of the sea. . . .

Quickly, rapaciously, with feudal fury, I inspected the domains of my view.

One puts the eye like that into a wide goblet full to the brim so that a mote will come out.

And I began to understand what the obligatory nature of color is—the excitement of sky blue and orange football shirts—and that color is nothing other than a sense of the start of a race, a sense tinged by distance and locked into its size.

Time circulated in the museum in accordance with an hourglass. The brick siftings would come running as the goblet emptied itself and there would be the same jet of golden simoom from the little case at the top to the bottle on the bottom.

Hello, Cézanne! Good old grandfather! A demon for work. The best acorn in the forests of France.

His painting was certified on the oak table of a village notary. He is as incontestable as a will executed by a man sound of mind and possessed of his memory.

But what captivated me was the old man's still life. Roses that must have been cut in the morning, solid and rolled tight, unusually young tea roses. Exactly like little scoops of yellow ice cream.

On the other hand, I took a dislike to Matisse, a rich man's artist. The red paint of his canvases fizzes like soda. He knows nothing of the joy of ripening fruits. His mighty brush doesn't heal the vision but gives it the strength of an ox, so that the eyes become bloodshot.

Enough already of this carpet chess and odalisques!

Persian whimsies of a Parisian *maître*!

The cheap vegetable pigments of Van Gogh were bought by accident for twenty sous.

Van Gogh spits blood like a suicide in furnished rooms. The floorboards in the night café are tilted and stream like a gutter in their electric fit. And the narrow trough of the billiard table looks like the manger of a coffin.

I never saw such barking colors!

And his streetcar conductor's vegetable-garden landscapes! The soot of suburban trains has just been wiped from them with a wet rag.

His canvases, smeared with the omelette of an accident, are as clear as visual aids—as the charts in a Berlitz School.

The visitors move about with little steps as though in church.

Each room has its own climate. In Claude Monet's room there is a river air. Looking at Renoir's water you feel blisters on your palm as though you'd been rowing.

Signac invented the maize sun.

The woman who lectures about the pictures leads the cultural workers behind her.

To look at them you'd say a magnet was attracting a duck.

Ozenfant worked out something surprising by using red chalk and gray slate squirrels on a black slate ground and modulating the forms of glass-blowing and fragile laboratory equipment.

But you also got a nod from Picasso's dark blue Jew and Pissarro's raspberry gray boulevards, flowing like the wheels of an immense lottery with their little boxes of hansom cabs, their fishing-pole whips pitched on their shoulders, and the shreds of splashed brain on the kiosks and chestnut trees.

But isn't that enough?

Generalization is already waiting, bored, at the door.

To anyone recuperating from the benign plague of naïve realism I would recommend the following method of looking at pictures.

Under no circumstances go in as if you were entering a chapel. Don't be thrilled or chilled, and don't get glued to the canvas. . . .

With the stride of a stroll on a boulevard: straight on!

Cut through the huge heat waves of the space of oil painting.

Calmly, with no excitement—the way little Tartars bathe their horses in Alushta—lower your eye into what will be for it a new material ambiance—and remember that the eye is a noble, but stubborn, animal.

Standing before a picture to which the body temperature of your vision has not yet adjusted itself, for which the crystalline lens has not yet found the one suitable accommodation, is like singing a serenade in a fur coat behind storm windows.

When this equilibrium has been achieved, and only then, begin the second stage of the restoration of the picture, the washing of it, the removal of its old peel, its external and late barbaric layer, which is the linking of it to sunny, solid reality.

With its extremely subtle acidic reactions, the eye, an organ possessed of hearing, which intensifies the value of the image, which multiplies its accomplishments by its sensual insults (which it fusses over like a child with a new toy), raises the picture to its own level; for painting is much more a matter of internal secretion than of apperception, that is, of external perceiving.

The material of painting is organized in such a way that it stands to lose nothing, and that is its distinction from nature. But the probability of the lottery is inversely proportional to its feasibility.

And only now does the third and last stage of entering the picture begin: when one confronts the intention behind it.

Now the traveling eye presents its ambassadorial credentials to the consciousness. Then a cold treaty is established between the viewer and the picture, something on the order of a diplomatic secret.

I left the embassy of painting and went out into the street.

So soon after having left the Frenchmen I found the sunlight to be a phase of some waning eclipse, and the sun to be wrapped up in foil.

Near the entrance of the cooperative stood a mother with her son. The boy was tabetic, respectful. Both were in mourning. The woman was sticking a bunch of radishes into her reticule.

The end of the street, seemingly crushed by binoculars, swerved off into a squinting lump; and all of this, distant and linden-lined, was stuffed into a string bag.

VI. *About the Naturalists*

Lamarck fought for the honor of living nature with a sword in his hands. You think he was as reconciled to evolution as the scientific savages of the nineteenth century? But I think that Lamarck's swarthy cheeks were burnt by embarrassment on nature's behalf. He could not forgive nature for a trifle called the variability of species.

Forward! *Aux armes!* Let us cleanse ourselves of the dishonor of evolution!

Reading the system-making naturalists (Linnaeus, Buffon, Pallas) has a splendid effect on the disposition, straightens out the eye, and communicates to the soul a mineral quartz tranquillity.

Here is Russia as depicted by that remarkable naturalist Pallas: old women distil the dye "mariona" from a mixture of birch leaves and alum; the bark of the linden tree peels off on its own to become bast, and be woven into sandals and baskets; peasants use a thick crude oil for medicinal purposes; Chuvash girls tinkle with trinkets in their tresses.

Whoever does not love Haydn, Glück, and Mozart will never understand a word of Pallas.

He transported the corporeal roundness and courtesy of German music to the plains of Russia. He collects Russian mushrooms with the white hands of a *Konzertmeister*. Damp chamois skin, rotted velvet—but when you break it open to look inside: azure.

Whoever does not love Haydn, Glück, and Mozart will never understand anything in Pallas!

Let us speak about the physiology of reading. It is a rich, inexhaustible and, it would seem, forbidden theme. Out of the whole material world, of all physical bodies, a book is the one object that inspires man with the greatest degree of confidence. When a book is firmly established on a reader's desk it is like a canvas stretched on a frame.

When we are completely immersed in the activity of reading, we mainly admire our generic attributes, we feel something like ecstasy at the classification of ourselves at various ages.

But if Linnaeus, Buffon, and Pallas have colored my mature years, it is to the whale that I am grateful for having awoken in me a childish astonishment at science.

In the zoological museum it's: drip . . . drip . . . drip. Nothing to speak of in the way of empirical experience.

Oh, turn off that tap!

Enough!

I have signed an armistice with Darwin and placed him on my imaginary bookstand next to Dickens. If they should dine together the third member of the party would be Mister Pickwick. One can't help being charmed by Darwin's good nature. He is an unintentional humorist. The humor of situation is habitual to him, follows him everywhere.

But is good nature a method of creative advance in knowledge, a worthy means of gaining a sense of life?

A greatness like that of Dante is in Lamarck's backward, descending movement down the ladder of living creatures. The lower forms of organic existence are the Hell of humanity.

The long gray antennae of this butterfly had an aristate structure and looked exactly like the little branches on a French academician's collar or like the silver palm fronds placed on a coffin. The thorax is strong, shaped like a little boat. An unimportant head, like a cat's.

Its wings with their big eyes were made of the exquisite old silk of an admiral who had been both at Cesme and at Trafalgar.

Suddenly I caught myself wildly desiring to have a look at nature through the painted eyes of that monster.

Lamarck feels the abysses between classes. He hears the pauses and syncopes of the evolutionary line.

Larmarck wept his eyes out over his magnifying glass. He is the one Shakespearean figure in natural science.

Look—that red-faced, half-respectable old man will run down the staircase of living creatures like a young man to whom a government minister has just shown some special kindness or who has just been made happy by his mistress.

No one, not even an inveterate mechanist, looks upon the growth of an organism as resulting from the variability of the external environment. That would be far too presumptuous. The environment merely invites the organism to grow. Its functions are expressed in a certain benevolence that is gradually and continually canceled by the severity that binds the living body together and finally rewards it with death.

So, for the environment, the organism is probability, desire, and expectation. For the organism, the environment is a force that invites. Not so much a covering as a challenge to a duel.

When the conductor pulls a theme out of the orchestra with his baton he is not the physical cause of the sound. The sound is already there in the score of the symphony, in the spontaneous collusion of the performers, in the populousness of the auditorium and in the arrangement of the musical instruments.

In Lamarck one finds beasts out of fables. They adapt themselves to the conditions of life. According to La Fontaine. The legs of the heron, the neck of the duck and swan, the tongue of the anteater, the asymmetrical and symmetrical position of the eyes in certain fish.

It was La Fontaine, if you like, who prepared the way for the doctrine of Lamarck. His philosophizing, moralizing, reasoning beasts were a splendid living material for evolution. They had already apportioned its mandates among themselves.

The artiodactylous reason of the mammals clothes their fingers with rounded horn.

The kangaroo moves with the leaps of logic.

As described by Lamarck, this marsupial consists of weak forelimbs, that is, limbs that have reconciled themselves to being useless; strongly developed hind extremities, that is, convinced of their importance; and a powerful thesis, called the tail.

Children have already settled down to play in the sand at the pedestal of the evolutionary theory of Grandfather Krylov, I mean to say, Lamarck-La Fontaine. When this theory had found refuge in the Luxembourg Gardens it became overgrown with balls and shuttlecocks.

And I love it when Lamarck deigns to be angry and smashes to smithereens all that Swiss pedagogical boredom. Into the concept of "nature" bursts the Marseillaise!

Male ruminants butt foreheads. They don't yet have horns.

But an internal feeling, born of anger, directs "fluids" to the forehead which aid in forming the substance of horn and bone.

I take off my hat. I let the teacher go first. May the youthful thunder of his eloquence never die away!

"Still" and "already" are the two shining points of Lamarckian thought, the spermatozoa of evolutionary glory and photography, the signalmen and pioneers of morphology.

He was one of the breed of old tuners who tinkle with their bony fingers on the pianos in other people's mansions. He was permitted only chromatic notes and childish arpeggios.

Napoleon allowed him to tune nature because he regarded it as the property of the Emperor.

In the zoological descriptions of Linnaeus it is impossible to overlook the successive relationship to, and a certain dependence upon, the menagerie of the county fair. The proprietor of the wandering show-booth or the hired charlatan who gave a guided tour of the animals strove to show off his wares to their best advantage. Drumming up business outside, the guides never dreamt that they were to play a certain role in developing the style of classical natural science. They were lying as if there were no tomorrow, talking rot on an empty stomach, but at the same time they were themselves fascinated by their art. Something always turned up to save them, and they were saved also by their professional experience and the lasting tradition of their craft.

As a child in the small town of Uppsala, Linnaeus could not have failed to go to the fair or listen with delight to the explanations offered in the wandering menagerie. Like boys everywhere, he swooned and melted before the knowledgeable big fellow with the boots and whip, that doctor of fabulous zoology, who would shower praises on the puma as he waved his huge red fists about.

In linking the important accomplishments of the Swedish naturalist to the eloquence of that loudmouth in the sideshow, I haven't the least intention of belittling Linnaeus. I only want to remind my reader that a naturalist is a professional teller of tales, a public demonstrator of new and interesting species.

The colored portraits of animals in Linnaeus's *Systema Naturae* might hang next to pictures of the Seven-Year War or an oleograph of the Prodigal Son.

Linnaeus colored his monkeys with the tenderest colonial colors. He would dip his brush in Chinese lacquers and paint with brown and red pepper, with saffron, olive oil, and cherry juice. And he managed his task with dexterity and gaiety, like a barber shaving the Burgermeister, or a Dutch housewife grinding coffee on her lap in a fat coffee mill.

Delightful—the Christopher-Columbus brilliancy of Linnaeus's monkey house.

It is Adam passing out certificates of merit to the mammals, aided by a sorcerer from Baghdad and a monk from China.

The Persian miniature squints its frightened, graceful almond eye.

Sinless and sensual, it convinces one like nothing else that life is a precious gift, inalienable.

I love the Moslem enamels and cameos!

To continue with my comparison: the beautiful woman's hot stallion eye comes down to the reader, aslant and merciful. The charred cabbage-stumps of the manuscripts crunch like the tobacco in Sukhum.

How much blood has been spilt on account of these touch-me-nots! What pleasure conquerers took in them!

Leopards have the sly ears of punished schoolboys.

The weeping willow has rolled up into a globe and now, floating, flows round.

Adam and Eve hold a consultation, dressed in the latest paradisal fashion.

The horizon has been abolished. There is no perspective. A charming slowness of wit. The vixen's noble ascent of the stairs, and the feeling of the gardener's inclination towards landscape and architecture.

Yesterday I was reading Firdousi[14] and it seemed to me that a bumblebee was sitting on the book sucking it.

In Persian poetry ambassadorial winds blow out of China like gifts.

It scoops up longevity with a silver ladle and endows whoever wants it with millennia by threes and fives. That is why the rulers of the Djemdjid dynasty live as long as parrots.

When they have been good for an incredibly long time, the favorites of Firdousi suddenly, for no reason on earth, become rogues and rascals in strict obedience to the author's luxuriously arbitrary fancy.

The earth and the sky in the book of *Shahnama* are afflicted with goiter—they are delightfully exophthalmic.

I got the Firdousi from the State Librarian of Armenia, Mamikon Artemevich Gevorkian. I was brought a whole pile of little blue volumes—eight, I think it was. The words of the noble prose translation—it was the French version of Von Mohl—were fragrant with attar of roses. Chewing his drooping gubernatorial lip, Mamikon sang me a few lines in Persian with the unpleasant voice of a camel.

Gevorkian is eloquent, clever, and courteous, but his erudition is exceedingly loud and pushy and his speech fat, like a lawyer's.

Readers are obliged to satisfy their curiosity right there in the Director's office, under his personal supervision, and books that are put on that satrap's table take on the taste of pink pheasant meat, bitter quails, musky venison, and roguish hare.

VII. *Ashtarak*

I managed to observe the clouds performing their devotions to Ararat.

It was the descending and ascending motion of cream when it is poured into a glass of ruddy tea and roils in all directions like cumulous tubers.

The sky in the land of Ararat gives little pleasure, however, to the Lord of Sabaoth; it was dreamed by the blue titmouse in the spirit of the most ancient atheism.

Coachman's Mountain glistening in the snow, a mole field, sown as if for some mocking purpose with stone teeth, the numbered barracks on construction sites, and a tin can packed to the brim with passengers: there you have the environs of Erevan.

Then suddenly a violin, sectioned into gardens and houses, divided up according to the system of the whatnot—with spreaders, interceptors, dowels, and bridges.

The village of Ashtarak hung on the purling of the water as on a framework of wire.[15] The stone baskets that were its gardens would make the most splendid gift for the coloratura soprano at a charity performance.

A place to stay the night was found in the large four-bedroom house that had belonged to some dispossessed kulaks. The collective farm administration had scattered the furnishings out of it and set it up as the village hotel. On a terrace that might have given refuge to all the seed of Abraham a lactifluous washstand was grieving.

The orchard was a dancing class for trees. The schoolgirl shyness of the apple trees, the vermilion competence of the cherry . . . look at their quadrilles, rilles, their ritornellos and rondos.

I was listening to the murmur of the kolkhoz accounts. In the mountains a drenching rain passed through, and the abysses of the street gutters ran more quickly than usual.

The water rang and welled up on all the stories and stands of Ashtarak—and permitted the camel to pass through the eye of the needle.

I have received your eighteen-page letter, completely covered in a hand straight and tall as an avenue of poplars, and here is my answer:

First sensual encounter with the material of an old Armenian church.

The eye looks for form, idea, waits for it; but it stumbles instead on a moldy loaf of nature or a stone pie.

The teeth of vision crumble and break when you first look at Armenian churches.

The Armenian language cannot be worn out; its boots are made of stone. And of course its word is thick-walled, its semivowels seamed with air. But is that all its charm? No! Then where does one's craving for it come from? How to explain it? Make sense of it?

I felt joy in pronouncing sounds forbidden to Russian lips, secret sounds, outcast—and perhaps, on some deep level, shameful.

There was some beautiful boiling water in a pewter teapot and suddenly a pinch of wonderful black tea was thrown into it.

That's how I felt about the Armenian language.

I have cultivated in myself a sixth sense, an "Ararat" sense: the sense of attraction to a mountain.

Now, no matter where fate may carry me, this sense already has a speculative existence and will remain with me.

The little church in Ashtarak is of the most ordinary kind and, for Armenia, meek. It is a little church in a six-sided headdress with a rope ornament along the cornices of the roof and the same sort of string eyebrows above the stingy mouths of its chinklike windows.

The door is quiet as a dormouse. I stood on tiptoe and peeped inside: but there was a cupola in there, a cupola!

A real one! Like the one in St. Peter's at Rome above the thronged thousands, the palms, the sea of candles, and the sedan chair.

There the recessed spheres of the apses sing like seashells. There are the four bakers: north, west, south, and east, who, their eyes plucked out, knock into the funnel-shaped niches, rummage among the hearths and the spaces between and cannot be at peace.

Whose idea was it to imprison space inside this wretched cellar, this low dungeon—in order to render it homage there worthy of the psalmist?

When the miller can't get to sleep, he goes out bareheaded to look over the millstones. Sometimes I wake up at night and rehearse the conjugations in the grammar of Marr.

Ashot the teacher is immured in his flat-walled house like the unfortunate personage in Victor Hugo's novel.

When he had tapped his finger on the case of his captain's barometer, he would go out into the courtyard to the reservoir and plot the curve of the precipitation on a chart of graph paper.

He cultivated the fruit of his small-commodity plot of ground, his tiny vineyard on its tenth of a hectare, baked into the stone-and-grape pie of Ashtarak, and, as an extra mouth to feed, was expelled from the collective farm.

In a hollow of his chest of drawers were preserved a university diploma, a school certificate, and a thinnish folder of watercolor sketches—an innocent test of character and talent.

He contained a low hum of the past imperfect.

A hard worker, wearing a black shirt theatrically open at the neck, with a heavy fire in his eyes, he retired into the perspective of historical painting, to the Scottish martyrs, the Stuarts.

The story of the tragedy of the semi-educated has not yet been written. I think that the biography of the village teacher might become the bedside book of our day, as *Werther* once was.

Ashtarak is a rich, snugly nested settlement and is older than many European cities. It was famous for its harvest festivals and for the songs of the Ashugs. People who are brought up in the vicinity of vineyards are fond of women, sociable, mocking, and tend to be touchy and idle. The people of Ashtarak are no exception.

Three apples fell from heaven: the first for the one who told the tale, the second for the one who listened, and the third for the one who understood. That is the way most Armenian fairy tales end. Many of them were written down in Ashtarak. The region around there is the folkloric granary of Armenia.

VIII. *Alagez*

Which tense do you want to live in?

—I want to live in the imperative of the future passive participle—in the "what ought to be."

I feel like breathing that way. That's what I like. There exists such a thing as mounted, bandit-band, equestrian honor. That's why I like the fine Latin "gerundive"—that verb on horseback.

Yes, the Latin genius, when it was young and greedy, created that form of imperative verbal traction as the prototype of our whole culture, and it was not the only thing that "ought to be" but the thing that "ought to be praised"—*laudatura est*—the thing we like. . . .

The above was a conversation that I carried on with myself as I rode on horseback among the natural boundaries, the nomads' territories, and the gigantic pastures of Alagez.[16]

In Erevan Alagez stood there before my eyes like "hello" and "goodbye." I saw its snowy crown melt from one day to the next and in good weather, especially in the morning, I saw its dyed slopes crunch like dry toast.

And I felt myself drawn to it over the mulberry trees and the earthen roofs of the houses.

A piece of Alagez lived right with me in the hotel. For some reason, a heavy specimen of the black volcanic glass called "obsidian" lay on the windowsill. A visiting card of half a ton left behind by some geological expedition.

The approaches to Alagez are not fatiguing, and it is no trouble at all on horseback, in spite of the 14,000 feet. The lava is contained in tumors that have swollen up on the ground and through which one rides with the greatest of ease.

As I looked out the window of my fifth floor room in the Erevan hotel, I formed a completely wrong notion of Alagez. I thought it was a monolithic ridge. But in fact it is a folded system and develops gradually—proportionately to the rise, the accordion of diorite rock comes untwisted like an alpine waltz.

It was a spacious day that fell to my lot!

Even now, when I think back on it, my heart throbs. I got tangled up in it as in a long shirt pulled out of one of the trunks of my forefather Jacob.

The village of Byurakan is celebrated for its baby chick hunt. They rolled about the floor like little yellow balls, doomed to be victims of our cannibal appetite.

We were joined in the school by a wandering carpenter—a skillful man who had seen much of life. Taking a swallow of cognac, he told us that he had no use either for artels or labor unions. His hands, he said, were golden, and he was so respected that he could find a place anywhere. He required no labor exchange to find a customer: he had a nose, an ear for guessing where his work was wanted.

I think he was Czech by birth, and he was the spit and image of the Pied Piper.

In Byurakan I bought a large clay salt cellar on account of which I had a great deal of trouble later on.

Imagine to yourself a crude form for the Easter cake—an old woman in a farthingale or hoopskirt, with a cat's head and a large round mouth right in the middle of the skirt where you could easily put all five fingers.

It was a lucky find from what was, by the way, a large family of such objects. But the symbolic power with which some primitive imagination had invested it did not escape even the most casual attention of the townsmen.

Everywhere there were peasant women with tearful faces, shuffling movements, red eyelids, and cracked lips. They had an ugly way of walking, as if they had the dropsy or had strained a tendon. They moved like hills of weary rags, stirring up the dust with their hems.

The flies eat the children, gathering in clusters at the corners of their eyes.

The smile of an elderly Armenian peasant woman is inexplicably beautiful—there is so much nobility, exhausted dignity, and a sort of solemn, married charm in it.

The horses walk among divans, step on the pillows, and trample the bolsters. You ride along feeling that you have an invitation from Tamerlane in your pocket.

I saw the tomb of a giant Kurd of fabulous dimensions, and took it for something quite normal.

The lead horse minted rubles with her hooves and her prodigality knew no bounds.

On the pommel of my saddle there bobbled an unplucked chicken, killed that morning in Byurakan.

Occasionally the horse would bend down to munch the grass, and its neck expressed its obedience to the Stubborns, a people older than the Romans.

A milky quietude ensued. The whey of silence curdled. The curds of the bells and the cranberries of the harness bells of various calibers muttered and banged. From every courtyard in the community came the cries of the karakul committee. It seemed that dozens of small circus owners had pitched their tents and show booths on the lice-ridden hill and, startled by the full house, taken unawares, now swarmed about in their camps, clattering the dairy dishes, cramming the lambs into their lairs, and rushing to lock up for their night in oxrealm the world-weary, steaming damp heads of cattle, each allotted its stall in barktown.

The camps of the Armenians and Kurds do not differ in their arrangements. They are cattle breeders' settlements on the terraces of Alagez, stopovers for villas, laid out in well-selected spots.

Stone borders indicate the plan of the tent and the small adjoining yard with a fence modeled out of dung. Abandoned or unoccupied camps look as if they had been swept by fire.

The guides from Byurakan were glad to stop overnight in Kamarlu: they had relatives there.

A childless old couple received us for the night into the bosom of their tent.

The old woman moved about with lachrymose, retiring, blessing motions as she prepared a smoky supper and the felt things for bedding:

"Here, take the felt! Here, take a blanket . . . and tell us something about Moscow."

Our hosts got ready for bed. An oil wick illuminated the tent, making it seem as high as a railway station. The wife took out a coarse nightshirt and invested her husband with it.

I felt as shy as if I were in a palace.

1. The body of Arshak[17] is unwashed and his beard has run wild.

2. The fingernails of the king are broken and wood-lice crawl over his face.

3. His ears have grown stupid from the silence but they once listened to Greek music.

4. His tongue is mangy from jailer's food but there was a time when it

pressed grapes against the roof of his mouth and was as agile as the tip of a flutist's tongue.

5. The seed of Arshak has withered in his scrotum and his voice is as reedy as the bleating of a sheep.

6. King Shapukh—thinks Arshak—has got the better of me and, worse than that, he has taken my air for himself.

7. The Assyrian has hold of my heart.

8. He commands my hair and my fingernails. He grows me my beard and swallows me my spit so accustomed has he grown to the thought that I am here in the fortress of Anyush.

9. The Kushan people rose up against Shapukh.

10. They broke through the border at an undefended place as through a silken cord.

11. The attack of the Kushani stabbed and disturbed King Shapukh like an eyelash in his eye.

12. The enemies fought and squinted their eyes so as not to see each other.

13. A certain Darmastat, the kindest and best educated of the eunuchs, was in the center of Shapukh's army, encouraged the commander of the cavalry, wormed his way into his master's favor, snatched him, like a chessman, out of danger, and all the while remained in full view.

14. He was governor of the province of Andekh in the days when Arshak used to give orders in his velvet voice.

15. Yesterday he was king but today he has fallen into a chink, huddles in the womb like a baby, warmed by lice, enjoying the itch.

16. When the time came for his reward Darmastat inserted into the Assyrian's keen ears a request that tickled like a feather:

17. Give me a pass to the fortress of Anyush. I want Arshak to spend one additional day full of hearing, taste, and smell, as it was before, when he amused himself with hunting and saw to the planting of trees.

Sleep is light in nomad camps. The body, exhausted by space, grows warm, stretches out straight, recalls the length of the trip. The paths of the mountain ridges run like shivers along the spine. The velvet meadows burden and tickle the eyelids. Bedsores of the ravines hollow out the sides. Sleep immures you, bricks you up. Last thought: have to ride around some ridge. . . .

Notes

Introduction: The Prose of Mandelstam

1. The reader should be aware that this essay was written in 1963–64 and published in 1965. An introduction to the present new and expanded edition is to be found on p. 63.

   If I retain intact these observations, with all their disadvantages of age, it is partly out of a no doubt selfish desire to keep straight certain matters of chronology. A quarter of a century ago, the student of Mandelstam found himself all but alone in a field now populous indeed, for which no other testimony is needed than the bibliography—and that only selected—to be found on p. 243. So extensive is the scholarship, much of it superior to anything of which I was or am capable, that latecomers to the study of Mandelstam may be excused for the occasional erroneous attribution to later authors of certain discoveries and opinions which first saw the light of day in these pages. Hence their reproduction without change.

2. George Stuckow (pseudonym), "The Fate of Osip Mandelṣtam," *Survey*, 46 (January 1963): 154f.

3. As this was being written, the journal *Moskva*, 8 (1964), 143–152, published a sympathetic memoir of Mandel'štam by Nikolaj Čukovskij and on pp. 153–155 a selection of eight poems.

4. "Moë znakomstvo s Mandel'štamom" [My Acquaintance with Mandel'-štam], *Novyj Žurnal* [The New Review], 49 (1957): 258–261.

5. *Portrety sovremennikov* [Portraits of Contemporaries] (New York, 1955), 377–379.

6. "Ital'janskie obrazy i motivy v poézii Osipa Mandel'štama" [Italian Images and Motifs in the Poetry of Osip Mandel'štam], in *Studi in onore di Ettore Lo Gatto e Giovanni Maver* (Rome, 1962), 601–614.

7. *Vstreča* [Meeting], 2 (1945), 30–31.

8. Karpovič, *loc. cit.* (note 4).

9. 12 (1958), 116–135.

10. "Kak ja ne stal poétom" [How I Did Not Become a Poet], *Oktjabr* [October], 10 (1959), 131.

11. *Panorama de la littérature russe contemporaine* (Paris, 1929): 265.

12. Preodolevšie simvolizm" [Those Who Have Overcome Symbolism], *Russkaja Mysl'* [Russian Thought], 12 (1916). Reprinted in the same author's *Voprosy teorii literatury* [Problems of Literary Theory] (Leningrad, 1928).

13. Il'ja Ehrenburg, *Ljudi, gody, žizn'* [People, Years, Life] (Moscow, 1961), 493–504; Marina Cvetaeva, "Istorija odnogo posvjaščenija" [The History of a Dedication], *Oxford Slavonic Papers*, XI (1964): 114–136.

14. *Ogonëk* [Little Light], 20 (12 August 1923).

15. Leningrad, 1931. This has recently been reprinted with a very useful intro-
     duction by Boris Filippov, Washington, D.C., 1964.

16. In all his writing Mandel'štam referred to his wife only once (in *Putešestvie
     v Armeniju* [Trip to Armenia]), and it was not until after the publication
     of his *Collected Works* in New York in 1955 that most of his friends, now
     émigrés in the West, even knew of his marriage. In disclosing the fact, Geor-
     gij Ivanov characteristically seasoned it with inventions of his own, such as
     that the marriage had been tragically unhappy and that a daughter, whose
     name he gave as Lipočka, had been born; see *Novyj Žurnal* [The New
     Review], XLIII (1955). Anna Axmatova, who knew Mandel'štam all his life,
     has now disclosed the falsity of these reports: there was never any daughter,
     and the Mandel'štams appear to have been a devoted couple. See her memoir
     in *Vozdušnye Puti* [Aerial Ways], IV (1965).

17. "Impressions of Boris Pasternak," *The New Reasoner*, 4 (1958): 88–89.
     The author of this memoir, who wishes to retain the anonymity under which
     it was published, writes with an authority upon which readers can rely.

18. Except for a few details, the following account of Mandel'štam's final years
     comes from information recently obtained by George Stuckow and pub-
     lished by him in *Survey*, 46 (January 1963): 151–155; *Mosty* [Bridges], 10
     (1963), 150–159; *Russkaja Mysl'* [Russian Thought (Paris)], 5 February
     1963; *Novoe Russkoe Slovo* [New Russian Word], 9 February 1963.

19. *Survey*, 46:154.

20. *NRS* (9 February 1963).

21. *Op. cit.*, p. 503.

22. N. Berkovskij, *Tekuščaja literatura* [Current Literature], (Moscow,
     1930), pp. 170–171.

23. "Smert' Luny" [The Death of Luna], trans. by Walter Morison in Richard
     Newnham (ed.), *Soviet Short Stories* (Baltimore, 1963), 17.

24. Cf. Berkovskij, 173f.

25. William E. Harkins, "The Pathetic Hero in Russian Seventeenth-Century
     Literature," *American Slavic and East European Review*, 4 (1955): 512–
     527.

26. F. M. Dostoevskij, *Sobranie sočinenij* [Collected Works] (Moscow, 1956),
     I:240.

27. *Ibid.*, p. 245.

28. Berkovskij, p. 177; the translation by Mirsky and Limbour, "Le timbre
     égyptien," appeared in *Commerce*, XXIV (1930): 119–168; Šklovskij, "Put'
     k setke" [Way to the Net], *Literaturnyj kritik* [Literary Critic], 5 (1933):
     115.

29. Berkovskij, p. 160.

30. *Polutoraglazyj strelec* [The One-and-a-Half-Eyed Archer] (Leningrad,
     1933), 264.

31. For the identification of Father Bruni I am indebted to the late Artur Lourié,
     who kindly shared with me many memories of his friend Mandel'štam.

32. For my knowledge of the real-life source of Parnok I am indebted first of all to a Soviet writer who requests anonymity. I must assure the reader that his authority is beyond question. For linking the brother of the poetess Parnok to the Parnax of Paris, and for other information about him, I am obliged to my colleague Nina Berberova.

33. The word *dantist* (dentist)—and also *farmacevt* (druggist)—could have additional meanings, undoubtedly of importance here. Poets and artists used them for literary hangers-on, "squares" or "tourists" who frequented the cafes as mere spectators; but since a great many dentists and druggists in St. Petersburg were Jews, the words are faintly anti-Semitic in connotation, suggesting specifically Jewish "squares."

34. Georgij Ivanov, *Peterburgskie zimy* [Petersburg Winters] (New York, 1952), 124–128. On Ivanov's inventions see my *Mandelstam* (Cambridge University Press, 1973), 13–16 *et passim*.

35. *Ibid.*, p. 114.

36. Berkovskij, p. 176, notes that *The Egyptian Stamp* is stylized in the manner of a manuscript containing two texts, the second consisting of "marginal notes," the autobiographical asides.

37. See Victor Erlich, *Russian Formalism: History—Doctrine* (The Hague, 1955), 150f.

38. *Skovz' literaturu* [Through Literature] (Leningrad, 1924), 256.

39. From a copy of the unpublished essay "Razgovor o Dante" [Conversation about Dante], kindly made available to me by Professor Gleb Struve.

40. "The Heuristic Value of Rhyme," *Selected Writings of Edward Sapir in Language, Culture and Personality* (Berkeley and Los Angeles, 1951), 496–499.

41. *Oeuvres complètes* (Paris, 1899), 1 : 15f.

42. M. Vitenson, "O 'pravde žizni,' o klassovoj bor'be v literature i o zadačax kritiki" [On "The Truth of Life," the Class Struggle in Literature, and the Tasks of Criticism], *Zvezda* [Star], 2 (1934): 171.

Introduction to the Second Edition

1. O. Mandel'štam, *Stixotvorenija* [Poems] (Leningrad: Sovetskij pisatel' [Soviet Writer Publishing House], 1973).

2. A partial English translation of this may be found in *Soviet Studies in Literature*, Vol. IX, No. 4 (Fall, 1973): 44–95. Dymshits does not deal with the prose, of course, but the article repays study as a capital instance of the contortions, half-truths, and evasions to which even decent people must resort if they wish to help in the rehabilitation of long-suppressed and hopelessly uncongenial writers.

3. Osip Mandel'štam, *Sobranie sočinenij* [Collected Works], 4 vols. Vols. I–III: Edited by Gleb Struve and Boris Filippov. New York: Inter-Language Literary Associates, 1964 1971. Vol. IV: Edited by Gleb Struve, Nikita Struve, and Boris Filippov. Paris: YMCA-Press, 1981.

Vol. I (Poetry). Introductions by Clarence Brown, Gleb Struve, and
E. M. Rais, 1964. Second edition, revised and expanded, 1967.

Vol. II (Prose). Introduction by Boris Filippov. 1966. Second edition,
revised and expanded, 1971.

Vol. III (Essays and Letters). Introductions by George Ivask, Nikita
Struve, and Boris Filippov, 1969.

Vol. IV (Supplementary), 1981.

4. A selected bibliography of works in English about the prose of Mandelstam
may be found on p. 243. A note of introduction to the new material of this
edition, *Fourth Prose* and *Journey to Armenia*, begins on p. 167.

The Noise of Time

1. *Gluxie gody*: The word *gluxoj* is rich in emotional associations and therefore
virtually untranslatable. It has the primary meaning "deaf," but it also can
mean "overgrown, wild; dead (of a season); suppressed, obscure, smolder-
ing; remote, out of the way, god-forsaken" and so on. The phrase *gluxie
gody* has, moreover, literary associations, since it recalls the poem by Aleksandr Blok which begins

> Roždënnye v goda gluxie
> Puti ne pomnjat svoego

[Those born in remote and desolate years do not remember their own path]
(*Sobranie sočinenij* [Collected Works], III [Moscow, 1960], 278). It is characteristic of Mandel'štam's relationship to Blok that he summons up the
older poet only to contradict him.

2. "Near the station is the large railway restaurant of Vauxhall . . .; popular
concerts with a good band every evening in summer (adm. free; reserved
seats 10–50 cop.)" (Baedeker's *Russia* [1914], 189).

3. Nikolaj Vladimirovič Galkin (1850–1906), violinist, conductor, teacher.
Between 1892–1903 Galkin conducted weekly concerts in Pavlovsk, where
the works of Russian composers were often given their first performance.

4. Nikolaj Nikolaevič Figner (1857–1918), tenor, soloist at the Mariinskij
from 1887–1907.

5. Gostinyj Dvor: "The Gostinyj Dvor, or Bazaar. . . , bounded on the E. by
the Sadovaja and on the S. by the Černyšov Pereulok, is an extensive building painted white and enclosing several courts. It was erected in 1761–85 by
Vallin de la Mothe and completely rebuilt at the end of the 19th century.
The arcades on the ground floor and the first floor contain about 200 shops,
which, however, are less elegant than the other shops on the Nevskij" (Baedeker, 104f). The building still stands, bears the same name, and serves the
same function in present-day Leningrad.

6. Engineers' Palace: "To the E. of the Mixajlovskij Garden lies the Engineers'
Palace, or Old Michael Palace. . . , built in a mediaeval style in the reign of

Paul I. between 1797 and 1800. . . . In 1822 the building was fitted up as an Engineering Academy (Nikolaevskaja inženernaja akademija)" (Baedeker, 118).

7. bullet-riddled banners: "On the pillars and walls are 103 banners and eagles captured from Napoleon, which give the church a military aspect" (Baedeker, 104).

8. Andrej Ivanovič Željabov (1850–81) was the founder of the People's Will, a group of revolutionaries responsible for the assassination of Alexander II. Sof'ja L'vovna Perovskaja (1853–81) was an adherent. Both were executed.

9. bathing houses: Wooden structures built in the water for the shelter of modest swimmers.

10. Narodnyj Dom: literally, People's House. Its full name was Narodnyj dom Imperatora Nikolaja II [People's House of Czar Nicholas II]. Located in the Alexander Park, on the north and east sides of the Kronwerk Canal, it contained a large theater of 4,000 seats. This was the most famous of a number of institutions with the name Narodnyj Dom in prerevolutionary Russia, which served as combined cultural and recreation centers.

11. Jewish quarter: This was the Kolomna District, which Baedeker treats in two brief paragraphs of reduced type and dismisses as "unattractive" (p. 124). The Litovskij (or Lithuanian) Castle was in fact the city prison.

12. Covetous Knight: The title and principal character of one of the little tragedies of Aleksandr Pushkin.

13. hares: This was the term for illegal passengers on streetcars, trains, and other forms of public transportation. It probably derives from their leaping on and off the moving vehicle between stops to avoid paying.

14. "Dubbeln, the oldest of the Riga bathing resorts, is (like Majorenhof) very noisy; among the visitors are many Jews" (Baedeker, 64).

15. sound recording device: *zvukopriëmnik*. I am not sure of this meaning. Mr. Alfred J. Swan (author of *Scriabin* [London, 1923]) informs me that it could not, as might be thought, be an error for the *clavier à lumière*, a huge reflector used for casting colored lights over the hall to the accompaniment of the music, since this innovation of Scriabin's *Prometheus* was never used at any performance that Mandel'štam could have witnessed.

16. Josef Casimir Hofmann (1876–1957). Jan Kubelik (1880–1940).

17. Hôtel d'Europe: At the time of which Mandel'štam writes, the Evropejskaja Gostinica, which is now one of the Intourist hotels in Leningrad, was known even to Russians by its French name.

18. Count Sergej Jul'evič Vitte [Witte] (1849–1915), Minister of Finance 1892–1903, Prime Minister 1903–06.

19. Pëtr Isaevič Vejnberg [Weinberg] (1831–1908), a Russian poet and translator. Mandel'štam for some reason reverses his first name and patronymic, making it Isaj Petrovič.

20. Maksim Maksimovič Kovalevskij (1851–1916), professor of constitutional law and, from 1909 to his death, editor of the journal *Vestnik Evropy* [Mes-

senger of Europe]. Ivan Il'ič Petrunkevič (1844–1928), a founder of the Constitutional Democratic Party and, from 1907, publisher of *Reč'* [Speech] and *Sovremennyj Mir* [The Contemporary World].

21. Fëdor Izmajlovič Rodičev (1856–1933), a leader and the principal spokesman of the Constitutional Democratic Party. Nikolaj Fëdorovič Annenskij (1843–1912), editor of *Russkoe Bogatstvo* [Russian Wealth] and a founder of the People's Socialist Party. Fëdor Dmitrievič Batjuškov (1857–1920), literary historian and critic, privatdocent in the University of St. Petersburg and editor of *Mir Božij* [God's World] 1902–1906. Dmitrij Nikolaevič Ovsjaniko-Kulikovskij (1853–1920), editor of a well-known history of Russian literature and one of the editors of *Vestnik Evropy* [Messenger of Europe].

22. Vladimir Nabokov (1899–1977), the author of *Lolita* and other novels and the translator of Pushkin's *Eugene Onegin*, attended the Tenishev School some ten years after Mandel'štam. He was driven to school in a limousine by a liveried chauffeur and presumably belonged to the "military, privileged, almost aristocratic undercurrent." Nabokov's memoirs in *Speak, Memory* (New York, 1947; original title, *Conclusive Evidence*), published in a Russian version as *Drugie berega* [Other Shores] (New York, 1954), provide a fascinatingly different slant on this remarkable institution.

23. Mixail Matveevič Stasjulevič (1826–1911), professor of history in St. Petersburg and one of the founders of the Party for Democratic Reforms. From 1866 to 1908 he was editor and publisher of *Vestnik Evropy*.

24. luminous personality: *svetlaja ličnost'*. Also on p. 81.

25. SR: Socialist Revolutionary, a political party formed in 1902 by various factions of the Populists. SD: Social Democratic (or, to give it the full title, Russian Social Democratic Labor Party), founded in 1898, was split in 1903 into two factions, the Mensheviks and Bolsheviks.

26. V.V.G.: Vladimir Vasil'evič Gippius (1876–1941). An early Symbolist poet and Mandel'štam's teacher in the Tenishev School, of which he was at one time director (see Chap. 14). He was the author of *Puškin i xristianstvo* [Pushkin and Christianity] (Petersburg, 1915) and wrote poetry under the pseudonyms V. Bestužev and V. Neledinskij. Memoirs of him can be found in Valerij Brjusov's *Dnevniki 1891–1910* [Journals] (Moscow, 1927).

27. chicken legs: A reference to line 11 of the prologue to Pushkin's *Ruslan and Ljudmila*: "Izbuška tam na kur'ix nožkax" [A hut (stands) there on chicken legs].

28. Viktor Mixajlovič Černov (1873–1952), a leader of the SR party and a disciple of Mixajlovskij. Nikolaj Konstantinovič Mixajlovskij (1842–1904), a leading literary critic and principal ideologist of Populism. Pëtr Lavrovič Lavrov (1823–1900), a leading Populist philosopher, wrote his major work, the *Historical Letters* (1868–69), under the pseudonym of P. L. Mirtov.

29. Konevskoj: Ivan Ivanovič Oreus (1877–1901), an early and now forgotten Symbolist, wrote under the name of I. Konevskoj.

30. Aleksej Vasil'evič Pešexonov (1867–1933), a leader of the People's Socialist

Party, formed in 1906 from the ranks of the right SR's. Venedikt Aleksandrovič Mjakotin (1867–1937). Mark Andreevič Natanson (1850–1919).

31. Lev Maksimovič Klejnbort [Kleinbort] (1875–1938), the editor of *Temy žizni* [Themes of Life], a weekly published in St. Petersburg in 1906–07, and the author of *Očerki narodnoj literatury* [Studies in the Literature of the People] (Leningrad, 1924). His real name was Lev Naumovič Klejnbort.

32. Franz Stuck (1863–1928), a German artist. The small satirical and grotesque sculptures of Innokentij Žukov depicted human sloth, pride, and so on, and were widely reproduced on postcards and elsewhere.

33. P. Ja.: Pëtr Filippovič Jakubovič (pseudo. L. Mel'šin) (1860–1911), a poet and revolutionary associated with the People's Will party. Mixail Larionovič Mixajlov (1826–65), revolutionary poet best known for his verse translations. Evgenij Mixailovič Tarasov (b. 1882), a revolutionary poet who gave up writing in 1909 and devoted himself thereafter to economics.

34. thick reviews: *tolstye žurnaly*, a term used of all the leading monthlies such as *Vestnik Evropy, Russkoe Bogatstvo*, etc.

35. According to Anna Axmatova's memoir in *Vozdušnye Puti* [Aerial Ways] IV (1965): 24, it was to Mandel'štam himself that this remark was made by the owner of the print shop where *Kamen'* [Stone] was published.

36. fighting organization: A semi-independent group within the SR party having as its function the commission of acts of terror against members of the government. It was led by the notorious Evno Fišelevič Azef (1869–1918), who proved to be a double agent.

37. Grigorij Aleksandrovič Geršuni (1870–1908). A revolutionary terrorist among the SR's, organizer of the "fighting organization" later led by Azef.

38. *raznočinec*: An intellectual associated with none of the principal social classes, such as the nobility, priesthood, merchants, etc.

39. Vera Fëdorovna Komissarževskaja (1864–1910).

40. Gippius: See note 26 above.

41. Konevskoj: See note 29 above. Aleksandr Mixajlovič Dobroljubov (1876–1944[?]). An early Symbolist poet, D. soon combined his poetry with religious fervor, became the leader of a small sect, and vanished "into the people."

42. Konevic (formerly Konevec), a large island in Lake Ladoga and the subject of a poem (1898) by Ivan Konevskoj.

43. Its house was a full cup: A Russian adage signifying abundance and plenty. It occurs again on p. 153, below.

44. Walsingham: A character in Pushkin's *Feast During the Plague*, translated from a scene in John Wilson's dramatic poem *The City of the Plague*.

Theodosia

1. Centrosojuz: Central'nyj sojuz potrebitel'skix obščestv [Central Union of Consumers' Cooperatives].

2.   Mixail Vasil'evič Mabo (1878–1961), a director of the Azov Bank, left the Soviet Union in 1921. I had the pleasure of an interview with him in Freehold, New Jersey, where he was living in retirement, a few weeks before his death in 1961. Mabo (or Mabo-Azovskij, to use his nom de plume) recorded some of his recollections of Mandel'štam in an article in the *Novoe Russkoe Slovo* (New York) for 14 January 1949. Perhaps it should be noted that Mabo remembers Aleksandr Sarandinaki to have been Harbor Master in Kerč', not in Feodosija, where the post was filled by a certain A. Novinskij. And, to fulfill a pledge made to Mabo, I should like to record that he did not write poems, as Mandel'štam says, but plays, and he was still writing them at the time of his death.

3.   bobbies: Mandel'štam's error for "tommies."

4.   railroad birds: I am trying to suggest Mandel'štam's pun on the resemblance between *kurjane* [residents of Kursk] and *kury* [chickens], which accounts for the image of their being taken down from a roost.

5.   OSVAG: *Osv*edomitel'noe *ag*entstvo, the information and propaganda section of the White Army.

6.   *sotnik*: A Cossack military rank (equivalent to lieutenant in the Russian army); originally, a commander of a unit of 100 men.

7.   the royal mantle of the Law: *Barmy zakona*. I take the English translation of this term from Vjačeslav Zavališin's *Early Soviet Writers* (New York, 1958), 55.

The Egyptian Stamp

1.   Giacomo Guarenghi (1744–1817), one of the number of great Italian architects who built the most beautiful buildings in St. Petersburg and its environs.

2.   *Kreščatik*: the name of the main street of Kiev. *Ščastie*: "happiness." Mandel'štam gives the pronunciation rather than the spelling, which is *sčast'e*. *Ščavel'*: "sorrel."

3.   Lucien Chardon de Rubempré is a character in Balzac's *Illusions perdues* and *Splendeurs et misères des courtisanes*.

4.   Alberto Santos-Dumont (1873–1932), Brazilian airship pioneer.

5.   Sands: the popular and unofficial name for a section of St. Petersburg that lay roughly at the juncture of the Litejnaja and Roždestvenskaja quarters.

6.   Nikolaj Aleksandrovič Bruni: See p. 48.

7.   Kerenskij summer: The summer between the February and October revolutions of 1917; from Aleksandr Fëdorovič Kerenskij (b. 1881), the president of the Provisional Government.

8.   Petersburg Side: The *Peterburgskaja storona* is the oldest quarter of the city, comprising the several islands between the Neva and the Bol'šaja Nevka. It contains the Fortress of SS. Peter and Paul.

9.   The Shiahs (or Shiites) constitute one of the two principal religious sects of

Islam. The feast day, more commonly spelled Šaxsej-Vaxsej and identical with the Ashura of English usage, commemorates the sufferings of the descendants of Ali who were killed in the Battle of Karbala in 680. Here, from a source that has a certain piquant appropriateness (see p. 47), is a further comment on this feast: "Aujourd'hui, pendant une fête musulmane, les Persans se portent eux-mêmes des coups de poignard et se réjouissent à la vue de leur sang qui coule à la gloire de leur dévotion. Cette coutume masochiste, connue sous le nom de Chakhsé-Vakhsé, persiste encore au Caucase" (Valentin Parnac, *Histoire de la danse* [Paris, 1932], 17).

10. Kalinkin: the name of a bridge across the Fontanka.

11. information booth: *adresnyj stol*—as in Leningrad today, a booth for obtaining addresses and telephone numbers. No general directory of private telephones is published.

12. hooks: *krjuki*, which can also refer to musical signs in ancient Russian notation.

13. Teodor Leszetycki (1830–1915).

14. The name "Marat" is suggested by the verb *marat'* [scribble], three lines above.

15. *Prosemenil Semën v proseminarij*. Said by the students in the Puškin seminar at the University of St. Petersburg about their professor, Semën Afanas'evič Vengerov, Mandel'štam's relative, in reference to his mincing gait (see pp. 58, 81). See Boris Ejxenbaum, *Moj vremennik* [My Journal] (Leningrad, 1929), 38.

16. "A house is a full cup." See note 43, *The Noise of Time*, above.

17. *järvi*: the Finnish word for lake.

18. Mon Repos: The country seat of Baron von Nikolai, said by Baedeker (207) to be "the finest point in the environs of Viborg."

19. Ejlers's flower shop: See p. 47f.

20. Kifared: The reference is to Innokentij Annenskij's tragedy *Famira Kifared* (1913), based on the myth of Thamyras, whose playing on the cythara was so accomplished that he challenged the Muses themselves to a contest and, defeated, was deprived of both his talent and his eyesight.

21. Nurmis: so in Mandel'štam's text, though it is probably an error for the name of Paavo Johannes Nurmi (b. 1897), the great Finnish athlete.

22. Angiolina Bosio (1830–59, according to *Grove's Dictionary of Music and Musicians* [London, 1954]), an Italian soprano, sang in the capitals of Europe, in America, and for four seasons, beginning in 1856, in the opera in St. Petersburg. She died in St. Petersburg 13 April 1859 of pneumonia and was buried in the Catholic cemetery there. It is worth noting that the death of Angiolina Bosio was also the subject of four of the most beautiful lines of the poet Nikolaj Nekrasov:

Vspomnim Bozio. Čvannyj Petropol'
Ne žalel ničego dlja neë,
No naprasno ty kutala v sobol'
Solov'inoe gorlo svoë.

[Let us remember Bosio. Arrogant Petropolis spared no pains on her behalf. But it was in vain that you wrapped your nightingale throat in sable.] This is from the poem "O pogode" [About the Weather], 1865. In the issue of *Zvezda* for December 1929 and in the first three issues for 1930 a novella by Osip Mandel'štam entitled "Smert' Bozio" [The Death of Bosio] was announced for publication in 1930. Oddly enough, during all of 1929 the name had appeared as "Borgia," and that was also the spelling in the three succeeding issues for 1930. By the time of number 7 for 1930, however, no further announcement appeared, and the novella itself, if indeed it was ever completed, has never been printed. The concluding paragraphs of Chap. VII were published in quotation marks and are, probably, a part of the lost work. See the editorial note in Mandel'štam, *Sobranie sočinenij* [Collected Works], (New York, 1955), 392.

23. Annuška: It may be that Mandel'štam chose this name as a reference to the maid of his friend Georgij Ivanov, about whom Irina Odoevceva, Ivanov's wife, wrote in her recollections of Mandel'štam in *Novyj Žurnal* [The New Review], 71 (March 1963): 15.

24. "The Lord God might have given more brains and money": The line is from Pushkin's *Mednyj vsadnik* [The Bronze Horseman], 1, 35–36: "Čto mog by Bog emu pribavit' / Uma i deneg" [That God might have given him more brains and money].

25. The original of this is an extended example of Mandel'štam's toponymic paronomasia: "Pod lebjaž'im, gagač'im, gagarinskim puxom—pod tučkovymi tučkami, pod francuzskim buše umirajuščix naberežnyx . . ." and so on. The Swan [*lebjažij*] Canal ran along the west side of the Summer Garden. The swan suggests down, which suggests the eider duck [*gaga*] from which down is commonly obtained, and the sound of this calls up Gagarin Street, not far from the Swan Canal and parallel to it. Gagarin Street leads into the French Embankment. Tučkov is the name of a bridge across the Little Neva. Other examples of this device are discussed above, p. 57f.

26. raspberries: There is an untranslatable play on the words *malina* [raspberries] and *malinnik* [raspberry patch] and Malinov, the name of the town.

A Note on Fourth Prose and Journey to Armenia

1. Thomas Mayne Reid (1818–1883), an Irish-born writer of rip-roaring adventure tales set in the American West, South Africa, and other marginal regions. Like other subliterary fictions of derring-do, his writings were immensely popular with the newly literate mass reader of the USSR. Mandel'štam's English was rudimentary. He worked from French versions (and might have had help from Nadežda, whose English was excellent), but letters from this period show how conscientiously he strove to present to his Russian audience the best possible text of a writer for whose work he could have felt little more than aversion.

2. See note 15, *Journey to Armenia* (p. 240).

Fourth Prose

1. A professor of mathematics at Moscow University. Because of his skill as a translator of mathematical literature, he was asked to be an arbitrator in the *Ulenspiegel* case.

2. I. B. Mandelstam, a translator, no relation to Osip Mandel'štam.

3. A name used for units of the Komsomol light cavalry that kept watch on organizations (and later on individuals) and reported evidence of suspicious behavior, disloyalty, "anti-Soviet" activity, and so on, to the authorities.

4. TSEKUBU: An acronym for the committee for the relief of scholars established in 1921.

5. Grin: pseudonym of A. S. Grinevskij (1880–1932), a writer of fantastic adventure novels and stories.

6. Herzen House: this building on Tverskoy Boulevard was at the time something like the headquarters of Soviet literature, since it housed the principal writers' organizations as well as numerous indigent writers and their families.

7. pockmarked devil: a phrase that would almost certainly have been taken as a reference to Stalin.

8. Askanaz Artem'evič Mravjan was Commissar of Foreign Affairs in Armenia in 1920–1921; from 1923 he headed the education ministry and served as Deputy Chairman of the Council of People's Commissars there.

9. Mixail Zoščenko (1895–1958), the best and most popular Soviet satirist.

10. A line by Sergej Esenin, whose suicide in 1925 is mentioned below.

11. Dmitrij Blagoj, one of the most prominent Soviet literary scholars.

12. Baron Georges D'Anthès killed Aleksandr Pushkin in a duel in 1837.

13. The writer Korolenko was editor of the journal *Russian Wealth*, to which Gornfeld contributed regularly.

14. A collection of Gornfeld's critical articles, first published in 1906.

15. Buxarin (1888–1938), whom Lenin called "the most valuable and greatest theoretician of the Party," was editor of *Pravda* [Truth] and a member of the Politburo. For his opposition to Stalin he was expelled from all his Party positions in 1929 and shot in 1938 after a "show trial" of the Great Purge.

16. Angiolina Bosio, an Italian soprano who sang for several seasons in St. Petersburg, where she died in 1859. There is evidence that Mandelstam once wrote or planned to write a novella entitled "The Death of Bosio." Whether he did is not known, but a passage of his *Egyptian Stamp* is devoted to her. See note 22, *The Egyptian Stamp*, above.

17. Herzen House; see note 6 above.

18. In N. A. Nekrasov's poem "Hey, Ivan!" a destitute wretch, brutally ordered about by everyone, yearns for the dignity of being addressed with a more respectable version of his name.

19. MSPO: initials of the Moscow Union of Consumers' Cooperatives.

20. Vij: the monster in Nikolai Gogol's story of the same name. Its eyelids reached to the ground.

Journey to Armenia

1. Sevan is an island (today actually a peninsula) in the lake of the same name. The lake was formerly called Gokcha. It is the largest in the Caucasus (557 sq. mi.) and lies (*pace* Mandelstam) 6315 feet above sea level. Baedeker recommends the trout fishing.

2. *Urartu* is the Assyrian name for what the Hebrews called Ararat and which later became Armenia.

3. N. Y. Marr (1864–1934) dominated Soviet linguistics for many years. He held that all the pre–Indo-European languages of Europe were related and belonged to a racial group which he called "Japhetic" after Noah's other son. Marr's theory was thought to be properly Marxist until no less a linguist than Stalin himself intervened, in an article in *Pravda* in 1950, to declare him utterly mistaken.

4. *Onguardist*: The journal *Na Postu* [On Guard] was the organ of a group of proletarian Soviet writers in the early Thirties.

5. *Zamoskvoreč'e*: Literally "beyond the Moscow River"—an old section of Moscow across the river from the Kremlin, fabled for the inelegance and spiritual narrowness of the inhabitants.

6. Centrosojuz: see *Theodosia*, note 1.

7. Boris Sergeevič Kuzin: Mandelstam's interest in what Nadežda calls *Naturphilosophie* (*Hope Against Hope*, p. 227) was greatly intensified by his meeting in Armenia with Kuzin ("B.S."), a biologist with a strong interest in literature, especially German. Mandel'štam's poem "To the German Language" is dedicated to him.

8. P. R. Kammerer conducted experiments intended to confirm Lamarck's doctrine of the transmissibility of acquired characteristics. A gripping account of his tragic life may be found in Arthur Koestler, *The Case of the Midwife Toad* (New York, 1971).

9. *termenvox*: A musical instrument (anticipating electronic music) invented by Lev Termen, a Russian who in the West called himself Leo Theremin and his device "Etherophone." Today it is generally known as the Theremin.

10. This sinner in the *second* (not seventh) ring of Dante's Hell is not named there. See *Inferno* XIII, 32–37.

11. Berija: If this is Lavrentij Pavlovič Berija (1889–1953), as seems likely, he was evidently not in 1930 quite the terrifying figure that he later became as head of Stalin's secret police and chief executive officer of the Great Purge.

12. Nikolaj Evreinov (1879–1953), one of the most talented Soviet dramatists and directors. Lived in the West from 1925.

13. Aleksandr Bezymenskij (1898–   ): a proletarian poet who once declared that he was first a Party member and only then a poet, a judgment without many dissenters. RAPP, of which he was a principal ornament, is the acronym for Russian words meaning Russian Association of Proletarian Writers.

14. Firdousi: Persian poet, author of the *Shahnamah* [Book of Kings], the national epic of Persia.

15. Ashtarak: a village some 30 kilometers NW of the capital city of Erevan and due south of the Alagez. An ancient center of Armenian spirituality.

16. Alagez, of which the modern name is Aragats, consists of four summits (highest 13,445 feet) about an extinct volcanic crater (1.25 miles in diameter). In 1914 Baedeker advised the traveler desirous of ascending Alagez to carry a revolver on account of the nomadic Kurds.

17. The prose poem that follows deals with the legendary struggle between the kings Arshak and Shapukh and can be understood as referring to Stalin's oppression. The censor so understood it, and forbade its publication. When Caesar Volpe, the editor who first published *Journey* in *Zvezda*, ignored the order, he was promptly fired.

Selected Bibliography

The following are works in English that deal in whole or in part with the prose of Mandelstam.

Books:

1. Mandelstam, Nadezhda. *Mozart and Salieri*. Trans. by Robert A. McLean. Ann Arbor: Ardis, 1973. [While not specifically about the prose, this small booklet is an insightful guide to many aspects of Mandelstam's creativity and should be considered a sort of appendix to the two volumes of her memoirs.]

2. Brown, Clarence. *Mandelstam*. Cambridge University Press, 1973.

3. Cohen, Arthur A. *Osip Emilievich Mandelstam: An Essay in Antiphon*. Ann Arbor: Ardis, 1974.

4. Monas, Sidney (ed. and trans.). *Osip Mandelstam: Selected Essays*. Austin: University of Texas Press, 1977.

5. Harris, Jane Gary (ed. and, with Constance Link, trans.). *Mandelstam: The Complete Critical Prose and Letters*. Ann Arbor: Ardis, 1979.

6. Mandelstam, Osip. *Journey to Armenia*. San Francisco: George F. Ritchie, 1979. [A reprint from 4 above with an excellent introduction by Henry Gifford.]

7. West, Daphne M. *Mandelstam: The Egyptian Stamp*. Birmingham [Eng.]: Department of Russian Language and Literature, University of Birmingham, 1980.

8. Avins, Carol. *Border Crossings: The West and Russian Identity in Soviet Literature, 1917–1934*. Berkeley: University of California Press, 1983.

Articles:

1. Harris, Jane Gary. "An Inquiry into the Use of Autobiography as a Stylistic Determinant of the Modernist Aspect of Osip Mandel'stam's Literary Prose." *American Contributions to the Eighth International Congress of Slavists, Vol. 2* (edited by Victor Terras). Columbus, Ohio: Slavica Publishers, 1978, pp. 237–59.

2. Isenberg, Charles. "Associative Chains in *Egipetskaja Marka [The Egyptian Stamp]*." *Russian Literature*, Vol. V, No. 3 (July 1977), pp. 257–76.

Index of Names

Note: The transliteration in the index of names is that used in the notes (see A Note on Transliteration, p. 11). In those cases where confusion might result, both forms are cited, e.g., Akhmatova, Axmatova. The index includes all proper names, both of real and imagined persons.